To my husband,
who tolerates my writing obsession
and only reads the smutty bits :)

Nestor Invest

Chapter 1

Shasa sank into her worn-out wingback chair and let out a deep sigh. Afternoon nap time. For the next ninety minutes, she could ignore the floor covered in dirty clothes and crumbs and just sit. She had nothing scheduled. Nothing but the scent of lemony green tea rising from her cup and a phone she could use to read her emails – if she had the stomach to open the last one.

The message was from Ollie, her partner and the father of her child. He'd spent the last two years working on the Greenpeace ship somewhere in the Pacific Ocean, extending his stay twice. In three weeks, he'd finally return to New Zealand. That was the plan, anyway.

Over the last two months, their relationship had become more and more strained. The distance between them felt longer than nine thousand kilometres of ocean. Now, this ominous email had landed in her inbox. Nothing good ever followed a subject line 'Something you should know'.

Shasa dropped the phone on the floor. She didn't need to know anything. Not yet. She could sit for a moment and admire how the afternoon sun played with her net curtains, exposing a sprinkling of mould, illuminating the dust particles dancing in the air. She focused on her breath, inhaling for one, two, three…

Before she reached 'four', someone knocked on the door, loudly enough to break her concentration and wake up her daughter. A hot burst of anger propelled Shasa out of her chair. Chorused by her daughter's high-pitched wail, she flung open the door.

"Hi! Mac MacCarthy. I'm here for the property evaluation. Were you expecting me?"

Damn! A week ago, she'd received a text from her property manager, informing her of the valuation. Why hadn't she marked it in her calendar?

Shasa looked at the guy standing at her doorstep. She already hated this jerk. His suit and tie exuded success. A branded pen stuck out of his pocket.

A real estate agent.

He had a stupid name, beautiful eyes and a dazzling smile, which quickly turned cheeky. His gaze dipped down, scanning her from head to toe, no doubt noting the over-grown dreadlocks and colourful bracelets. It wasn't a style fit for a 32-year-old, her mum had announced during one of their

Skype calls, later sending her a gift card for the hairdresser. The rest of her outfit was equally questionable. Shasa wrapped her arms around her chest to cover the threadbare, food-stained tank top from the guy's roaming gaze. Was he here to evaluate the house or her?

Lilla's cries grew louder, demanding attention.

Shasa nodded towards the bedroom. "That's my daughter."

The agent's eyebrows shot up in an animated show of sympathy that bordered on excitement. "Poor little one!"

Shasa glared at him. "*You* woke her."

He didn't have the decency to look uncomfortable. "Don't worry, this won't take long. She can go back to sleep in a jiffy."

"No, she can't. She takes ages to fall asleep." The low hiss of Shasa's exhale sounded like a tiny Darth Vader. If only she had a scary mask and were two feet taller. Being petite meant guys tended to underestimate her.

Shasa spun on her heels and hurried to the bedroom along the borer-eaten wood floor. Her three-year-old, Lilla, stood in her cot, her doll face contorted in despair, wailing like she'd been abandoned on a desert island. She had her father's blue eyes and Shasa's dark, wavy hair, self-styled with far too many pink and purple clips.

Bracing her back, Shasa scooped the girl up and carried her to the lounge. Even if the ritual of bum-patting and water-bottle-suckling worked to put her to sleep the second time, she'd only get another half-an-hour at best. With a stranger snooping around the house, nap time was officially over.

Lilla was a waif of a thing, but she wasn't a baby anymore and was becoming too heavy to carry. Shasa adjusted the skinny legs on her waist, letting her shoulder get slimy from the child's tears, and strolled around the house. The old villa had long hallways that connected to create a loop. Gradually, Lilla's wailing turned into sniffling, allowing Shasa to hear another sound.

The real estate agent cleared his throat, still at the doorway, right behind her. Couldn't the dude just do whatever he was here to do and get out of her way?

"What?" Shasa barked.

The guy flashed her a bright smile. "Is it okay if I look around now? Or would you rather reschedule?"

"I'd rather you were done already."

Sensing an intruder, Lilla halted her sniffling. Her arms tightened around Shasa's neck, and her head lifted in curiosity.

The agent beamed at her. "Hi, there! Sorry I woke you."

Shivering at his sugary voice, Shasa backed away from the door. Lilla, the traitor that she was, decided she was done with hugs and squirmed off her arms, onto the floor. She followed Mac-whatever down the hallway, straight into the laundry. A sight to behold. The mountain of dirty clothes had grown to the point where it could no longer be contained by the cupboard-sized room and spilled freely into the narrow corridor, meeting a row of recycling containers lined up along the wall.

Hurdling a heap of washed Styrofoam, Mac nearly stepped on a pair of dirty undies. Shasa shuddered, squeezing her eyes shut. She was desperate to run away, but first, she had to catch Lilla. The girl had attached herself to Mac's side, fascinated by the stranger taking photos of their laundry pile.

"Mummy's panties," she explained, lifting the frayed, purple underwear.

Shasa wanted to die.

"You're right," Mac replied, nodding appreciatively.

Was he actually looking at them? Shasa leapt in, grabbed the panties out of her daughter's hand and stashed them behind a bag of dirty towels.

"Look—" the girl picked up a T-shirt with a big spaghetti stain "—My unicorn shirt. It's dirty."

"Yes, I'm sure your mummy will wash it, at some point."

Shasa's fingers curled into tight fists. For the last two weeks, she'd worked long hours at the community house to make up for the lack of volunteers. She'd stayed behind to pack food parcels and call local businesses to secure more donations. With no family around, she always had her child with her, sometimes even at work. If she didn't have time to tackle laundry, so be it. Who was this guy to pass judgment?

Mac reached into his jacket pocket and pulled out a bag of chocolate frogs. He glanced at Shasa. "Do you mind if I give her one?"

Shasa huffed her consent, her brow so knitted it was giving her a headache. Anyone who showed a child a treat *before* asking the parent was playing a dirty game. How could she say no? Her daughter was so excited she practically levitated towards the chocolates.

"Say thank you," she grumbled, grabbing Lilla's non-chocolate-holding hand, pulling her to the kitchen. "Do you want a snack?"

Lilla wrinkled her button nose. "You have scary eyes."

Shasa tried to relax her face. "Can you save that chocolate for later? Have some kiwi fruit first."

Lilla shook her head. By the time Shasa had peeled the kiwi fruit, the chocolate was gone and Lilla accepted the healthier snack. Watching her daughter munch on fruit, Shasa relaxed. She fetched her previous teacup, now lukewarm, and settled at the table. For a glorious moment, she forgot about the intruder – until she saw him outside the window, holding a tape measure.

A layer of cold sweat formed on Shasa's neck. The landlord had sent property valuers before, so he could borrow more money from the bank. The last one had only checked that the house hadn't burnt down. So why was the real estate agent strolling around her backyard with a tape measure, recording the width of her driveway, the distance from the boundary to her garden shed, the girth of the magnolia tree? Property valuations weren't based on the circumference of trees, were they?

Shasa knew she paid way below market rent. She had a lot of space – two bedrooms, a study and a huge, fenced backyard. Last summer, her blueberry bush had produced the first good crop. She'd planted it five years ago when they'd first moved in. This year, she was planning to stock the community pantry at her workplace. Blueberries were so expensive in the shops.

From behind the curtain, Shasa kept her eye on Mac. He stopped in the middle of the lawn and typed something on his phone, a self-satisfied smirk on his face. She wanted him gone, but she needed answers. Was the owner planning to sell the house?

It would be easier to confront him outside, without the dirty laundry or carpet stains casting judgment on her.

She wiped her daughter's mouth and hands with a tea towel. "Get your shoes, let's go outside!"

Opening the back door, Shasa located Mac by the rear boundary, partially hidden by the compost bin and their abandoned chicken coop. They'd given up the chickens when Ollie had gone vegan, dragging them all in with him. The day he'd left for his first voyage, she'd driven to the supermarket to buy eggs and yogurt. With no grandparents around, it was hard enough to be a single mum without maintaining complicated shopping and meal planning.

Lilla stuck her feet into her glittery ballet shoes. "Swing?"

She loved the swing they'd hung off the magnolia tree. In

the spring, huge, floppy flowers formed a magical, pink ceiling. Now, in late summer, the ceiling was green, contrasting with the yellow grass that had seen little rain in weeks. The council didn't charge for water, but Ollie had always been adamant they shouldn't waste town water on the garden. Right now, the collection barrels were empty, and Shasa only used the hose for her blueberries. When Ollie returned, she hoped he'd see the yellow lawn as a sign of her dedication and would forgive her for not sticking to a vegan diet. *If* he returned. That ominous email still sat on her phone, unopened.

Lilla ran to the swing and yelled, "Push me!" before even sitting down.

Shasa followed Lilla and gave her a couple of shoves. Leaving her squealing with delight, she approached Mac, who was now taking a photo of her house, and as it appeared, her child.

"What are you doing?"

Mac jumped at her voice. "Don't worry, these are just for reference."

"Why are you taking measurements? Is the house going on the market?"

"I'm just here to do a valuation."

"Don't bullshit me. I need to know what's going on!"

He tapped on his phone, avoiding eye contact. "If your landlord's planning to sell, he has to give you a ninety-day notice. Or, if they're not getting new tenants, forty-two days.

Either way, you'll be notified."

"Forty-two days is nothing! There are hardly any rentals out there and rents have gone up so much! I'm a single mum on a part-time salary. I'll be in deep shit."

"Calm down, you'll be fine." A stock standard answer. A brush off.

Mac took another photo and typed something.

Panic swirled in Shasa's stomach. She had to get through to this guy. "It's all about making money for you and your clients, right? Nobody gives a damn about the tenant."

Mac looked up at her with mild amusement. "I don't make money. Money makes money, you just have to make it work for you."

Shasa stared at him, dumbfounded. "What if you don't have any money?"

He shrugged. "Plenty of people start with nothing and make millions."

Shasa's blood boiled. "And millions of people start with nothing and make nothing! The system's not fair!"

"Life's not fair! Doesn't mean you give up, sit on your bum and whine about it."

"I'm not whining! I'm asking you to tell me what you know, so we can avoid becoming homeless. Isn't that what I'm supposed to do in your capitalist utopia?"

He turned back to his phone, his mouth a straight line. "I'm sorry. We don't discuss property deals with tenants."

Shasa drew a deep breath. "Even if you believe you need

to stomp on other people to get ahead, stomping on me gets you nowhere! I haven't even reached the first rung of your precious property ladder. Giving me fair warning about what's happening to our home takes nothing away from you!"

Mac slipped his phone into his pocket and turned up his palms in surrender. "Oh my God, calm down! If you must know, my client's looking at developing. It's a good-sized section, enough for several high-end townhouses. Makes more sense than trying to renovate … that." He gestured at the old villa with disdain. "The location's perfect. Close to town, close to the lake, on a popular street. You're right, Hamilton is short of rentals. When you think about it, this is great for everyone. Multiple apartments instead of one."

Great for everyone? Shasa's stomach roiled. This was her worst nightmare. She stared at her perfect garden, all the fight seeping out of her. "Is it final yet?"

Mac shrugged. "It's looking good. The house is on stilts, easy to move. No reason it wouldn't go through."

Shasa's gaze landed on her big blueberry bush, surrounded by nets she'd painstakingly installed last summer. "Do you think they'll destroy the whole garden? The blueberries, the fruit trees, everything?"

Mac gave her an odd look. "Why? You won't be here."

"I know. But I've put in so much work, I don't want to see it all die." She bit down on her lip to stop it from quivering. This was the worst news, and she hadn't even read Ollie's email yet.

Mac looked at the blueberries. "If the garden's in the way, it has to go."

Lilla shouted from the swing, asking for someone to push her. Shasa tried to move, but the devastation of the news nailed her to the ground. She fought the sting behind her eyes, but it only got worse. Mac stepped in and gave her daughter a good shove and she erupted in giggles.

Mac turned to Shasa, lowering his voice. "Okay. I was going to take one more look inside, but..."

Shasa squeezed her eyes shut, tears now flowing freely. "I think it's best you leave."

"Yeah. I was thinking the same thing." She heard the discomfort in his voice. He probably couldn't wait to get off the property, away from her.

"Thanks for having me, I guess," Mac said. "And not that it makes any difference, but I don't stomp on people to get ahead."

Through her tears, Shasa watched him get behind the wheel of a huge black pickup truck and tear away. She could only hope she'd never see him again.

Lilla took her hand. "What is it mummy?"

Shasa wiped her eyes, trying to calm down. "Just a hard day, baby. But we'll figure it out."

How, she had no idea.

Chapter 2

Shasa stretched out on her bed and turned on her pink vintage nightlight. Lilla snuggled up against her like a heat-seeking missile. The girl accepted her cot for afternoon naps but slept next to Shasa at night. Shasa didn't mind. Without Ollie, she no longer needed privacy. This way, she felt less alone.

Shasa's arms ached. After the real estate agent had left, she'd cleaned the house. She needed to prove to herself that the state of her home had been temporary, that he'd just happened to step in moments before her weekly – okay, monthly – clean. By clearing the tabletops and mopping the laundry room floor, she'd been redeemed.

Yet sleep eluded her. She had to read that email. Shasa grabbed her phone and brought up the message.

It began with well wishes and greetings to Lilla, his little bean. Shasa wondered if Ollie called her that because the last time he'd really bonded with his daughter, she'd been the size of a bean. He'd been great during the pregnancy, but once they entered the daily grind of looking after a baby, his interest waned, his feet itched.

Shasa kept reading, her heart in free fall. Ollie always wrote eloquently, but his beautiful words couldn't hide his intent. He wasn't coming back. On the ship, he felt like he was finally contributing in a meaningful way. As much as he'd miss Lilla, he needed to do this for the planet, for their future. And he didn't want to *stop Shasa from realising her dreams*.

Shasa shrank as though someone had sucked the air out of her lungs. She struggled to take a deep breath and read the message again, imagining his tone of voice. She could hear the undertones. He'd already let her go.

Shasa hugged her knees, willing for her churning gut to settle. Nothing would change, she told herself; she'd practically been a single mother for two years, only now it was official. She was officially alone.

At college, her own parents had split up and returned to their respective home countries, Finland and South Africa, while she remained in New Zealand. They stayed in touch over Skype but visited infrequently. Ollie's parents lived in the South Island, too far to be of any help.

Shasa looked at her wrists, covered in colourful, woven bracelets. Some were from second-hand shops; others Ollie

had given her during his brief visits. She'd worn them proud-
ly, happy for the way they brightened her wardrobe and connected her to him and his causes. Just like the dreadlocks.
Hers were dark to Ollie's dirty blond, but they matched,
signalling to the world that they belonged together. She sat
up on the bed, running her fingers through the thick, woolly
strands. That was it. If he let go of her, she'd let go of the
hair.

A petty thought, but it gave her a sense of control. Shasa
tiptoed into the kitchen, looking for scissors. The threads
were overgrown, so she wouldn't have to do a close shave,
only snip them off one by one. It would look terrible, but she
could get someone to tidy it up later. Until then, she'd wear
a hat.

After twenty minutes of frantic scissor work, she had
a sink full of matted hair and the most awkward pixie cut
ever seen. But it was all hers. Nothing to do with Ollie. Shasa
looked into the mirror, picturing the horror on Ollie's face.
She'd always fallen short of his standards – veganism, plas-
tic-free life, exclusive breastfeeding. The chopped off hair
was the perfect cherry on top of her half-hearted efforts. It
made her look exactly how she felt – someone who didn't fit
in anywhere.

Shasa scooped the loose hair into a paper bag, wondering
how to dispose of it. She'd heard it could be used to clean
up oil spills, but how? Maybe she could compost it. Without
Ollie, did she still care about the planet? Would she aban-

don the compost bin? Buy a packet of plastic spoons? Shasa shook her head. That was the truly hard part. She agreed with most of what Ollie said: there was too much plastic in the world. Recycling made sense. Helping the less fortunate was important. It was part of her job, too. As much as she hated Ollie right now, she couldn't align herself with greedy, self-serving people like that Mac-something, who bought and sold properties for maximum profit, never mind the tenants. After all, she had a conscience. She hadn't lopped her principles off with the dreadlocks.

Shasa marvelled at how light and cool her head felt as she returned to the bedroom. Sliding under the covers, she snuggled against Lilla's warm back, taking solace in her daughter's soft breathing. Shasa would find her own way, a way of doing the right thing without Ollie's nagging voice in her ear. She didn't need him. She didn't need a man at all. Men couldn't be trusted – as fathers or anything else. She needed a village. Shasa wrapped her arm around her daughter and imagined them lying on a floating raft in the middle of the ocean with no land in sight. Ollie had just thrown them overboard, and they needed to find land. A place to anchor.

Chapter 3

Mac stepped into the buzzing cafe on Victoria Street and ordered two drinks. A flat white for him, a short black for Rick, his friend and business partner, who was running late. Again. Mac suspected Rick's perpetual lateness was part sloppiness, part power play – a game Mac refused to engage in. If he did, they'd never actually meet. Besides, he was happy to wait for Rick as long as necessary.

Three years ago, Rick gave him a start as a property developer, letting him in on a deal that made a year's wages in only a couple of months. Mac could still remember the thrill of it, the moment he'd realised he wouldn't need to toil away on a property manager's salary anymore. He could invest and grow his wealth, just like Rick. The more money you had, the more money you could make. No matter what his parents told him, money wasn't evil. It made things possible. If he ever wanted to do something good on a larger scale, he needed money.

Stepping on the cafe terrace, Mac spotted a greasy stain on his shirt and folded his sleeve to hide it. Why did he eat a pie in the car? Things like that, old habits from his less than luxurious upbringing, gave him away. He wasn't all class like Rick, but he was hard-working and smart. Fortunately, Rick had recognized those qualities and asked him to join his business venture, allowing him to leave his job at the property management company. Even with the couple of missteps Mac made since then, he counted himself lucky.

Mac sat on the aluminium chair and balanced three folders, a phone and a laptop on the wobbly table. The sun still shone hot, but it didn't change the fact that summer was already waning. They were running late finishing drawings for buildings that had to be weather tight before the rain started to pour. Every cloudless day that went by was a perfect construction day wasted. It hadn't really rained for weeks, which made him nervous about the future.

Only twenty minutes late, Rick arrived as their drinks were served. His attire was smart casual, but had an expensive sheen. Even his black leather shoes glinted in the sunlight, recently polished. Rick exuded wealth in a fashionable and understated way, that was also blatantly obvious, a skill Mac knew he should master. Growing up, he'd never held an interest in fashion or had enough money to buy the right gear. At home, he usually reverted to jeans and T-shirts – he lived alone and kept busy with work, rarely having anyone over, so there was no need to keep up appearances for empty walls. It was a relief, really.

"How's my prodigy?" Rick grinned, baring a set of pearly whites that could have featured on a dentist billboard. "Are you making progress?"

"I am." Mac opened the top folder and handed over a pile of smudgy scans he'd obtained from the council. "Everything looks good. It's freehold, you can build one point five metres from the boundary, two levels up. The soil has never been tested, but there shouldn't be any issues."

Rick lowered his voice. "And the owner?"

"He's on board, we should settle quickly. But I don't want to push it, he might get suspicious."

"Of what?" Rick raised his brow in mock innocence. "We're paying market price, saving him agent fees and a lot of the trouble."

"Yeah, I just meant ... Never mind." Mac slid the papers back in the folder and tried to smile.

It wasn't shady. They'd offered a good price, on par with what a first-home buyer would have been able to pay. But if the vendor knew what he stood to make, he'd feel duped. This project was a license to print money – something Mac desperately needed after a fiasco involving a leaky town-house. He'd learned his lesson and wouldn't make the same mistake twice; he wouldn't touch an old house with a ten-foot pole. It was far safer, not to mention more profitable, to build new with reputable companies.

"How's it going on the ranch?" Mac asked.

Rick rolled his eyes. "Missus wants to get chickens." Rick's family lived on a vast lifestyle property just out of town.

"And ... you don't want chickens?"

"They destroy the lawn and we're hosting the balloon this year. Every man and their dog will be there. I don't want the place to be full of chicken shit."

Rick's company sponsored Hamilton's annual hot-air balloon festival, the highlight of the year for local families and for Mac. Rick made fun of his passion, but he didn't care. As much as he wanted to win in business, he couldn't limit himself to the kind of life Rick led, picture perfect and conservative, surrounded by other wealthy people.

Mac flashed a cheeky smile. "If I get my own balloon, can I park it at your house too?"

Rick waved his hand. "You'll have your own land by then. And a family?"

Mac forced a laugh. It's not that he didn't want a family, but women were high maintenance. The last one had driven him absolutely bonkers. He wanted to make money but navigating the social scene of the wealthy drained his energy. With Charlotte, it had sucked the life out of him. They had to be seen at every event, wearing the right labels, dropping tasteful hints of his success. Every room they entered, his girlfriend sized up the competition, to later serve him with an assessment of their current standing, delighting in anyone else's misfortune. She'd insisted she was looking out for him, but he didn't want a never-ending makeover, or someone to help him throw out old towels. He wanted a relationship.

Rick's wife was great, but even she expected diamonds a couple of times a year. Mac sighed. Casual relationships were definitely easier. It must have been his upbringing, having a mother who never expected more than a hand drawn card from her children, or her husband. There was something sweet about that, something he wanted for his family. If that wasn't available, he'd gladly stay away from commitment.

"The kids must be excited about the balloon?" he said, hoping to steer the conversation back to Rick.

"You have no idea."

Mac had met the nippers, but still found it hard to imagine Rick with children. He never had ketchup stains on his clothes.

Rick finished his coffee with one gulp, stood up and grabbed the folder off the table. "Cheers. I'll look it over and let you know if I notice anything. But I think it's solid. This'll get you into the big leagues."

Mac swallowed. "I just got lucky."

Rick shook his head. "Luck is when preparation meets opportunity."

Mac wished he could sound as confident. He hated how much was riding on this. Sleep at night was becoming elusive.

"You haven't spoken to anyone about this, right?" Rick asked.

Mac shook his head. "No."

It was only after Rick had left that Mac thought about the tenant. No, she wasn't worth mentioning. Her biggest concern was finding another rental. He could see why. After he'd left the house, he'd checked with the vendor. The girl was paying at least a hundred dollars below market rent. She'd find nothing decent for that price. It was a shame, but he couldn't get sentimental about every poor person he came across. He had to look at the big picture. If he made this work, in a couple of years, he could achieve something far better than helping one tenant. That was the plan, anyway.

She was cute though, he had to admit, even with those horrid dreadlocks and harem pants. He hadn't been able to stop staring at her huge eyes and her perfectly formed breasts moving under the threadbare tank top she'd probably picked up from an opportunity shop bin – or a good-ol' rubbish bin. The sight of her figure had helped him overlook the weird stuff she'd said. What kind of tenant got so attached to their garden? The best thing about renting was the freedom not to worry about cultivating the land. Why on earth would she put in all that effort to raise the value of someone else's investment? Mac shook his head, looking across the cafe table to the busy downtown street.

Still, the little girl had been absolutely adorable. For her sake, Mac hoped the tenant would find a decent new home.

Chapter 4

Shasa gave a grateful smile as Marnie slid a steaming cup of tea across the desk and sat down next to her.

"We'll figure it out," Marnie whispered in her most soothing tone.

They kept their voices down so as not disturb the ladies' Pilates class in the community room on the other side of an open doorway. The class focused on breathing, targeted at elderly visitors with limited mobility. Marnie sipped her coffee, a distracted look on her face.

Shasa could tell she was listening to the instructions, breathing out and squeezing her pelvic floor, as the instructor's serene voice told them to imagine sucking a blueberry up in their vaginas.

Shasa took her tea and adjusted the headscarf that concealed her homemade haircut. The late summer heat made it far too hot for a scarf, or hot drinks, but the latter was a ritual she relied on, especially in stressful times and especially with Marnie, her best friend and colleague who ran the community house with her. Soft and curvy, with a penchant for drop earrings that frequently got tangled in her chestnut perm, she was one of the best people Shasa knew. They were chalk and cheese, sometimes mistaken for mother and daughter. Marnie was only six years older but favoured long tunics and orthopaedic shoes. Despite their differences, they'd formed a friendship that made the poorly paid work a million times better.

Shasa stirred her peppermint tea. "I think they're a couple of weeks away from finalising the sale, so I should have more than forty-two days to find a new rental."

"It'll be more than that! Those things always take time," Marnie reassured her as she reached for a muffin.

Shasa sighed. "I just thought next time we'd move into our own place, not another rental. I saved everything Ollie sent us. We've been lucky to have such low rent, most people can't save anything. But it was such a pipe dream."

Marnie straightened up. "Are you sure? With the interest rates this low..."

"Prices are going up faster than my savings. And my pay is too low."

Marnie nodded, carefully removing a white chocolate chunk from a piece of muffin before popping it in her mouth.

After a moment, she lifted her chin, eyes wide. "What

about that cohousing thing?"

A month ago, they'd hosted the chief architect of a new cohousing community in Auckland. She'd shown countless slides of the building process and the finished village with its community garden and rammed earth houses. The houses were beautiful and solid, a far cry from the standard new builds in Hamilton.

Shasa let out a wistful sigh. "It looked amazing, but did you hear how long it took?"

"Eight years? But..." Marnie lowered her voice, "I reckon it was because they couldn't agree on anything. They came up with that coloured card system just to manage people talking at meetings. Our parliament's more agreeable than that lot."

Shasa chuckled. The cohousing community reminded her of the mix of characters they saw at the community house. Some were all about the environment, others protected cultural heritage, followed religious or dietary rules, or complained about the cost of anything that wasn't free. How anyone could build houses with a group like that was beyond her.

"It's human nature," she said. "If you have thirty people all putting in their life savings, it gets complicated."

Marnie threw up her hands, nearly knocking over her teacup. "That's it! Scale it right back! You don't have to do it with thirty people. Do it with ... I don't know ... five? You can still get a larger piece of land and design the space the way you want. It's much easier to get five people to agree on things."

"True." A flicker of hope woke up in the pit of her stomach.

Was it possible? Could she get some people together to buy and build something?

Marnie beamed. "You already have one."

"One what?"

"One person who agrees with you and thinks you'd be the perfect project lead. And who'd happily move into one of the houses to get away from a certain ex-mother-in-law."

Marnie's divorce had left her in the family home with her two teenagers. The downside? Her ex-mother-in-law lived right next door. Not by accident. They'd paid good money to buy the neighbouring property, hoping to get regular babysitting help. Instead, the demented grandmother of her children now wandered over daily, firmly believing Marnie and Steve were still married. Steve didn't want her mother in a nursing home, but he had the luxury of living in another town with his new girlfriend.

Marnie sighed. "I'd move right in! Since Tom's in college, I'm thinking of downsizing. Tanya and I can fit in a two-beddie, easy! Even if we built some smaller townhouses, I'd be keen."

"Seriously? If we built like ... four or five apartments and leave space for a shared garden?"

"Totally! I was going to put the house on the market and was looking at those new townhouses in Greenhill Park, but honestly, I can't afford anything in there. This could be my chance, too! I'm sick of that old house, it's falling apart and Steve's not there to do any maintenance. I hate it."

Shasa's heart leapt as she considered the possibility.

Marnie tilted her head, catching her earring on her jumper, pulling loops out of the loose knit. "Just promise me I won't have to raise a blue card to make a suggestion."

Shasa rolled her eyes. "Or a red one for a toilet break? And no meal roster or community house!"

"Don't we already have one?" Marnie gestured the surrounding space.

"Exactly." Shasa sighed, the smile lingering on her lips. It felt good to dream about something, even if it was completely unattainable.

Her fingers drummed the teacup. "Would any bank touch it?"

"Why not? They funded those mud houses in Auckland."

"Rammed earth houses," Shasa corrected, suppressing a giggle. "Remember the spreadsheets, though! They had those really complicated calculations, I mean budgets ... that's not my strong suit." Her shoulders dropped.

"I can help with that. Plus, we can let the builders and the bank worry about the numbers. That's their job."

Shasa loosened her headscarf to let in some air. "Okay."

Marnie rested her hand on Shasa's arm. "Promise me, you'll think about this. It'd be so good for your family to finally get out of renting."

Her family. She attempted to smile, tears in her eyes.

Her friend frowned. "What is it?"

Shasa fidgeted in her seat. "Ollie. He's not coming back.

He's signing another contract, for another year."

"And…"

How did she know there was an 'and'?

Shasa inhaled a lungful of warm, stuffy air. "He's breaking up with me."

"Oh, girl!" Marnie pulled her in a side hug. "I knew there was something else to this new haircut."

Shasa offered a weak smile. "I meant what I said. I am tired of maintaining it. But yeah, when I read that email … he couldn't even come and tell me face to face, he's just starting another contract, staying at sea."

"Is there someone else? Another activist?" She spat out the word 'activist' like they were talking about child molesters.

"He didn't say anything about … anyone. I hate the way he worded that email, like he was being charitable, thinking of what's best for me. He said he wants to 'release me' to live my life in total freedom with whoever I wish."

Marnie's expression shifted. "Okay. So, he's already embracing his own freedom with someone."

Shasa winced. It made sense. Why hadn't she thought of that?

She finished her tea and got up. "Lucky me, I'll have something else to focus on. I get to worry about becoming homeless."

"Oh, shush now! If you run out of time, you can always move in with me."

"Thank you."

Although a lovely sentiment, the thought of sharing Marnie's small house with her moody teenage girl made her heart heavy. It wouldn't be home.

Marnie picked up her cup and the plate of muffins and followed Shasa to the staff kitchen. Afternoon sun streamed through the small window above the sink, heating anything it touched.

Marnie stopped at the window, staring into the distance. Shasa recognized her plotting face; she'd seen it many times before. Marnie wrote romance novels set in faraway locations. To escape, she said. She was so good at it that she'd replaced her ailing marriage with an imaginary love life. No dating, no heartbreaks. An example Shasa was tempted to follow, if only she could write.

Marnie rinsed their cups and began stacking the tray that was waiting to go into the industrial dishwasher. "Ollie would make a great villain. I mean … he's a daft prick, but thinks he's saving the bloody world. Can I use him in my book, please?"

Shasa shrugged. "Just make sure you include a self-righteous lecture – a page-long monologue about tuna and dolphins."

"Will do! You'll have to help me with that, though."

Shasa laughed despite the stab of pain. "I'm not sure I can survive another lecture. If he ever comes for a visit, you should see him. Bring a can of Sealord." She chuckled at the horrible thought, wringing a dish cloth over the sink.

"I can finish up here," Marnie said, nodding at the pile of

dishes sitting in the sink. "Leave early, take Lilla out for an ice cream? Maybe get a proper haircut?"

Shasa smiled, fighting the stubborn tear that tried to squeeze out of the corner of her eye. Marnie had a way of lightening to the mood. Her solutions were often food-based but surprisingly effective.

Shasa set the dish cloth on the counter. The heat made her harem pants stick to her sweaty legs. Ice cream sounded heavenly, and Marnie was probably right about the haircut. Shasa picked up her canvas bag off the floor and leant her weight on the swing door, edging herself out of the kitchen.

"Thank you," she said from the doorway, as her smiling friend waved to usher her away.

At the front door, she bumped into the ladies who were leaving the Pilates class. Ladies and one middle-aged man. Lando had a physique of a racehorse, dressed in tight bike shorts that left little to imagination. He did odd jobs, mostly landscaping, and had a lot of time on his hands.

"They let me join the ladies' class. I did pelvic floor exercises!" he gushed without a hint of embarrassment.

Shasa laughed as he blew kisses to the giggling women and jogged towards his car. So, he hadn't even ridden a bike today. The shorts must have been for the ladies' benefit.

Chapter 5

Next morning, Shasa arrived at work early. Bracing the hot, stuffy air the building had bottled overnight, she headed straight to the computer. She had to create some flyers before the community house officially opened. They needed to get the word out about the first cohousing meeting as soon as possible.

The schedule was ambitious. To be able to approach the bank about a loan, they needed three other buyers for new townhouse units, a builder, and a section that was big enough for the build. With all this, and the deadline of Shasa's impending house move, they'd decided to hold the first open cohousing meeting the following Tuesday night, which only gave them one weekend to spread the word.

The plan was stupidly optimistic, yet it suddenly seemed possible. She'd spent the previous night with Marnie, planning and writing notes over a bottle of wine. For the first time in months, Shasa felt like putting up a fight. She wanted to see this through, even if it didn't work. If this project kept her mind off Ollie, that in itself was a big win.

Shasa fired up the old PC and the one-colour laser printer. Fifteen minutes later, she had something a generous person might have called a poster, with the title 'COHOUSING MEETING'.

She scanned their noticeboard brimming with government messages about smoking cessation, cervical screening and rheumatic fever, mixed with yellowing personal ads from people looking for flatmates and lost cats. The board didn't have very good reach. She'd have to go wider, distribute some flyers and posters around town and post on Facebook.

Shasa pushed 'print' on fifty copies just in time. Behind the glass doors, she spotted Bridget, their resident law advisor, making her way across the parking lot, her flowery tunic flapping in the wind. Her style had become more flamboyant since retirement.

"Good morning!" Shasa called.

Bridget manoeuvred her large frame through the door and placed her laptop on the reception desk. "Oh, I'm so hot! When's this going to end?" She flapped her arms to get some air under the tunic.

The weather was warm, but nowhere near as hot and muggy as it had been in early February. The cooler nights were a welcome relief, since the only places Shasa could enjoy air con were the mall and the local library.

The printer finished warming up and started churning out the posters. Bridget picked one up and studied it. She'd been at the cohousing presentation they'd hosted with the Auckland group, asking questions about the legal side of things. Bridget was a big supporter of anything community-led and empowering. 'Empowering' was probably her favourite word.

"Oh, great! I was hoping someone would do this in Hamilton. Such an empowering concept. Are you leading this?"

Shasa stiffened. "Ye … es."

"Brilliant! This'll stir the pot for sure. Good on you!"

"Stir the pot? Why?"

Bridget shrugged. "It goes against the grain, doesn't it? Buyers don't even know this is an option. Once word gets out, people will start questioning the way things are done. Everyone will have to take notice. The council, developers. It's a good thing."

"It's not going to be at that scale. We're only looking at building one block of townhouses. It's hardly even cohousing, more like what they call a pocket neighbourhood. I doubt anyone will notice." Shasa rambled, blushing in shame. She should have been changing the landscape of the city and challenging the status quo, but in honesty, she just wanted to get out of renting and live next door to her friend. Besides, she couldn't afford to buy anything nice any other way. She wasn't a social justice warrior; she was selfish, or desperate, or maybe both.

"Well, good luck! I'll just go get a glass of water to start with. Hope someone shows up today. I'm bored." Bridget took a copy of the poster and made her way to the kitchen.

Shasa collapsed back in her chair, emptying her lungs. It was official now. She wasn't just dreaming up things with her friend, she was leading a building project. Could she do this? How far could she get before everyone noticed she knew nothing about real estate? She thought about Mac, the slick guy with the million-dollar smile. Could Marnie and she really do things differently, or did the business itself turn people into greedy, selfish assholes? Shasa had a feeling she was about to find out.

Chapter 6

Elsie Joyce took one last look in the mirror and adjusted her Lululemon top. At sixty-two, she needed her daily walk around Hamilton Lake to keep her spirits up and her figure slim. Her Dachshund, Stina, needed it too. The old girl had a healthy appetite and a potbelly that hung dangerously close to the ground.

Snapping a lead on Stina's collar, Elsie made her way across the manicured front yard and through her cast iron gate. Behind a row of pitched roofs, the lake glistened. She'd chosen the building site for its position, perched on top of a hill, the highest point across the flat Waikato landscape. It was her universe, the crux of her new independence, furnished and styled exactly to her liking. During the divorce, they'd sold the sprawling lifestyle property on the outskirts of town. After decades of pleasing her husband, she was finally free to choose for herself. There wasn't a single chesterfield couch, entertainment unit, or an 80-inch TV in her current home.

Stina pulled her towards the lakeside path. It was Saturday, and the playground was packed. The recently opened outdoor gym attracted youths and fitness junkies. Elsie studied the two girls spinning on a carousel, so happy and carefree. Yet, she couldn't enjoy their smiles, not with the cloud of regret hovering over her. She was a childless woman – not by choice. As much as the thought still stung, she'd been saved from a lot of heartache. Her sister had lost a child in a driveway incident. Her bottomless sorrow had been Elsie's consolation. She'd never experience that pain. Nor would she ever know what it was like to love someone that much.

It is what it is, Elsie told herself firmly. That's what the therapist had said. *It is what it is.* So simple, so underwhelming, but in the end the thought comforted her. She had to let go of things she couldn't change. The horrible thing about the divorce at her age was the space it created for introspection. For so long, she'd been consumed by Jeff, his business ventures, his goals, his legal battles. Without Jeff, she had to look at her own life. What did she want to do? Who did she want to be? It was terrifying.

Elsie picked up speed, and Stina complied, her potbelly wobbling from side to side. Pounding the pavement always helped. She could almost outrun the darkness. A bead of sweat trickled between her shoulder blades. The morning was gorgeous. Everything was possible. She could get into volunteer work, do something good. She could be remembered from something in her own right, not as the discarded ex-wife of property guru Jeffrey Alders.

Elsie's thoughts were cut off by a flash of green and a flurry of giant, square snowflakes. She hit the asphalt and tasted blood.

It took her several seconds to put together the chain of events that led to her fall. The green was a speeding Lime scooter. The snowflakes were white papers belonging to a young woman with a man's haircut, who was duct taping notices onto the brick feature wall when the scooter had driven around it.

The young woman helped Elsie up. "Are you okay?"

Elsie brushed her clothes, embarrassment running through her veins. Had anyone seen that? There was nobody else in close vicinity, thank God.

Where was Stina?

The lead was still in her hand and the dog seemed fine, moving about her feet. Her face hurt. Had she actually hit the ground? She'd landed on her hands and knees; she was fairly certain of that.

The young woman looked at her with a strange expression, as if searching for words.

"What is it?" Elsie demanded.

The woman rummaged through a purse that looked like some kind of Middle Eastern camel saddlebag and pulled out a packet of tissues. "Here. You're ... bleeding."

Elsie accepted the tissues. The packet was opened, but they seemed unused. A mirror. Was there a mirror somewhere?

As if reading her mind, the woman returned to the saddle-bag and found a scratched-up powder container. The 'vegan makeup' advertised on the cover was all but gone, but Elsie wiped the mirror with a tissue and peered in.

"Oh, my God." The side of her cheek was bleeding. She dabbed the blood with a tissue, revealing a long graze along the left side. She felt like she'd just been punched in the face; it would probably turn into an almighty bruise.

The young woman nodded. "I think he hit you with the scooter handlebar. He should've stopped. But he was under-aged, maybe twelve. They're not allowed on Lime scooters, so they're scared to get caught riding them."

Was this woman making excuses for the rascal who ran her over? Elsie huffed in disdain and handed back the sorry excuse for makeup. She exhaled and turned around, ready to return home. Maybe after a strong cup of tea and a thick coat of makeup, she might be able to show her face in public again.

Elsie pulled on Stina's lead to get the old girl moving, but found her dog stretched out on the lawn, enjoying enthusiastic attention from a young girl with dark ringlets.

The young woman urged her child to say goodbye to the dog. "Lilla, sweetie, let's go. You can help mummy hang all these posters."

Elsie wondered how she'd missed the child. She must have been there the whole time. Thank goodness she hadn't been in the path of the wretched scooter.

"She's so cute, I love her," the girl gushed, trying to give Stina an awkward hug.

Elsie had to admire the dog's patience. She didn't seem the least bit bothered by the smothering display of affection.

The young woman picked up the last one of her discarded papers, sliding the pile back inside her bag. She wore a pair of colourful parachute pants that looked ridiculous on non-ethnic women. She must have been one of those alternative types, the kind that believed in vibrations and burned incense in every room. Elsie eyed the little girl's colourful outfit – pink, purple, yellow and green. Would anyone teach her how to dress, how to walk in heels or choose the right hairdresser? The mother's haircut looked suspiciously home-made.

The young woman smiled and handed her one of the papers. "I work at the nearby community house. We're putting up flyers about this cohousing meet up. It's the first one, we're just gauging interest."

Maybe it was the recent hit in the head or her sudden affection for the little girl, but Elsie didn't do her usual gracious hand wave, the one she used to stop the fundraisers and campaigners in their tracks.

"Uh huh." Elsie glanced at the flyer. Why an earth would she be interested in something like that? She could easily afford to live on her own. In all honestly, she could afford several houses, but couldn't be bothered with property investment, the field her ex-husband had dominated, so she'd put most of her money in conservative funds. Yet here she was, reading a home-printed flyer on cohousing. The absurdity of the situation was almost amusing.

The young woman, encouraged by the smile she'd misinterpreted as interest, spoke with enthusiasm. "It's such a great idea, building houses to serve the community rather than the other way around. Have you ever thought about how the property developers get to decide everything? They aren't the ones living in those houses, but they make all the choices. What if I don't want a double garage? What if I want to have a safe play area for my kids, instead?"

Elsie smiled. "Aren't they making decisions based on what sells, what the consumers want?" That was exactly what Jeff would have said, she thought with a shiver. Had she any thoughts of her own?

The girl flicked a short strand of hair away from her eyes. "How would they know? If the only type of house available is the one with a double garage, surrounded by a two-metre fence, that's what people buy. I never thought there could be a better way until I heard about this village in Auckland..."

"Okay, okay." Elsie waved her hand to shut down the marketing speech. "I appreciate your enthusiasm, it sounds lovely. But I have my own home, which I've designed to my liking. I suppose I'm very lucky to be that comfortable." She tried to sound gracious, with a magnanimous smile, but the pain on her face made it difficult.

The young woman stepped back, matching her smile. "That's great. You don't happen to know anything about property development? We could really use someone with expertise."

The throwaway comment carried such underlying exasperation that Elsie felt a tug in her gut. Hadn't she just thought about doing something good, volunteering? She did have expertise, and she had to admit, the idea of helping others by sharing her knowledge was rather appealing.

"I was in the property business for two decades, with my ex-husband."

The young woman's eyes widened as she took in her tentative admission. "Wow! You'd be a treasure trove to us. Would you please consider coming along, even just once? We have so many questions..."

Elsie carefully folded the piece of paper. "I'll think about it."

Ten minutes later, as she opened the door to her empty house, she'd made up her mind. She would join this meeting. If it worked out, she could end up doing something worthwhile, something memorable. This could be her legacy, advising young people on how to get onto the property ladder. She wouldn't be a rich, old divorcee, wasting long days with a book and a glass of wine. She was going to achieve something.

Chapter 7

Mac pulled up in his parents' driveway, cringing at the way the loose gravel battered the bottom of his car. Would his father ever budge to get it sealed?

The best thing about visiting his parents was the food. On Sundays, delicious scents filled the house, covering the mouldy odour lurking underneath. Mac smelled lamb and roast potatoes from outside. He reached the door at the same time as two of the neighbourhood kids, probably also drawn in by the smell.

"Tawhiri! Manaia! What up?"

He high-fived the boys and let them in ahead of him. Mac was used to his mother feeding half the neighbourhood. He could never quite understand how she did it with his father's modest pension after a lifetime of pastoring a small church. His mother earned next to nothing, having stayed home with the kids.

"Elijah!" Mac's mother, Sue, was the only one who called him by his Christian name. She hugged him, holding up a spatula covered in chocolate cake batter.

Mac made a mental note to check the back of his T-shirt for batter stains. Not that he ever wore his best clothes for the Sunday lunch. Even leaning on the wall was dangerous in this house. Many a sticky hand had left their mark on the curling wallpaper. I'll tear it all down soon, he promised himself, looking around the dim dining-slash-living area and its flowery, thread-bare carpet.

The table was set for ten. What his parents lacked in number of children, they more than made up for with neighbours. After Tawhiri and Manaia were seated, four more kids showed up. Mac knew his mum would say the empty seat was for Jesus. Sometimes, her preachiness was overbearing. So much so, that his younger brother Isaiah had excused himself on account of 'being stuck in the edit suite' for his new film. He'd carefully avoided calling it work – it was better to be held hostage in a basement than admit to working on a Sunday. Mac didn't mind. He had to come this week, so he'd typed an enthusiastic response in the family Facebook chat, letting Izzy off the hook.

As everyone took a seat, Mac's father, John, strode in from outside. "The prodigal son!" he called to Mac, peeling off a pair of greasy gloves.

He must have just wheeled himself from under the car. In

his retirement, Mac's dad had become a self-taught mechanic. He never seemed to fix the car, as it kept breaking down, but that may have been more about the car itself, a nineties Volkswagen.

Mac narrowed his eyes. "What's wrong with it now?"

"The petrol meter stopped working. Left me on the road this week, had to call AA. The tank might have a dent in it."

"You ran out of petrol?"

"Well, yeah. I thought I had heaps, but the needle just stopped moving."

"He thought God was making the same petrol go longer," Sue chimed in, her eyes wide with amusement as she carried a tray of roasted potatoes and carrots to the table.

"But he wasn't?" Mac asked in mock horror, as he sat at the table.

Mac's father rolled his eyes as he reached the kitchen sink to wash his hands. "I think he was teaching me about the importance of renewing my AA membership. And now I get to learn about petrol tanks."

"Exciting," Mac said with a wry smile. He took it as an encouraging sign that his father, at age seventy-three, still had his mental faculties and a curiosity to learn – even if he was rapidly losing the last of his hair.

"I'll say grace," Sue announced, taking her seat.

After a long-winded freestyle prayer that mentioned each child and their families by name, she opened her eyes at Mac. He mouthed 'Amen', making sure Mum noticed his participation.

Mac finished early, licked his plate clean and went to the kitchen to wash it. The sink was already filled with soapy water, ready for the kids to 'do their part'. The window from above the sink overlooked the backyard.

Mum joined him, peering at the weathered planter boxes. "We have a beehive now. See that box at the back?"

"What? Seriously?" Mac feigned interest in the beehive to create an opportunity to talk to his mum in private. "How does it work?" He stepped out the back door and wandered in the direction of the white box.

Mum followed, chattering about bees and their quirks.

Once they reached the buzzing hive, Mac turned to face the house. From the back of the property, it looked even worse than from the front.

He took a deep breath. "Mum, I need to talk to you about something. An opportunity has come up, a once in a lifetime kind of deal. You might have heard about those neighbours in Auckland teaming up, selling their properties together and making a huge profit?"

Mum cocked her head. "I saw it in the paper. Can't really see why anyone would pay that much, but Auckland's a bit crazy, isn't it?"

"It makes sense for developers. Trust me. If you can combine the sections and put fifteen apartments on them, you make it back pretty quickly. Those homeowners thought they were getting a good deal, but the developers are the ones winning big."

His mum shrugged. "I suppose you know these things. Did you know bees can—"

"Mum, listen. Your neighbour's house is going on the market. I'm talking to the owner and he's interested in selling together with you."

His mum's eyes widened. "But this street is our—"

"Mission field? I know. That's the best part! You wouldn't have to move away. You could move into one of the new townhouses, right here! I'd make sure you get a good deal and the best views. You'd still be here, only in a house that's new and healthy to live in!"

Mac studied his mother's face as she transitioned from dismissive head-shaking to disbelief. Finally, he spotted a flicker of interest.

He pressed on. "Wouldn't it be nice to wake up in the winter without seeing your breath? Not having to constantly bleach the bathroom walls and curtains? You wear a beanie to bed!"

"I'm more sensitive to the cold than your father. It's just a genetic thing..."

"No! It's a sign of poor housing!" Heat rose in Mac's chest. He hated the defeatist attitude of fellow Kiwis, explaining away living conditions that wouldn't have been acceptable anywhere else in the developed world.

Mum patted Mac's arm. "I hear you. Thanks for thinking of us, but I don't think your father would ever go for that.

Where would we live while you're building the new houses? And what would happen to the garden, the bees?"

Mac tried to keep the frustration out of his voice. "A part of the garden would need to be redone, but I'm pretty sure the bees could stay for the time being."

"Which neighbour's selling? The apartments?" Mum's voice rose in concern as she looked at the rundown apartment block where some of her beloved neighbourhood kids lived.

"No, not that one. The other side." As they moved closer to it, the ground sloped up. "If we build on two levels, you'll have lake views! Joining these sections will open up a big, beautiful yard. It'll look much better than ... this."

Through a gap in the ramshackle fence, Mac saw a slice of the blueberry bush the feisty tenant had protected so fiercely. His mind wandered to the girl, and the way her breasts had moved as she'd yelled at him. If he had to be yelled at, which in his line of work was inevitable, he wished it always came with a see-through tank top.

Mum joined him at the fence and peered through it. "Look at the blueberries! It's grown so much!" She turned to Mac. "What's going to happen to Shasa and Lilla?"

Mac frowned. He wasn't surprised that Mum knew the feisty girl and her daughter, although he'd rather hoped that lifestyle or political differences had kept them apart. His mother had commented on the dreadlock-couple and their poor child when they'd first moved in, but she'd never mentioned them since. Based on his ill-fated visit earlier that week, it seemed the woman was now sans a partner.

"They're tenants, they'll move to another rental."

"What about her blueberries? It's a shame, such a beautiful bush. She shared some with us last summer. That's when I learnt her name. Such an odd name, isn't it? But she's a lovely girl."

Mac nodded, trying to keep a straight face.

A sound startled them.

"Hello!" The little girl, standing on the other side of the fence, wedged her head in the narrow gap, eager to get their attention.

His mum gasped. "Oh dear, Lilla! Don't do that, you'll get stuck!"

Too late.

The girl's eyes flashed with panic as she tried to move her head. "I'm stuck!"

Sue tried to wiggle the girl's head free and ended up pulling her through the gap on their side. The girl's hair stuck out at the back. She was wearing another unicorn shirt, this one purple.

"Silly girl! What did you do that for?" Mum combed the girl's dark curls with her fingers.

Mac pointed at her shirt. "You really like unicorns, don't you?"

She nodded in earnest and pointed at the gap in the fence. "Can you push me on the swing?"

Mac laughed. "Sweetie, we're not going to fit through there. And it seems neither can you. Let's take you back through the gate, shall we?"

He led the girl along the fence, to the front of the house. He expected Mum to follow, but she swerved towards the back door. "I have to serve dessert!"

Lilla turned around, her eyes like saucers. "Dessert!"

Mum glanced at Mac, then at the neighbour's house. "Ask her mum if she can join us, will you?"

Mac bit down on his lip. Mum didn't need to know he'd already visited the neighbour's house, or how that visit had gone. The thought of going back to that door made him break out in a cold sweat. Mac took a breath. He dealt with all kinds of uncooperative idiots all day long, he could take one mouthy hippy. Filling his lungs with warm, thick summer air, he let Lilla pull him along the footpath towards the run-down villa she called home.

Chapter 8

Shasa pulled a tray of mini quiches out of the oven and set them on the kitchen counter to cool. Later, she'd put them in the freezer until Tuesday night for the cohousing meeting. They hadn't advertised catering, but now she'd invited the fancy, rich lady, she had to make an effort.

Inhaling the fresh baking aroma, Shasa glanced out of the window to check Lilla was still on the swing. The sight jolted her. The backyard was empty, the swing still. Shasa dropped her oven mitts and ran outside, her heart pounding in her chest. The instant flood of adrenaline that flowed whenever she suspected something had happened to her daughter always surprised her. She urged herself to calm down. Her girl was in a fenced backyard she knew inside out – a safe environment they'd soon have to exchange for a set of unfamiliar hazards. The painful thought squeezed her chest as she meticulously checked each of Lilla's usual hiding spots. No sign of her. The girl had vanished.

A faint knocking made her freeze. It came from the house. Was someone at the door? Lilla couldn't possibly have reached that side of the house. She couldn't scale a six-foot fence.

Shasa ran through the gate into the front yard to be greeted by a double whammy surprise. Lilla ran down the steps from the front door, and close behind her, the smarmy real estate guy, Mac-something, flashed his pearly whites and waved his hand like they were old buddies.

"Hi! I found your daughter."

"Mum! Can I have dessert? Please!" Lilla yanked at her sleeve.

Shasa ignored her. "Mac? What are you doing here? Where did you find her?"

"She got through a gap in the fence."

Lilla jumped up and down, pointing at the neighbour's house. "Mum! Dessert! Can I go?"

Shasa's brain kicked up a gear, trying to piece together what was going on. At least her daughter was safe, if a bit hyper.

"Mac, tell her!" Lilla demanded. "Dessert." She folded her arms, expectant.

Shasa raised her brows at Mac.

He shifted his weight. "Erm ... my mum's serving dessert to the neighbourhood kids. She thought Lilla might want to join?"

Shasa's mouth fell open as she put two and two together.

Her elderly neighbours were Mac's parents! "Your mum?" A small smile crept up her face.

Mac flushed. "Yes, my parents live next door."

This was more than a little coincidental. "Does this have something to do with the property valuation?"

A hint of alarm crossed Mac's face before he regained his composure. "Of course not."

He was lying, Shasa was sure of it. "So, how did you meet my landlord? Coincidence?"

Mac looked annoyed. "Clients find us through many channels. We have a website, email, a phone..."

Shasa studied his face for any further clues, but there was nothing. He must have been taught slippery sliminess at the real estate academy – or wherever they trained these douche bags.

"Dessert!" The child's voice hit a new pitch.

"Okay, let's go then," Shasa sighed and took Lilla's hand.

Together they marched towards the neighbour's house. She heard Mac trailing a few steps behind them. He'd probably expected her to say yay or nay and not get involved, but she couldn't just let a three-year-old run out in the street, could she? Even going to the neighbour's house involved getting on the footpath. If only they lived in a cohousing community where children didn't have to navigate cars or driveways.

It seemed like such a pipe dream, but maybe that's what she needed right now. Anything to take her mind off the fact that she was officially a single mum. She'd finally replied to Ollie with a short, polite, cryptic email she knew would drive him crazy. It was only fair. If he didn't have the balls to come home and talk to her face to face, she didn't have to engage. Besides, if they got into an argument, it would only prove what Ollie claimed to be true – that they were a terrible match and couldn't live under the same roof. Ultimately, that would sooth his conscience, and Shasa wasn't going to give him that. He could live in his happy ship-bubble with this new ship-girlfriend, but she wanted him to know, in his heart, that he'd abandoned his family.

Shasa sighed again, her heart heavy. She'd always known, deep down, that Ollie and she were a terrible match – partly because she'd been faking it. She'd never been a true activist like him. He'd been the one doing research late at night, pulling her into that world. While she agreed with him, she didn't have the capacity to maintain outrage over what was happening on the other side of the world. Having someone like Ollie in her life had made her even lazier. If she looked after their daughter while he fought for the environment, surely that made her good enough by association?

Lilla sprinted ahead of her, through the open doorway to the neighbour's sixties brick house. Neither of them had ever been inside it, but Lilla seemed to know where to go. She took her place at the long, cloth-covered dining table, along with several other kids who were either finished or licking their plates. Shasa remained by the doorway watching.

Mac's mother appeared from the kitchen, smiling brightly in a colourful apron that featured native plants. She placed a piece of chocolate mud cake on the table. "Here you go, Lilla."

She noticed Shasa and Mac at the doorway. "Oh, hi! Come on in! We've met before, haven't we? I'm Sue." She gave Shasa's hand a firm shake. "It's always great to meet the parents. I like your new hair!"

Shasa nodded, her hand brushing her short pixie cut. A visit to the hairdresser had improved it, but she wasn't used to it yet. She glanced at Mac and caught him staring.

"What?" she asked, suddenly self-conscious.

"Nothing. It looks great."

Shasa settled by the doorway to wait for her child to finish eating.

"Would you like some?" Sue asked, lifting another plate of mud cake in her direction. "Plenty to go around."

Shasa shook her head with a polite smile.

"I'll have it." Mac brushed past her and grabbed the plate. He took a seat at the table, right next to Lilla.

"Good, eh?" he said.

Her mouth full, Lilla nodded with the largest range of motion her neck allowed. They looked so cosy together, like old friends. How was it possible? Last time Shasa had arranged a Skype call with Ollie, Lilla had wandered away after a couple of minutes. Then again, she couldn't really expect a three-year-old to engage with a two-dimensional person on a computer screen. They hadn't had any three-dimensional males around, not since Ollie's last visit three months ago, which had only lasted three days. Enough to remind Lilla of his existence, but not enough to close the distance. This real estate jerk was the first man her daughter had connected with in months. Shasa's chest tightened at the thought.

Sue came back from the kitchen as the kids started getting up. "I'll take care of the plates, don't worry. Just go play!"

Lilla's head whipped from side to side as she watched her newly discovered friends run out the door. Shasa could tell she wanted to follow them but didn't want to leave her dessert.

"How about I push you on the swing after?" Mac suggested.

He looked up at Shasa as if he'd just remembered the child was tethered to this annoying adult. Shasa felt weird standing at the doorway, so she joined them at the table.

Mac flashed her a charming smile. "Is that okay with you?"

Shasa narrowed her eyes. "Are you sure you don't have anything more important to do? Like open homes, or inspections?"

"You mean appraisals?"

"Whatever."

"No. I'm enjoying a Sunday lunch at my parent's place."

He seemed infuriatingly relaxed, leaning against the table as he shovelled down mud cake. His close-fitting T-shirt exposed muscular forearms. Without a tie, he seemed more relatable, like someone you could be mates with, not someone you'd slam a door in the face of, which is what Shasa always felt like doing to property managers, real estate agents and door-to-door salespeople.

"Don't real estate agents work all weekend? Gotta get your commissions and so on, to get ahead? It's a dog-eat-dog world, right?" She was being deliberately argumentative, but she didn't care. She hated that she couldn't tear her eyes off his muscles. They made her all wobbly inside, reawakening buried sensations.

Mac licked his spoon, studying her face. "Okay. I can tell you have issues with real estate agents, but maybe you should take up those issues with, you know, real estate agents. Not me."

Shasa frowned. She thought back to their first meeting. He'd worn a tie with those colours, and that pen with a logo. What was it? "Harcourts! You work for Hartcourts!"

Mac looked dumbstruck. "Never worked for them in my life."

"No, seriously. You had a pen sticking out of your jacket. I saw the logo. Dark blue and light blue..."

"Like this one?"

Mac set down his spoon, found a wallet out of his back pocket and pulled out a business card. It was indeed navy blue with light blue stripes, but the company was MacCarthy Developments.

"Maybe it's not the most original branding," he admitted. "But we didn't copy Harcourts, not intentionally at least."

Shasa's cheeks flamed. "So, you're a property developer?"

The corner of his mouth tugged upwards. "I get the feeling you're not a fan of those either?"

Shasa bit her lip, not wanting to start another argument. "I suppose you're a necessary evil."

He laughed. "Wow, that's ... encouraging."

Shasa smiled along, wishing she could swipe the last piece of cake off his plate. "I just think people should have more of a say on how their living spaces are designed, which materials are used..."

Mac looked baffled. "You can always buy a section and design your own house."

"How many people have that option? Houses are so expensive, even the bog-standard ones you guys do."

"How do you know what I do?"

Shasa felt hot. "Well, generally speaking..."

Mac picked up his and Lilla's empty plates and stood up. "I build what sells. You know why it sells? Because people want it."

Shasa stood up as well, though she couldn't match his height. "Want it for themselves, or as investment properties?"

"What difference does it make?"

"When people buy for themselves, there has to be a backyard and a nice big deck. If it's for tenants, a tiny patio with nothing green is fine, right?" Anger seeped into her voice despite her best efforts to suppress it.

To her surprise, Mac shrugged his shoulders and smiled.

"That's true, I suppose. And it's not always nice to the tenants, like you."

His tender voice melted her anger, replacing it with an unsettling shiver.

"Can you push me on the swing?" Lilla piped up, sliding off her chair.

Mac cast Shasa a questioning look, and she nodded, happy that he still wanted to hang out with them. For her daughter's sake, and maybe a bit for herself. He was so different to anyone else she knew. A window to a strange world.

Mac carried the plates to the kitchen and joined them at the door. Lilla insisted on taking his hand as they walked back home, through the gate to the backyard. Mac helped Lilla on the swing and gave her a gentle push.

"Higher!" Lilla yelled.

"I don't want to freak out your mum." Mac turned to Shasa.

Shasa sighed. "Just make sure she stays in one piece, okay?"

Sunlight filtered through the leaves overhead. The sweet scent of ripening blueberries wafted on the breeze. The crop was going to be amazing. The last crop.

Looking at Mac standing in her garden reminded Shasa of their first meeting. "Wait. You're a property developer, but you spoke about the buyer, or a client, or something like that. Who's buying this house?"

Mac hesitated before replying, "My company."

"And how many people are in your company?"

"Um … one. But I have a business partner."

Shasa arched her eyebrow. "So, you? You're buying my house to turn it into some tiny flats with no backyards?"

"Not tiny! And they will have backyards…"

"Whatever! You misled me."

Mac raised his arms in surrender. "I didn't tell you everything because it's none of your business. I told you about the plans because you were so upset about moving. We don't usually discuss these deals with tenants at all."

A wave of conflicting emotions washed through Shasa. He was the one turning her life upside down.

Mac stared back into her flaming eyes. "Why does it matter who's buying the property and building on it?"

Shasa bit her lip, considering the question. If she expected honesty, she had to be honest, too. "I don't know. It gives me someone to blame, I suppose."

Mac shook his head. "Go ahead. Hate me. But I can't cancel a multi-million-dollar deal because of a blueberry bush."

He gave Lilla another big push on the swing.

"Higher, Mac!" She giggled in delight.

Shasa could swear the girl had cartoon hearts in her eyes.

She stepped closer and lowered her voice, making sure Lilla couldn't hear. "I don't really understand what you're doing here. Do you always push little girls on a swing before you make them homeless?"

Standing next to him, she caught his scent, so masculine, so real, that it made every hair on her body stand up.

Mac matched her soft voice, his mouth so close that she sensed his breath on her ear. "The way I see it, I'm spending time with my parents' neighbours. Where I grew up, which was literally next door, that's completely normal."

Shasa hadn't considered that the neighbour's house was Mac's childhood home. She didn't know how to respond. Maybe she would have if she weren't inhaling his scent, his warm breath tickling her cheek. She lived in an all-female household and spent her days at a mostly female workplace. The way her body reacted to being around a red-blooded male was mortifying. She needed to bottle that scent and use it daily in smaller doses, to build up a resistance.

"And I'm not making your homeless," Mac continued, with a smile in his gruff voice. "If you get stuck, I have a couple of rentals vacating soon. Unless it's against your principles to accept help from the necessary evil?"

Was she imagining things, or did he draw out the words? She could swear his voice lingered in her ear. His every breath sent a heatwave down her spine, gathering more warmth down south. Holy crap. She needed to get rid of this guy before she did something she'd regret. Something worse than offending him, or even letting him witness her disastrous housekeeping skills.

Shasa's face flushed. "Why would you help us?"

"How about, yes please? Or thank you?"

"But why?"

Mac flung out his arms in mock outrage. "Can't a guy

help a girl in need?" he bellowed. "And the girl's annoying
mother?"

The stupid joke caught Shasa off guard, and she burst into
laughter. She felt lighter, distracted by his gorgeous grin.

Sunshine kissed her face, warming her, making her see
purple floaters. Lilla leaned her weight back and forth to
keep the swing going. Shasa could tell her daughter was happy. Why couldn't she herself be happy, just for a moment?

Mac's gaze hovered on her lips so briefly she wasn't sure
if she'd imagined it, but she couldn't stop imagining. What
would it be like to kiss him? His hands looked strong, like
they could easily lift her off the ground. Heat rose up her
body, all the way to her hairline. The air between them vibrated. Did he notice it?

Lilla's scream brought her back to reality. She'd fallen off
the swing.

Guilt squeezing her gut, Shasa ran to her daughter. "Where
does it hurt?"

Lilla wailed. A sound of shock, more than pain. The girl
stared at Mac through her tears. "You fell me!"

Shasa hugged Lilla to her chest, probably harder than was
necessary.

Mac lowered himself to their eye-level. "I did. I'm so
sorry."

Shasa glanced at him. "She'll be fine. Just go." Her raw
voice betrayed her. She'd been the one daydreaming. She'd
let her daughter fall.

Mac nodded, getting up. "If you want to talk about the rentals," he said, placing one of the blue business cards in her hand.

The sound of his footsteps faded as he disappeared through the gate. Shasa stared at the card, wondering if she could afford anything he had on offer. Would he negotiate on price? And, most importantly, did she have the nerve to ask?

Chapter 9

"Where do you want these?" Lando asked, carrying two folding tables in the community hall. He'd volunteered to set up the hall for the cohousing meeting in his full cycling gear, including a helmet.

"In the far corner," Shasa instructed. "That way, if you want the food, you have to come all the way in, right? No snacking at the doorway."

"I'd never snack at the doorway! I participate," Lando grinned and began setting up the tables, eyeing the food over his shoulder.

Shasa had dug up an old Edmond's cookbook and baked far more than she'd planned. Lilla had been overjoyed with the spread of cinnamon swirls, scones and cookies. With Ollie, baking had always had an agenda. They made oat milk because it was the best ecological choice. They used hemp protein because hemp could be grown without pesticides.

Lilla perched on a chair next to the catering table, waiting for the treats to be set out. Marnie would let her eat anything she desired. For a woman not yet in her forties, she acted more like a grandmother, maybe because her own kids were all grown up.

Shasa left to boil another jug of water to fill up the pump thermoses. She should have been excited; she'd put in a lot of effort, distributing posters and baking. The previous night, she'd spent hours preparing her presentation. Yet, her mind wandered, repeatedly landing on that moment before Lilla had fallen off the swing. Nothing had happened, she reminded herself. Just a daydreamy moment, a silly urge she hadn't acted on. Although if *he* had, she wasn't sure what she'd have done. Of course, he hadn't. It was all in her head. She'd been alone for too long, and her current reality was depressing. Was it any wonder her mind cooked up delusions? She could certainly appreciate why Marnie preferred fictional men to real ones.

As Shasa returned to the hall with the full thermos, she heard a commotion from the front door – the first guests, an Indian family with three teenagers. She urged them to find seats in the neat semi circles of old classroom chairs.

Three more ladies arrived, holding an animated conversation about kids or dogs. Their bubbly laughter filled the space.

Lando prepared a cup of chamomile tea, his tight, shiny

ass framed by a bumbag. Shasa wondered if the man owned any pants. She also wondered if her long dry spell would eventually make her consider Lando as a romantic prospect. She had to admit the guy was in an impressive shape, even if he did resemble a horse, down to his long face and hairy nostrils, which quivered when he spoke.

"You must be ... Sasha?"

Shasa turned around and stifled a gasp. The rich lady from the park stood right behind her, wearing a crispy white shirt and the most luxurious pair of pants she'd ever seen. The soft fabric moved about her like a curtain in the summer breeze.

Shasa cleared her throat. "It's Shasa."

"Shasa, of course! I'm Elsie." The woman's handshake was tight and cold.

Shasa couldn't stop staring at her diamond watch. "I'm so glad you made it. Can I get you a cup of tea?"

Everyone else had made tea for themselves, but Shasa suspected Elsie was used to being waited on.

"That would be lovely." Elsie smiled and chose a seat in the back corner.

Shasa brought her a cup of black tea with a dash of milk, as instructed. She offered her the baking, but the lady politely refused each item. Maybe she was worried about getting greasy crumbs on her expensive outfit. Well, all the more for Lilla; as Shasa left the catering table, her daughter reached for her umpteenth cinnamon roll.

Once the traffic at the doorway had ceased, and everyone was seated, Shasa picked up her notes and stood up the front. She didn't hate public speaking. At work, she regularly made announcements and ran events, but this wasn't work. She was representing herself, and that notion woke the butterflies in her stomach. She took a deep breath to centre herself. It was good to be nervous, to have that sizzle of energy.

"Welcome everyone! I'm so glad you all made it. Tonight, we plan to go over some basics of cohousing and discuss a possible building project for those who are ready to move on in the near future. We're looking to kick-start with a smaller scale one, something called a pocket neighbourhood..."

From the corner of her eye, she caught Marnie giving her a thumbs-up. She had Lilla in her lap, focused on her phone.

Worried about boring people, Shasa rushed ahead with her presentation, flicking through slides of images she'd found online of other cohousing communities. They came in all shapes and sizes, from tall apartment buildings to individual cabins in a rural setting. Once she made it to one of favourite subjects, the carparks, Shasa relaxed.

"You may have noticed the lack of garages. It's not by accident. Many cohousing communities chose to leave their cars at the edge of the property and keep the grounds completely car-free. This makes it safe for the kids to play in the common areas and saves space."

One of the visitors, a middle-aged man in a Ramones T-shirt, raised his hand. "How do you get groceries to the house? Or deliveries?"

"I understand most people just carry their groceries. If it's a larger cohousing village, they might have a cart they use, or a bike. And if someone needs to get a larger item delivered, the houses are usually accessible by car."

The man said, "But, what if—"

"My sister lost her child to a driveway accident."

Elsie's commanding voice echoed in the hall. Everyone fell quiet, staring at her.

She kept her chin up, unfazed by the attention. "I used to think we just needed to keep kids in fenced backyards. But kids want to visit their friends, and the little ones follow the big ones. New Zealand has the highest reported rate of driveway accidents in the world. Our current model doesn't work. We've chosen our own convenience over our children's lives."

The Ramones man sat down, his mouth hanging. Surprised by the impromptu speech, Shasa shot a smile at Elsie and flicked onto the next slide, continuing about how most cohousing communities were run. When she got to the last slide, her stomach lurched. What now? She didn't know many of these people from a bar of soap. How could she start talking about building a house together?

As if sensing that she needed help, Marnie shifted Lilla onto another seat and stood up. "Thank you, Shasa, for preparing this amazing presentation, and introducing us to these inspiring housing projects! Let's give Shasa a big hand."

After a wave of scattered clapping, Marnie explained that

they were planning a small-scale cohousing project. Having once been a teacher, she still had her teacher voice, one that always soothed Shasa. Her heart swelled as she listened to her friend describe the pocket neighbourhood of urban townhouses they'd envisioned together on that first night.

"So, if you're interested and ready to take the next step, please stay back and let's chat," Marnie finished with an enthusiastic smile.

The room fell silent. Shasa's heart hammered so loudly she was sure everyone could hear it.

The Ramones man stood up. "Yeah, that's all good, thanks. I'm not looking at buying right now, so..." He made his way to the door, followed by the Indian family and a couple of others.

With only two people left, Shasa's shoulders sagged. One of them was Lando, who she knew had nothing to his name. She watched him bag two mini quiches in his bumbag and head out the door.

The other was a young woman in a tight ponytail and a bright blue blazer, who approached them, sticking out her hand. "Barbara Bell, Waikato Times. Once you get this project off the ground, I'd like to interview you. It'd make a great story."

Shasa shook her hand, trying to hide her disappointment. The woman handed them a business card and left, her heels clicking against the hardwood floor.

The door slammed behind her, and it was suddenly very

quiet. Shasa looked at Elsie and Marnie with Lilla in her lap. So that was it? A big, fat zero.

Elsie cleared her throat. "You asked me here to advise, so ... There's a real shortage of large sections in the city, and you're competing with the property developers. I wouldn't worry too much about finding the people. Securing a section is the first step."

Shasa perked up, thinking of her conversation with Mac.

"My rental! It's on a large section and it's for sale. The developer's going to build apartments on it. I don't think the sale's finalised yet. Is it possible to, you know, swoop in and make an offer?" Shasa explained the location, the state of the current house, and what she'd found out from Mac.

Elsie's eyebrows lifted at the mention of his name. "Mac McCarthy? He's done some high-profile deals. Frankly, I'm surprised he's told you that much about his plans."

Shasa flushed. "He probably didn't think it would matter, since I'm just the tenant."

Elsie looked into the distance like she was calculating something. "Mac has done business with my ex. It sounds like he's trying to keep this on the down low and not get into a bidding war. Maybe he's made a low-ball offer? That could give us an opportunity."

Shasa took a deep breath, a flicker of hope in her heart. "Could we save the garden?"

Elsie nodded. "Maybe. Having a good architect will help. I happen to know a great one."

Shasa smiled and turned off the projector. It must have been lovely to have such confidence. Lilla yawned, leaning on Marnie's chest.

Shasa gestured at the girl. "I need to take her home."

Elsie held up her hand. "Before you go ... I wasn't planning to get involved, but a lot of what you said tonight really resonated with me. It never occurred to me to challenge the way houses are built, even after my nephew died..." She took a moment to compose herself. "I like the concept. I couldn't live in a two-bedroom unit, but I'd be happy to invest, especially if we can secure a section on Marama Street."

Marnie straightened up. "So, you wouldn't buy one of the units, but you'd own part of the entire property?"

"Something like that. We can suss it out with the lawyers."

"And you'd be part of the decision-making?" Shasa asked.

Elsie smiled. "As an advisor, not to overrule you."

Shasa glanced at Marnie. Was this for real? Could they trust this lady? Her friend gave her a slight nod.

Shasa sighed from relief. "Honestly, that sounds wonderful."

"What are the next steps?" Marnie asked.

Elsie stood up. "Council. We should go and find out as much as we can about the section."

Shasa took a deep breath. "Would it possible to go together? I'm not sure I'll ask the right questions."

Elsie reached out her hand, as if to pat her on the arm, but before she made contact, her fingers curled up and she grasped a fistful of air. Her smile didn't waver. "Of course."

Chapter 10

Shasa held Lilla's hand as they stepped through the sliding doors into the deserted council lobby. Lilla let out a high-pitched cheer, excited by the vast, empty space. Shasa cast an apologetic glance at Elsie, who offered her a quick smile and headed straight to the receptionist.

"Is the town planner available?" she asked, leaning over the counter.

The receptionist removed her headphones and smiled. "Morning, Mrs. Alders! Yes, he is. Go ahead."

Mrs? Wasn't she divorced?

Elsie led them down the corridor, through an open doorway.

An elderly man behind a messy desk looked up from his computer screen. "Come in." His face was weary, but his eyes kind.

Shasa sat down with Lilla on her lap, leaving the other chair for Elsie.

The town planner only had eyes for Elsie. "Mrs. Alders."

"Hi, Earl," Elsie spoke softly. "It's Miss Joyce now."

"Right. Right. What can I do you for?"

Elsie reached a pack of post-it notes on his desk and wrote down Shasa's address. "We're looking at building on this section and need to check the basics."

Earl typed on his computer. "How have you been?"

"Very well, thank you. You?"

"Busy. Grandchild number four should be born any day now."

"Wonderful!"

"So, here's the section..." Earl angled the screen so they could see the aerial map. He talked at length about water, power and wastewater connections, pointing at various co-loured lines crisscrossing the map.

Shasa held onto Lilla, who fidgeted in her lap.

"I'll print these out for you," Earl said, then lowered his voice at Elsie. "Are you ... needing the neighbouring section as well?"

Shasa opened her mouth to answer, but Elsie placed her hand on hers. "Yes, that would be great," she replied with a charming smile.

The printer whirred to life. Shasa whipped her head left and right, trying to figure out what was going on. They were only looking at buying one section, right? But Elsie's cold, firm hand remained on hers, keeping her silent.

The printer churned out a pile of maps and documents, most of which had distorted text and dark edges, like they'd been scanned from ancient microfilms and then xeroxed to death.

Moments later, they stepped out of the sliding doors.

"What was that?" Shasa drew a deep breath, like she'd just surfaced from underwater.

Elsie urged them away from the door, towards the lifts leading to the underground carpark. "Let's talk in the car."

The lift smelled like fresh urine. Lilla held her breath with such determination Shasa feared she'd pass out.

Finally, they all sat in Elsie's car, inhaling the scent of leather interior and elegant perfume.

Elsie navigated out of the carpark. Once she turned on the road, she pointed at the pile of papers in Shasa's lap. "Earl and I know each other from a long time ago. He ... um ... he's been watching out for me. My ex-husband Jeffrey and I have different approaches to business. He does calculations, I trust my instinct. Jeff started keeping things from me and I'd find out when it was too late, so I asked Earl to let me know which properties Jeff enquired about. As a public servant, he was uncomfortable about it, so we came up with a shorthand. I'd see him about a property, and he'd ask if I wanted to print out *the other one* I'd enquired about earlier, and that would be the one Jeff had seen him about."

A sizeable lump took residence in Shasa's throat. "Oh, my

God! Is your ex-husband buying the house next door?"

Elsie slowed down to stop at traffic lights and turned to face her. "I don't know. He has a connection to Mac, which makes me suspicious. But they haven't done business together for a while. Not since Mac started his own company..."

"Wait! Which neighbour is it?" Shasa flipped through the papers in her lap and uncovered the two maps. "Mac's parents' house! Of course!"

"What?" Elsie glared at her.

Shasa's cheeks flushed. How had she missed this? She should have told Elsie about it from the start. This made it sound like she was covering something up. If they were going to do business together, she had to be more transparent. She couldn't be like Jeffrey, who sounded like a self-important jerk.

"Mac's my friend! He pushed me on the swing," Lilla announced happily from the back seat.

Shasa took a breath and explained how Mac had shown up with her daughter the second time, and how they'd ended up eating dessert.

"Then he pushed me on the swing!" Lilla yelled out again.

Elsie smiled. "If I didn't know better, I'd say he was infatuated with you."

"But you *do* know better?" Shasa blushed at her own question. Did it really matter what the property developer thought about her? Still, she couldn't help her stomach tightening as she studied Elsie's face for clues.

Her new friend's hands tightened around the steering wheel. "If he's anything like my husband, he most likely has an ulterior motive."

Shasa's cheeks blazed. "You mean like ... getting me into bed?"

Elsie laughed. "No! Don't get me wrong, you're a pretty girl and all, but you're not really his type. I mean, maybe he's looking at you as a prospective tenant for one of his properties. It's hard to find reliable tenants and sounds like you've done a lot of gardening. You're not a drug user, and you have a job."

Shasa shuddered. She'd thought Mac had offered to help them find a new rental as a favour, wondering if he cared about her. She was the most gullible person alive. Why had she even suggested he'd be after her? That moment in the garden had definitely happened purely in her head.

"So, what happens next?" she asked Elsie. "Do we just make an offer?"

"First, we need a solid plan and buyers who are ready to sign a contract. Maybe you should hold another meeting at the community house, cast the net wider?"

"But what if Mac buys the section?"

"Give me your landlord's details, and I'll make sure he knows there's another interested buyer. He won't sign anything if he thinks he can get more."

As agreed, Elsie parked outside Lilla's day care, down the road from her house. From there, Shasa only had a ten-minute walk to the community house, something she now appreciated more than ever. What if they had to move to the outskirts of town and drive everywhere? She barely had enough money to keep her car on the road. If she had to start filling up the tank twice a week, she'd have to dip into her meagre house deposit.

After helping Lilla and her temporary booster seat out of the car, she turned back to Elsie.

"Thank you so much! I'll set up the next meeting. How about this weekend? People might be more available on a Sunday afternoon."

"Sounds good. Send me the details, and I'll be there. Let me know if I can help distribute the flyers. I can do it when I walk Stina."

Shasa blinked, attempting to keep a straight face. She couldn't imagine Elsie putting up posters in public, but she wasn't going to refuse any help.

They made plans to do a walk together, so Lilla could play with the dog. As Shasa waved goodbye to Elsie's shiny Maserati, she couldn't help wondering if her new friend also had an ulterior motive. Either way, she wasn't really in a position to look the gift horse in the mouth. She'd already pinned her hopes on this crazy plan. Shasa took a wobbly step towards the kindergarten's gates, squeezing her daughter's hand. She really hoped this would work.

Lilli Amanda

Chapter 11

"Shit. Shit. Shit." Rick's voice blasted from Mac's earpiece. "This is a disaster! How did she find out?"

Mac focused all his energy into emitting the correct emotion. Baffled. Flabbergasted. Absolutely stunned. "I honestly have no idea. She must have psychic abilities."

It sounded convincing, at least over the phone. Rick couldn't see the sweat stains under his armpits or the panic in his eyes.

"Elsie Alders?" Rick repeated.

"Not Alders. They divorced last year."

"Fuck! So, she owns half the empire now? We can't even go to Jeff?"

He was right. Jeff might have been willing to negotiate, but Elsie was a different story. From what he'd found out online, the divorce had been acrimonious. She wouldn't pander to her ex-husband's business partners.

Mac stopped at the traffic lights and picked up his take-away cup. Empty. Coffee. He needed more coffee.

"Don't worry," he told Rick. "I'll figure it out. I'll take care of this."

Rick's voice rose an octave. "How?"

"I ... have an idea."

He ended the phone call with a sick feeling. There was no question. The pixie-haired tenant had blabbed about his plans. He found it hard to believe she knew someone like Elsie, but anything was possible.

After a few minutes, Mac turned onto Marama Street. He slowed down well before the house and parked behind a van. He wasn't sure how he was going to take care of anything, but this was the logical place to start. The chick knew something, and he had to find out what it was. Shasa. A ridiculous name. He'd double checked the spelling from the tenancy agreement, not trusting his mum's pronunciation.

Just as Mac got out of the car, the gate opened, and Shasa stepped out, holding her daughter's hand. She wore a pair of what seemed to be an infinite selection of those brightly coloured harem pants. Maybe she didn't own any regular pants, like jeans. The inside of her house had looked like an ethnic second-hand shop.

Mac considered confronting her, but Shasa turned in the other direction and headed towards the lake. In her free hand, she held a stack of papers. Mac took a few steps to keep the girls in his sights. It wasn't hard; her bright red pants flapped in the breeze, catching the golden evening sun like they were actually on fire. She had a nice ass under all that draping. Mac trailed behind the duo as they arrived on the lakeside path and turned left towards the playground. The dusk horizon glowed pink with clouds of sandflies on the move.

Shasa stopped and scooted in front of a rubbish bin. Was she really a dumpster diver? Mac cringed, unable to look away like watching a roadside accident. If she pulled out a half-eaten pizza, he'd die. To his relief, Shasa didn't stick her hand in the bin but attached a piece of paper to it. When done, she got up and chased after her daughter, who'd run ahead of her. Mac waited for them to disappear behind a cluster of huge gum trees and approached the rubbish bin. What could the poster be about? A lost cat? A new rental? That would make sense, but surely it was better to just do a search online than to tape posters on bins around town. These alternative types were into all kinds of weird shit, though. Maybe she was scared of wi-fi.

When Mac finally reached reading distance, the penny dropped. This was the answer he'd been looking for, and he knew exactly what to do.

Chapter 12

Shasa arrived at the community house an hour early on Sunday to air out the hall. She had no idea how many people to expect. They'd distributed twice as many flyers and posted in a couple of community Facebook groups. The Facebook event showed ten confirmed guests and another fifteen 'maybes', but she knew better than to trust Facebook commitment.

Lilla ran in ahead of her, dancing to music only she could hear. Shasa went to the kitchen to boil the jug. This time, she'd kept the catering to a minimum – tea and biscuits.

Twenty minutes later, Marnie arrived, closely followed by Elsie. Five minutes to four p.m., the chairs were set up and Shasa spotted the first attendee. Lando. His smile waned as he eyed the catering table. A steady crowd followed him, a mix of ethnicities, old and young. A buzz of conversation filled the room.

Shasa took her place by the projector, feeling more comfortable than the first time. She knew her presentation inside out. They had a plan, and it was all thanks to Elsie. She'd briefed in her architect and had spoken to Shasa's landlord, who'd agreed to wait two weeks to hear their offer. Elsie's confidence was contagious. For the first time in months, Shasa felt excited.

Her excitement must have taunted fate, because that's when he entered. Mac McCarthy – the man who could throw her instantly off kilter. In worn jeans and a soft T-shirt, he looked like he was in a disguise.

Elsie appeared by Shasa's side, her eyes wide. They had no time to voice the questions hanging in the air as Mac strolled across the floor to greet them.

"Ladies." He touched the brim of an imaginary hat.

"Mac!" Lilla shouted from the other side of the room and ran to him. She hugged his legs and looked up with practised doe-eyes. "Will you play with me?"

She raised her arms and Mac picked her up, cradling the girl on his hip like the favourite uncle.

Shasa found her voice. "What are you doing here?"

Mac's eyebrows arched in perfect innocence. "I saw a flyer taped on a rubbish bin and it piqued my curiosity."

Shasa huffed. The whole thing stank to high heaven. "Seriously. What's going on?"

"Am I not welcome?" Mac's voice had an edge. He dug up

one of their flyers and pointed at it. "It says here 'everyone welcome' but I guess that's just marketing talk?"

Shasa filled her lungs, ready to give him a piece of her mind, but Elsie stepped in. "Of course you're welcome, Mac. Have a seat. Would you like a cup of tea or a biscuit?"

Mac responded to her honeyed, commanding tone and followed her to a seat at the far end of the front row.

With Mac just out of earshot, Elsie returned to Shasa. "Don't panic. Just do your presentation the way you planned. I'll handle the bit after, okay?"

Shasa nodded, still holding her breath. Her earlier confidence had been drowned by a surge of nerves. Could she do this with him watching? Part of her brain worked on connecting the dots. Why was he here? Why was he dressed like that? But she had no time to find the answers, she had to focus on the presentation.

Marnie gestured at the light switch, casting Shasa a questioning look. Shasa nodded, so Marnie dimmed the lights and took her place in the front row, coaxing Lilla to sit next to her.

Was the energy in the room different, or was it just her? Shasa fumbled with her notes, her fingers sticky. The projector whirred to life, blasting its light on the blank wall, leaving the rest of the room in relative darkness. Better. She couldn't see anyone.

She settled on a slower pace than the first time, lingering on the best photos and ideas from existing cohousing projects, especially the community gardens, safe play areas and the lack of garages. She doubted Mac had ever built anything without a garage.

After a while, she almost forgot about him, until she arrived at the last slide and powered down the projector. Marnie ran to turn the lights back on, and Shasa took in the small crowd, which looked at her expectantly, as if waiting for her to finish a sentence. All except Mac, who leant back in his chair, an inscrutable expression on his face.

To Shasa's relief, Elsie stood up and took the stage. "Let's thank Shasa for her wonderful presentation on cohousing!"

The applause was more pronounced than the first time, making Shasa's cheeks flush. She took a seat next to Lilla, who was curled up sideways, staring at something on Marnie's phone.

Elsie joined the clapping. "I know it's a lot to take in. We're inviting you to think differently about living and building community. The next part is only for those who are further along in your journey and looking for the right community to invest in. If you're ready to talk numbers, please stay. For everyone else, thank you for coming!"

Shasa sighed. They'd originally planned to pitch their building project to the entire group straight after the slideshow, but this was better. The faster they got everyone out, including Mac, the better.

As people began trickling out of the room, Shasa looked pointedly at Mac. He sat back as if he had no intention of leaving. Soon, he was the only one left.

Shasa's shoulders sagged. The dream that had kept her up at night was slowly slipping out of her grasp. The only silver lining was that they could now get rid of Mac without revealing any details of their plan.

Elsie approached him. "I'm sorry. It looks like we have to cancel the next part. Thank you for coming."

Mac looked around the empty room, widening his eyes in mock sympathy. "Can't believe no one's interested. How many investors are you after?"

Elsie held up her hand. "Come on, Mac. You're not going to get anything more out of us. It's time to go home."

"Wait, is this Mac?" Marnie asked, finally catching on.

Shasa cast her friend an apologetic look. She'd forgotten Marnie had never met the guy.

Mac got up and offered his hand to Marnie. "Mac McCarthy, pleasure to meet you." His gaze lingered.

What was he doing? Flirting with her friend? Judging by Marnie's blush, it appeared so.

Mac turned to Shasa. "And thank you for the lovely presentation."

He blinked slowly, like he was taking a screenshot of her. The strange gesture threw Shasa, and she blinked back in confusion.

"Bye, Mac!" Lilla shouted, hugging his knees.

Mac picked her up again. "Another unicorn shirt? How many do you have?"

Lilla showed up three fingers, then five, then seven, staring at them in confusion. "A fifteen hundred million," she announced with all the confidence of a three-year-old. She was likely to be as bad at math as her mother.

Laughing, Mac lowered the girl back on the floor, waved, and left.

They stood in stunned silence, waiting for the front door to click shut.

Marnie's eyes were huge. "What was that about?"

Elsie shrugged. "Your landlord must have told him about my phone call and somehow he's figured out what's going on."

Shasa groaned. "Why does he need two sections, anyway? We're building on one, can't he just build on the other?"

She started stacking the chairs and Marnie joined her.

Elsie's soothing voice filled the room. "It makes sense. If you combine the two sections, you can combine the driveways and take away the fence. It creates the effect of extra land. These luxury lakeside condos take up a lot of space. This way, he makes a better profit."

Marnie stopped mid-task. "Wait! Which side section is he after?"

Shasa gave her an odd look. "I thought you knew. The brown brick house on the left where his parents live."

Marnie's eyes widened in shock. "Sue and John are his parents?"

"You know them?" Shasa asked.

"Everyone knows them! I'm sorry I didn't connect the dots. I just assumed it was the other side. I never imagined he could be Sue's son. They're so ... different."

Elsie's eyes moved fast, like she was calculating a chess move. "How do you know his mum?"

"She used to volunteer at KidsCan. Probably still does." Marnie's previous job, before the community house, equipped kids in lower decile schools with food and clothes. "I've bumped into her a couple of times outside your house since then. She's always so lovely."

Shasa's heart sank. "Does that mean we can't go ahead? We don't want to mess up things for John and Sue."

Marnie pursed her lips. "If Mac wants to build a new house for his parents, he can do that on their section. If we stop him buying yours, it just means he can't build all those condos and make a huge amount of money."

Shasa nodded. "Okay. We'll keep going, but no more public meetings. We'll find the right people some other way."

"Online?" Marnie offered. "I can do some scouting."

Shasa shot her a grateful look. It meant so much that Marnie was on her side.

Elsie's eyes sharpened. "We should also try to find out as much as we can about Mac's plans."

Shasa narrowed her eyes. "Why?"

"If we find out how much he's offered for the section, we can outbid him without overpaying."

"We could talk to the people he hangs out with," Marnie

suggested.

Shasa frowned. "How would we find them?"

"If we find out his hobbies..." Marnie trailed off, a blank look on her face.

"I have an idea!" They all turned around to see Lando standing at the doorway, smiling.

"I thought you left," Shasa remarked.

Lando grinned. "Nah, I just went to the loo. I told you I can't invest, but I'm hoping you might hire me to do the landscaping, so I wanted to stay in the loop." He crossed the floor to get closer. "You're talking about Mac? The guy who was here?"

"Yeah," Marnie confirmed. "You know him?"

Lando reached the catering table and swiped the last biscuit. "You know I have a lot of time on my hands, and I'm big on personal development—"

Shasa's mouth twitched. "You'll join any class or group, as long as it's free?" She'd heard him say that before, asking about the next term schedule at the community house.

Lando offered her a good-natured smile. "Very much so. As soon as that guy stepped in, I knew I'd seen him before. I was racking my brain to remember where, but then you said his name and it all came back."

Smiling at his rapt audience, Lando wrapped his biscuit in a napkin, hid it in his bumbag, and launched into a story.

Within five minutes, Shasa knew what they had to do. The idea scared the life out of her, but she steeled her nerves. It was time for Mac to taste his own medicine.

Chapter 13

Mac was the first to arrive. The black theatre stage with one spotlight beckoned him like a magnet. He revelled in its otherworldliness, craving the way it could transport him to another reality. Especially today. The open doors and the spotlight told him Gareth was already there, probably having a smoke by the back door.

It was only Wednesday, but the week seemed endless. He could tolerate risk, but the stakes were too high. He had investors lined up and bills to pay. The leaky houses were sucking up money faster than he could make it. He had to fix them before the problems escalated.

Mac sighed. He jogged across the floor and hopped onto the stage. It would all work out, as long as they secured both sections and the council didn't sit on their plans for too long. Maybe the sweet deal had made him over-confident. He'd borrowed against two of his biggest assets – a huge risk, but the potential rewards were huge. He had to just keep calm and carry on.

Listening for other people, Mac peeled off his hoodie and sneakers and did a few jumps on and off the stage to warm up. Some people approached improv as something they did purely with their minds, but he involved his whole body. He loved the adrenaline boost.

Mac had landed in the group by accident. He'd come with his brother Izzy once, for moral support. Izzy had since transitioned into filmmaking behind the camera, but Mac kept coming. Improv was his secret weapon, one he credited for his career success. He'd learned to observe people, listen more intently, and respond to 'prompts' just like on stage. No more flawed assumptions or negotiating against himself. The more comfortable he became in his own skin, more he noticed how uncomfortable others were, their attention stolen by the inner critic whispering in their ear.

After breaking a light sweat by jumping, Mac heard the back door click and hopped off the stage. Gareth arrived in a cloud of cigarette smoke. Their acting coach was in his fifties, taller than average and surprisingly nimble for someone who carried so much excess weight. He had a fleshy face and a deep, resonant voice.

"Mac! Always the first one, eh?" Gareth slapped him on the back.

The front door opened, and Teana and her friend Brooke

entered. Teana was gorgeous. If it weren't for her blind ambition and appetite for dating anyone higher up in the show biz food chain, Mac might have been interested. Brooke, on the other hand, had a criminal record and viewed acting as one of her last remaining career options. Too bad she had no natural talent. Doing a scene with her was like acting with a vacuum cleaner. She made a lot of noise, but in the end, just sucked.

The girls dropped their handbags as Gareth motioned them to gather on the stage.

"Mac! How're you?" asked Teana.

The door opened again, and the nauseating giggle of two lovers told him it was Hills and April, the couple who did everything together. Hills had been a lot more fun before he'd started bringing his girlfriend. Mac hoped the relationship was short-lived.

Like a 200-kilo gazelle, Gareth lowered his frame down on the stage and patted the floor next to him. "Let's get started!"

As he said it, Mac noticed him glancing at the door. Were they expecting someone new? Now and then they had a visitor, but most people never returned. Mac preferred a bit of turnover. Seeing the same people every week meant getting to know them. He didn't want to be known. Despite several months of weekly practice, Mac had never told anyone else what he did for a living or where he lived. He knew that the minute they saw his car, or his house, he'd no longer be one of them. So, when others discussed their flat inspections and odd jobs, he just listened. Gareth was the only one who knew a bit more about him. A successful director and acting coach, he was hardly a starving artist himself and respected Mac's privacy.

Gareth turned to Teana. "What's on top?"

Teana launched into a detailed account of her flatmate's antics, and her own struggles with employment at a homeware store. "No matter what I do, they only give me two hours a day. Driving there for a two-hour shift, it's just ... I almost quit this week. But I don't have anything else lined up."

Mac nodded along with everyone else. Some days, he only worked two hours by choice. In his world, work hours didn't really line up with money earned. Sometimes, he wished he could tell these people how money really worked, but he doubted any of them had what it took to succeed. People craved security and were willing to trade their time and freedom to achieve it.

"Should we skip you, Mac?" Gareth mused.

"I had a great week," Mac replied. "Met this three-year-old girl who stole my heart. Not in a creepy way."

They laughed at the joke, and that's when the door opened. Before she stepped into the light, he recognised her silhouette. Shasa.

Why was she here? How did she even know about the improv group? They didn't advertise. Watching her diminutive frame approach, Mac felt both violated and impressed. He'd crashed her meeting – now she was crashing his.

Gareth jumped up, extending his hand. "Welcome aboard!

You must be Shasa."

"I am."

Gareth asked Shasa to join their circle on the stage. She chose the spot furthest away from Mac and folded her legs under her body. For once, she wasn't wearing harem pants. In a loose tee and cotton tights, she looked like she was dressed for the gym at YMCA. Shasa wasn't someone who expected diamonds. The thought snuck up on him, twisting his insides. Without the dreadlocks and overload of cheap jewellery, he could see the woman underneath. Understated, yet gorgeous.

The room fell quiet, everyone studying the newcomer with palpable curiosity. Mac wanted to ask her a million questions but couldn't catch her eye.

Gareth cleared his throat. "We were just finishing up our 'what's on top' round. Sharing highlights from the past week. What's been on top for you? You don't have to go into any detail, we just want to know what kind of emotions you've been dealing with."

Shasa looked up, her doe-eyes enormous. Mac almost felt bad for her.

***

Oh, God. What was she supposed to say? Shasa blinked again, hoping for some magical insight to drop into her brain from the shadowy surrounds. Was it necessary for the lighting to be this spooky? Surely people could act little skits or whatever they were doing in a less dramatic setting?

Shasa took a breath. She'd never met any of the others, but Gareth seemed genuinely nice. Sometimes, it was easier to be honest with a group of strangers. "I ... can't say it's been an easy week. A while ago, I was told the house we live in is going to be demolished. On Sunday, we held a meeting for people interested in cohousing, to see if we could get this project off the ground, but ... it didn't go very well."

She waited for Mac to interject, but he simply stared at her, so she continued recounting the trials of trying to establish a cohousing community. "I suppose it wasn't meant to be. Now I have to find another rental and this ... developer ... will knock down our home and build his condos." Her shoulder slumped in defeat.

She had to sell it, make him believe their plan had crashed and burned, and he had nothing to worry about. Maybe then he'd lower his guard and reveal something.

The beautiful Māori girl on her left let out a frustrated growl. "What a jerk! Those guys think they can do whatever they want, eh?"

Others joined in, expressing the same sentiment, grumbling about the wealth gap, a whole generation being priced out of the property market and a few greedy guys who exploited the system to endlessly grow their portfolios. Shasa glanced at Mac, watching his face for any signs of discomfort. He gazed back at her, a tiny smile tugging at the corner of his mouth. Shameless.

Gareth raised his hand, halting the conversation. "Okay, let's move on."

They went around the circle and each person introduced themselves to Shasa. Two of them, Hills and April, were a couple, and a clingy one at that, leaning on each other and holding hands. A girl with a neck tattoo was Brooke, the gorgeous Māori girl Teana. Shasa was disappointed she'd missed the proper catch-up round. Lilla hadn't been too keen to part with her. She'd spent fifteen minutes bargaining with her daughter, hoping to leave without the screaming. In the end, she'd made a dash for the door while Marnie distracted the girl with chocolate.

Gareth gathered himself off the floor. "Okay, let's see if we can get your minds off all that stuff, shall we? Everyone, please get up!"

He turned to Shasa. "Would you be more comfortable just watching at first? If this is your first time?"

Yes! A million times, yes!

Before she could answer, Mac cut in. "No, no! I've seen her on stage. She's not shy. She's here to do improv, and she told me she's dying to jump in." An evil grin spread across his face.

Shasa swallowed a lump rising in her throat. She could have argued or made excuses, but the silent challenge in Mac's eyes strengthened her resolve. She wouldn't give him the pleasure of seeing her back down.

"Happy to go first," she said, her jaw tight.

Gareth cocked his head, his gaze darting between the two of them, assessing the situation.

He shrugged. "Okay. You go first. And it sounds like Mac just volunteered to pair up with you. Let's go."

The others moved off the stage, taking seats in the front row.

Gareth explained he'd give them a prompt, and they'd have to improvise a scene, accepting each other's suggestions. "That's the most important thing to remember. Always say yes."

Shasa stared at Mac. Had she ever said yes to him before? Taking a deep breath, she squared herself to face him. Her whole body bristled, like she'd been dead, and someone had suddenly put in charged batteries. Adrenaline coursed through her veins, clearing her mind.

Gareth browsed something on his phone, then looked up at them. "You're in the waiting room of the doctor's office, and someone just farted."

Mac pulled two chairs from the side of the stage and she sat down next to him. He sniffed the air and looked away, as if embarrassed for her.

She straightened her back, her tone dignified. "It's called irritable bowel syndrome."

Mac looked genuinely shocked. "I'm ... sorry to hear that."

She wrinkled her nose. "You're sorry to hear the sound of someone passing gas? I'd think the smell is a rather more unpleasant."

"Oh, no! I'm here for a cancerous growth in my ... um ... nasal area. I can't smell a thing, but the sound of farting offends me. It reminds me of my disability."

Shasa managed to keep a straight face, but they were interrupted by Gareth's howling laughter. "Okay, okay! Next! You are ... selling shoes at a leper colony."

Shasa took off her sneaker and lifted it up to Mac. "This ground-breaking technology allows you to turn the shoe inside out to easily scrape off any flesh that's left behind when you remove the footwear."

He took the shoe from her and turned it in his hands. "That's fantastic. I've been using a spoon, and it takes me hours."

"Ugh, disgusting!" April yelled, burying her face in Hills' shirt. "Come on, Gareth. Something a bit nicer, please?"

Teana rolled her eyes, but Gareth shrugged. "Okay. You're on a date. One of you is nervous to propose. The other one wants to get a puppy. Go!"

Shasa locked eyes with Mac, heat rising in her chest. She was fine with joking or trying to gross each other out, but this was nauseating. Why couldn't Gareth just assign them roles? Why did they have to figure it out?

Before she could decide what to do, Mac dropped down on one knee. He cleared his throat.

She waited, but he didn't say anything.

Eventually, she threw out her arms. "What are you doing down there?"

He turned his attention to his shoelaces. "I just need to tie these. I think my shoes are coming off."

"Is your leprosy acting up again, darling? Because on those days when your flesh is falling off, wouldn't it be nice to have a bit of help? Someone who could fetch your slippers or bring the newspaper?"

Mac got up and turned his chair to face her, like they were sitting around a small table.

"You mean, like a butler?" he asked, cutting an imaginary steak.

"Yes! Like a butler ... dog."

"You're right, I've been thinking ... on those days when my flesh is falling off—" he paused to give her a meaningful look, while the group giggled in the background "—I'd love to know there was someone in my life I could count on. I feel like everyone's leaving me. My family, my friends, my flesh ... It's very difficult. You're the—"

"That's exactly what I mean! Dogs are so faithful! A well-trained labradoodle would never leave your side."

"But what if it eats the bits that fall off? I was rather thinking ... another human ... someone as principled and self-sacrificing as you could be a better companion. If you'd consider..."

He reached his hand across the imaginary table and took hers. The sensation released a fresh batch of butterflies into her stomach. She couldn't escape his gaze, and it churned her insides. He was good. She almost believed him.

'I love you,' he mouthed at her, a pleading look on his face.

The laughter in the background had ceased. The whole scene was ridiculous, yet something in his eyes held her captive. Maybe it was the freedom of make-believe, the commitment she'd made to going along with the story.

Who would back down first?

Shasa got up and circled the invisible table, angling herself so that the audience could see them both. She took his face into her hands. "I can't believe I never noticed ... you have puppy dog eyes!"

"Woof!" He blinked, fanning her with the most impressive fringe of eyelashes she'd ever seen. She could actually feel the breeze on her face.

"Oh, my God. Don't do that! I can't resist..."

He dropped down on one knee again, and lifted his hands up like paws, curling them under his chin. "Will you marry me?"

"Yes!"

Shasa laughed, expecting Gareth to call 'cut' or someone else to stop them, stop the madness. The room was silent.

Mac stood and gathered her in his arms. "I'd kiss you, but my lips may fall off. Oh, what the hell!"

He curled his hands around her neck and pulled her into a kiss. Soft and hot, absorbing. For a split second, she forgot about the group, the stage and everything else. She was engulfed by fire, white and hot—

"Thank you." Gareth's baritone brought them back to

reality.

Mac let go of her and hopped off the stage. She didn't catch his eyes before he disappeared into the shadow. Was he as flustered as she was? Probably not. He must have been used to this.

Shasa wanted to rush off the stage, but she didn't want to appear embarrassed. She flashed a cheeky smile and curtsied. Whatever had gone down, she'd own it. The group applauded her, and Brooke whistled.

Her cheeks slightly burning, Shasa clambered off the stage, looking for a vacant seat. The only one left was at the end of the row, next to Mac. She briefly considered going for the second row. No. She couldn't. If she was going to own it, she had to sit next to him.

As she settled in the plastic chair, Gareth cleared his throat. "Thank you, Mac and Shasa. That was ... interesting. Great commitment. Let's move on. How about Teana and Hills?"

Hills peeled himself off his other half and hopped on the stage. His girlfriend resettled in her seat, squirming like she'd lost a limb.

Shasa let out a long sigh, grateful for the reprieve. It was such a treat to sit in the dark and watch other people embarrass themselves. She could almost relax. If only she were sitting further away from Mac. Her whole body was hyper aware of him – his knee nearly touching hers, his wide shoulders encroaching into her space. She could smell his shower fresh hair, mixed with a hint of perspiration. Had their scene caused him to break sweat? Maybe he wasn't as cool as she'd thought. Shasa smiled to herself, reliving the kiss from moments ago. It had felt so real, so delicious... She had to stop thinking about it.

Hills and Teana acted out a scene involving Mr and Mrs Santa on a desert island. It fell a bit flat, but Shasa enjoyed watching April flinch every time the other woman stepped closer to her boyfriend.

When they stepped off the stage, Brooke got up.

"April, could you go with Brooke?" Gareth asked.

"I'm not feeling well."

She didn't sound that unwell, but Hills wrapped his arm protectively around her.

"Okay," Gareth nodded. "Who wants to go again?"

He cast an appealing look at Mac, who seemed reluctant but made his way on stage.

Within two minutes, Shasa understood why. Brooke was the worst actor she'd ever seen. Wooden, slow and loud, as if she was performing her own show, completely unrelated to her acting partner. Gareth seemed to know her limitations and kept the prompts simple.

"You are two astronauts floating in space. Go!"

Brooke flailed her arms and made a loud moo like a herd of distressed cattle.

"Is that space sickness?" Mac asked.

She thrust her body as if she'd been knocked by a gust of

wind. "My life is flashing before my eyes like a film. I can see all the important things that ever happened to me!" Her voice echoed from the back of the theatre.

Mac looked like he was trying to suppress a laugh. "Turn off the video feed. There's a button on the side of your helmet."

Everyone giggled. Happy with the response, Brooke stopped the animal noises and broke character, waving at Teana. Then she went back to flailing her arms a like she was falling from the sky.

Mac matched her spastic performance, down to the guttural sounds. "How odd that we're experiencing such strong winds here in outer space. We must be near a black hole or something."

He was a good sport, distracting them from the horror of Brooke's acting, allowing everyone to laugh with them.

After their performance, Brooke beamed and gave him a hug. "Cheers!"

Gareth glanced at his watch. "I'm sorry, I was hoping to do one more round, but we're running quite late, so I'm afraid we'll have to wrap it up. I have a dinner date."

With happy chatter, they filed out the door. Mac veered towards a Lime scooter lying in the middle of the footpath.

Shasa was about to head in the opposite direction, when Gareth's giant hand landed on her shoulder. "Thank you so much for joining us tonight! I hope you come again?"

"Sure, I'd love that!" The excitement in her voice surprised her. She'd enjoyed herself more than she'd expected, but how could she come back? What would Elsie or Marnie think? The thought hit her. The plan! She'd failed to find out anything useful about Mac or his plans with the section. Instead, she'd kissed him on stage and was now under some evil spell, unable to think straight. She was the worst spy in the history of espionage.

Heart hammering in her chest, Shasa hurried away from the theatre, letting the cool evening air fill her lungs. Hopefully, the fifteen-minute walk to Marnie's place would clear her head.

Chapter 14

Mac had just scanned the Lime scooter when Gareth caught up to him.

"Wait up! Can I have a word?"

Mac glanced at his phone screen. "It'll cost you thirty cents a minute."

Gareth laughed. "I'll be brief. I'm running late, anyway. About the girl you sparred with tonight. Shasa. She's got it."

"Agreed."

"You know I'm directing a play at Clarence Street, *Roman Holiday*, based on the old film, a timeless classic. It's been done as a musical before, but never as a dramatic play. The long-term plan is to take it to the new theatre they're building in the CBD. It'll be big."

"Yeah?" Mac held his breath.

Gareth stared at him, dead serious. "I want you to audition

for the lead role."

"Seriously?"

"Seriously."

Mac shook his head. "You know I'm in the property business. This is just a hobby."

"Bullshit." Gareth's expression didn't give in an inch.

Mac loved acting far more than he cared to admit. He couldn't pass on a chance like this. "You want me to audition?" He ran his fingers through his hair.

"I want you and her. You as Joe, Shasa as Anya. The producers are only looking at established actors, but you're my dark horse. I want to prep you two. We'll practice for a couple of weeks, then organise an extra audition after hours, blow their socks off. You in?"

His enthusiasm gave Mac a jolt. But him and Shasa? She wasn't an actor. He was pretty sure she'd come along as pay back for the way he'd crashed their meeting. She was snooping on him like he'd snooped on her. Not that she'd ever find out anything. He knew how to keep his mouth shut.

Mac wondered if Shasa now considered them even. They'd let him sit through their slideshow, dunking biscuits in a cup of tea. He'd put Shasa on the stage. But if you joined an improv group, you had to do improv. And he had to agree with Gareth, the girl had held her own. Shasa had raw talent, a good stage voice and a delicate, expressive face he couldn't stop staring, even if she was a pain-in-the-ass bleeding heart meddling with his business. Mac hadn't bought her spiel about the cohousing project failing. The vendor was still undecided, which meant something was going on.

Mac glanced at his phone. He was out four dollars. Oh, well. "I'm in. But I can't speak for her."

"Find out, will you, and let me know. We'd have to start rehearsing this week."

Mac gulped. "I will."

Gareth jogged towards his car. Mac hopped on the scooter and turned the handle. He could only hope the connection he'd felt with Shasa on stage was mutual. She had every reason to dislike him, but during those moments he'd noticed something else, a heat burning under the surface. The moment they'd touched, a surge of energy had shot through him, forcing him to fight for balance. He hoped there was more to it. He'd need any help he could get to win her over in this timeframe.

Chapter 15

"You did what?!" Marnie's eyes showed way too much white, matching the fridge in her kitchen.

Shasa's face felt hot. "It was just a stage kiss, part of the scene. Isn't that common?"

Marnie shook her head, her earrings whipping. "I don't think so. It was an improv class, right? Where you like ... goof around and make each other laugh?"

Shasa took Lilla's banana to finish it for her. The girl was whiny and tired; they needed to leave before she had a major meltdown.

"It wasn't exactly a romantic storyline," she argued, mouth full of banana. "Farts, flesh-eating bacteria ... it was gross."

Lilla giggled. "Mummy said fart!"

Shasa nodded at her daughter. "See? Comedy gold."

Marnie narrowed her eyes. "And you got from that to kissing, how?"

Shasa took a breath of cool evening air, focusing on the collection of colour-coordinated mugs hanging on chrome hooks. Marnie's place was homey in an old-fashioned way.

"I can't remember. It just ... went like that." Had she steered the scene in that direction? Maybe, but he could have backed out at any moment. If she were complicit, so was he.

Marnie broke into a conspiratorial smile. "So, was he into it?"

"What? No! We were just acting. Honestly, I think he just wanted to wind me up. I could tell he was annoyed I'd crashed his group."

Marnie lowered her voice. "Is he a good kisser?"

Shasa's face burned. Mac was a good kisser. So good that she'd slipped up. For an instant, she'd forgotten everything else, and responded like it was a real kiss, sneaking a brief taste of him. He hadn't pulled away, but she'd been the one to exceed the stage kiss.

"I'm going to take that as a yes." Marnie's face turned serious. "But remember, we're not on the same side here. I know he's hot, but he's in it to win it."

"I know." Shasa swallowed the rest of Lilla's banana to lubricate her throat. "I don't like his type at all. I think I like acting, but that has nothing to do with him, right?"

"Right. You should do an acting class. Maybe we can organise one at the community house?"

Shasa's shoulders relaxed. "Great idea!"

That's what she needed. The night had thrown her into a whirlwind of emotions, and finally something made sense. She liked acting, and she could pursue that on her own. It had nothing to do with Mac or his kissing skills.

Shasa lifted her daughter off the chair, onto her hip. They crossed the kitchen to the front door. Marnie's place had such a lovely feel, so grown up and nostalgic. The fresh tea towels and hanging baskets of fruit always made her feel like a teenager. Her own house was like a student flat she'd decorated on a budget.

"Are those curtains new?"

Marnie smiled. "They were on special. I also got new bathroom rugs and hand towels."

"What's the occasion?" She didn't expect there to be one, so Marnie's telling smile took her by surprise. "There *is* a special occasion? Spill!"

Marnie fiddled with her greenstone necklace. "No, nothing."

"What?"

"The writing group's meeting at my place next time, so I wanted to spruce things up."

Something didn't add up. "Anyone new in the group?"

"You know we haven't had any males since gay Dan left? I heard there's a new guy coming. Someone my age, Berta said. I think the ladies are setting us up, so I'm freaking out a bit."

"You've never met him?"

Marnie blushed. "I saw a photo, and … he's dreamy! I know I'm too old to talk like this, but I can't help it."

"You're not old!"

Shasa glanced at her friend's flowery top and white capri pants. Although no expert in mainstream fashion, she had a feeling Marnie could shave ten years off her age by changing clothes. Based on a group photo she'd seen on Facebook, Marnie dressed exactly like the sixty-year-old ladies in her writing group. One day she'd find a way to bring it up, gently.

They approached the door, Lilla dozing off against Shasa's shoulder.

Marnie stroked a brown curl hanging over the girl's face. "You know what I just realised? We're both single. At the same time!"

"Single mums." The term made Shasa shiver.

"It's not that bad," Marnie assured her, turning on the porch light. "Everybody has baggage these days."

They nearly bumped into the lone character emerging from the darkness. Marnie's ex-mother-in-law, Nanette. Her chignon was partly undone, her eyes wild. "Someone's in my garden. Someone's stealing my tomatoes."

Shasa cast a sympathetic look at her friend, mouthing 'good luck'. Marnie had the patience of a saint.

As she left, Shasa heard her friend's firm and reassuring voice, "You didn't plant tomatoes this year, remember?"

Chapter 16

Elsie was buttering a sandwich for a late dinner when her phone rang. It never rang in the evening and the sound made her jump. She didn't recognise the number and hesitated for a moment before picking up.

"Elsie speaking."

"Hello! It's Earl, from the council. I'm sorry to bother you at home so late." He sounded out of breath, like he'd been running.

Elsie stretched her mouth into a smile, hoping it made her voice friendlier. "Earl! What a surprise."

"I'm just leaving work and was wondering ... I have something that might interest you, a couple of printouts. I'm driving past your house, so I could drop them off at your door or maybe in your mailbox if it's too late?"

Elsie looked at the clock. Seven-thirty p.m. What kind of

nana did he take her for? "No, I was just making a cup of tea. Text me when you're at the gate, and I'll buzz you in."

"Great. I'll be there in fifteen minutes."

Elsie put the phone down, perplexed. She'd never spoken to Earl outside the council building. She was fairly certain town planners didn't make house calls, so this was unorthodox. Something to do with the section, no doubt.

She picked up her phone again and brought up Shasa's number. It was still saved under 'Audrey' as she'd first thought of her. Shasa was such a strange name, and the girl looked a lot like young Audrey Hepburn. At least she would if she'd ditch the ethnic wardrobe for a classier one. She had the figure.

Shasa picked up on the second ring. Elsie explained that Earl was coming over with some papers and asked if she and Marnie wanted to join them. "Just a quick cup of tea at my place, if that suits?"

She heard the little girl talking in the background. Thank goodness she was still up. Elsie hadn't even thought of that. Three-year-olds went to bed really early, didn't they?

"Sounds good. We're just leaving Marnie's. She's got her hands full with her mother-in-law at the moment, but we could stop at yours on the way home. You're somewhere on the other side of the lake, right?"

Elsie gave her the address and ended the call. The phone still in her hand, she sat down in her Eames armchair. What was going on? She rarely had visitors, especially at night. Her social life had shrivelled after the divorce, and she'd been contemplating ways to improve it. Now, it had all happened effortlessly, without any advance planning. Ann Holdaway, her nosy neighbour, wouldn't be able to peel herself off the window when the cars started arriving.

Entering her kitchen, Elsie arranged some Afghan biscuits on a tray anyway, along with cheese and crackers. She also filled Stina's bowl and tried to wake up the napping dog. She feared the old girl wouldn't be much fun to play with.

After a moment, her phone beeped, and she opened the gate to Earl's Hyundai. It was strange to see him here. Standing in the open doorway, she waited for him to cross the yard. He looked as hapless as ever in a cheap, wrinkled collar shirt and shiny polyester pants. If he'd attempted to comb his fluffy hair, the effort was undone by the gentle breeze blowing from the lake. He smoothed his hair with his free hand as the other one gripped a pale-yellow manila envelope.

"Come on in!" she said.

He bowed his head as he stepped in, like visiting a temple.

She led him to the lounge. "It's good to see you."

Earl took a seat on the couch next to Stina. He rested his hand on the dog and stroked her fur, relaxing a little.

Elsie sat in her armchair and indicated at the tray of tea and biscuits on the coffee table. "Tea?"

"Thank you."

She fixed him a cup according to his preference and placed it on a coaster in front of him.

As he sipped the black tea, she picked up the folder. "What's this? It must be important?"

Earl cleared his throat. "It's ... nothing, really. Just an old soil report I dug up. You know how I said there wasn't one? Well, this is old, but it might save you a bit of money." She'd never seen him like this, with a hint of colour on his cheeks, almost school-boyish.

"That's lovely, thank you. Is that all?"

"I know it's not urgent, I'm sorry if I misled you. It's just ... I was just..." He seemed to have lost his ability to speak.

Elsie waited, biting her lip. She'd heard she was intimidating. She wanted to change, but it wasn't easy. People had to work with her, show some courage. Right now, Earl had to take a breath and explain himself.

The doorbell rang.

"That must be Shasa."

Earl looked startled. "Who?"

"One of the people organising this cohousing the project. She was at the council with me, remember? When you told me you're bringing important papers, I invited her along."

Earl's face fell, but he covered it quickly with a smile. "Yes, of course."

Elsie left to get the door, wondering if she'd disappointed him. Had he been expecting to be alone with her? Was there something else in that manila folder – something he wasn't happy to share with a stranger?

The tired toddler hung off Shasa's slight frame like a koala.

"Your place is so beautiful," Shasa said, adjusting the girl onto her hip.

Elsie smiled at her sincere reaction.

"Where's doggy?" Lilla asked, lifting her groggy head.

Elsie led them to the lounge to meet Earl, who was now standing, either out of courtesy or because he was keen to leave. He shuffled his feet, greeted the arrivals and sat down in the same spot.

Shasa chose the opposite couch, her tie-dyed pants flaring like a parachute as she sat down. Elsie couldn't understand her fashion sense, but then again, she didn't really get how that whole generation dressed – denim shirts with hoods, tennis socks in plastic slippers and people shopping barefoot in the supermarket. In her own weird way, Shasa at least made an effort.

Lilla had her hair secured with a host of pink clips, and her eyes nearly crossed from tiredness. She climbed on the sofa with her mother and curled up against the sleeping dog, falling asleep in seconds.

Elsie looked at the sleepers. "I'm sorry I called you in so late. Let's keep this brief."

She turned to Earl, expecting him to continue where he'd left off. It was easier to study him like this, with other people present. He was slim and slightly hunched with thinning hair, but his eyes were bright and youthful, like he was hiding his vitality under a layer of office dust.

Earl twisted the manila envelope in his hands. Instead of

opening it, he got to his feet, addressing Shasa as he spoke. "I'm sorry you got brought into this. I don't have any important information, only a soil report which I easily could've emailed. The reason I came over ... I suppose I was just hoping to catch up with an old friend. I now realise I should've been more open about that. I'm quite rusty. Apologies."

He turned to leave, then swivelled back to drop the envelope on the coffee table and turned once more in an awkward pirouette. Elsie was so stunned she took several seconds to follow him to the door. By then, he was already in his car with the engine humming, waiting for her to open the gates. Elsie stepped outside, trying to catch his eye, but he stared ahead, knuckles white around the steering wheel. She swallowed and pressed the button on her remote, allowing him to drive away.

Shasa appeared behind her. "Oh, poor Earl," she said, her eyes full of compassion.

"Poor Earl?"

"He's obviously in love with you, and then we showed up."

Elsie shook her head in disbelief. They returned inside and sat down. Lilla slept peacefully, her hand around Stina's neck.

"We should ... probably go, too." Shasa cast her an uncertain look.

Elsie pointed at the tray. "Since you're already here will you have a cup of tea? I'd rather not be abandoned by two people on one night."

Shasa smiled, biting into a biscuit. "You must get that a lot. Lovesick men showing up with flimsy excuses?"

"Excuse me?" Elsie raised her brow.

"I just mean, you're gorgeous, wealthy. You must be fighting them off."

Elsie exhaled. "I'm really not. I think they're too scared to try." Earl must have been terrified but had still showed up. He hadn't reeked of booze either, like some men who approached her at the club. She had to respect that.

Shasa poured herself a cup of lemon and ginger tea and lifted it to her nose to inhale the steam. "Can I ask, how do you feel about him?"

The question made Elsie nervous. She'd never been with anyone like Earl. A few years ago, she'd have instantly dismissed him as a submissive beta male. Working as a Hamilton City town planner wasn't the career path of a winner. He'd been in the same role, sitting behind the same desk, for as long as she could remember.

"He's a fine friend," she replied. "I never realised he fancied me. I thought we just had a common enemy, my husband."

"What did your husband think about him?"

Elsie laughed. "Jeffrey wouldn't have noticed him. Earl was one of his minions. Not someone he'd consider ... competition."

She could have had an affair with Earl without Jeff suspecting a thing, she thought with amusement. Not that she'd ever considered cheating. That was Jeff's domain.

She'd been too busy trying to secure her position as the first lady, the one who couldn't be replaced. And for what?

Elsie sighed, pouring herself another cup of tea. It was lovely to talk to someone other than her dog. She pulled a soft throw over her legs, relaxing into the chair. "For a long time, I thought if I lost my marriage, I'd lose everything – my place in the society, my friends. Everything was tied up with Jeffrey – his connections, his businesses. We made friends with other so-called power couples, and every social inter-action was an opportunity to advance his business deals. It was exhausting."

"And what happened? I mean, after the divorce."

"It all came true. I lost most of my friends and connec-tions." The only ones left were Kerry and Rita, divorcees with whom she did Zumba and had occasional drinks. And now, she had Shasa and Marnie. They were a window to a foreign world. Maybe it was because of them that she could even contemplate getting to know someone like Earl. Her world was getting a little bigger, a little more colourful.

"It's not all bad," she said, a smile bubbling under the sur-face. "I got half his money. Well, half of what he failed to hide. I built my own house, my own way. It's quite enjoyable, you'll see." She gestured around her. Being in this room al-ways made her feel zen.

Shasa gazed up at ceiling. "I hope so. Even if our budget is a lot smaller."

"You'll have to be creative. The most expensive choice is

not always the best. There's a lot of tacky, hideous stuff you can waste money on. I've seen it far too many times."

Shasa finished her tea and stroked Lilla's back. "I better take her home to sleep."

She picked up her daughter carried her to her sardine can of a car, which was parked on the road. Elsie held the car door open and helped her fasten the seatbelt, trying to get the limp rag doll to sit straight enough on her booster seat. Her peaceful, sleeping face brought up the dark cloud again, but it felt more like an old friend, someone she might get used to. She placed a soft kiss on the girl's forehead.

As she closed the car door, she found Shasa behind her, a smile tugging at her lips.

"It's probably not my place, but I just wanted to say that I really like Earl. He seems like a thoroughly nice guy."

"Duly noted, little matchmaker." Elsie couldn't help smiling.

A thoroughly nice guy. No one had ever said that about Jeffrey. Maybe it wasn't the worst idea to get to know some-one different, like Earl. Except that she'd humiliated the poor man. He'd likely never contact her again. If she wanted to see him again, she'd have to take the first step. But what kind of step?

Chapter 17

Mac approached Shasa's house with trepidation. It was past eight o'clock. He'd tried to pick a time when the little girl would be in bed, but not so late he'd risk waking Shasa. In his experience, women were grouchy when aroused from sleep.

He'd left his car at home and grabbed a scooter. Parking anywhere near his parents' house ran the risk of his mum spotting him.

Shasa's banged-up nana Toyota was in the driveway. A light was on in the kitchen, although he couldn't see any movement. Mac left the scooter on the footpath and snuck through the front gate. He was grateful the porch light was broken, so he wouldn't be lit up for the neighbours to see. He knocked on the door as softly as possible and waited.

After a moment, he heard footsteps.

Shasa cracked the door, peering at him over the tightly

stretched security chain. "What are you doing here?"

"Hi! Is this a bad time? I have something to discuss with you." He glanced at his parents' house and noticed a curtain moving. "In private, please?"

She shook her head, her eyes bewildered. "I don't think we should be talking at all."

"It has nothing to do with real estate, I promise. And I really need to use the loo. You don't want me to pee on your front lawn, do you?"

That worked. Shasa sighed and opened the door. Just in time. As Mac stepped inside, he heard the sound of his parents' front door, followed by footsteps, probably his dad going into the garage.

Once inside, he flashed Shasa an apologetic smile. "That was a lie, sorry. I don't need to pee. But before you toss me out, can I have a quick word?"

She stared at him like she could hardly believe her eyes. "You're ... you're..."

"Charming?" he suggested.

She huffed, spun on her heels and marched into the kitchen.

He took it as an invitation and followed her. The house was tidier than last time, although no amount of cleaning was going to make the old place shine. He liked her thoughtful touches though, the hand-painted flowerpots and ink-dipped curtains. She used a lot of colour and combined it in ways he'd never seen before. It would work on stage, down to her own mustard yellow top and flowery pants. He thought about going out with her, being seen together. He almost wanted to just to see Rick's reaction.

Shasa sat down at the small, round dining table, and nodded at the seat on the other side. "What do you want?" She sounded exasperated.

He watched for signs of weakness, fine cracks in her armour he'd noticed earlier. She'd loved being on stage, he was sure of that.

Mac sat down and made eye contact. "Gareth's directing a play. He wants you to audition for the lead role."

She took a moment to process his words, slowly shaking her head. "I'm not an actor."

He caught the glimmer of a smile as she said it. At least she wasn't outraged.

"Gareth said he'd get us a private audition after hours. We'd be the wild card or something like that."

She laughed. "It's wild alright."

After a few seconds, her laugh dried up, her eyes sharpened. "Us? You said us?"

"There are two lead roles. It's a play based on an old comedy film, *Roman Holiday*. Have you seen it?"

Shasa shook her head.

"Me, neither. We can watch it. I mean, you can watch it on your own, and I can watch it somewhere else, some other time."

"Because you could never sit next to me for ninety minutes straight?"

He matched her cheeky tone. "That's not fair! You've made it clear you can't stand the sight of me. I was just trying to offer you an acceptable alternative."

She got up and went into the kitchen. "Tea?" she asked, turning on the kettle.

"Do you have coffee?"

"Only instant."

"God, no." He immediately regretted his gut reaction. He should have just accepted whatever tree bark juice she was serving.

Mac rubbed his temples, watching her back as she silently prepared a cup of tea for herself. She sat down at the table, a weary look in her eyes. "I don't have a lot of time for hobbies. I have a kid."

"Is ... Lilla asleep?" he asked.

"No, she's out with friends smoking ganja." She rolled her eyes. "Yes, of course she's asleep."

Mac sucked in his lips, along with the next stupid retort that was about to escape. "Look, if it weren't for this play, and what Gareth said about us playing so well off each other, I'd leave you alone. But ... you're great on stage. I suppose I was hoping we could put a pin on the other stuff and pursue this play together. No matter what happens with ... you know."

"The house?" She shot him a challenging gaze.

Mac took a breath. "The house. The section. Your blueberries..."

Her look softened, and he congratulated himself for remembering the bloody bush in the backyard.

"You like acting, don't you?" he said. He caught her eyes and saw the spark.

"I do."

"Then, do it for yourself!"

She stirred her tea. "But I'd have to do it with *you*. Someone who's putting us out of our home and trying to sabotage..."

"Hey, hey! I'm not trying to sabotage anything! It's all business, nothing personal. It was pretty straight forward before you gathered your leftie troops to buy the same section and sabotage *my* plans!"

Her eyes flashed. "I'm just trying to make an omelette when the eggs are already broken! There are no decent rentals in this town. Somebody has to fight for those who aren't already on that damn property ladder and buying up half the town!"

"And you couldn't do that on any other section?"

He noticed a glimpse of shame as she stood up and said, "I need a bathroom break."

She rushed into the hallway, leaving him staring at her steaming cup.

***

Shasa stared into the bathroom mirror, trying to calm down. She hated this guy. She hated everything he represented. Why couldn't she just ask him to leave?

Of course, she could use this audition opportunity to find

out more about Mac's plans. That's what she was supposed to do. He'd admitted they were messing up his business. Had he meant to say it? If she kept him talking, maybe he'd let something else slip.

She splashed cold water on her face to cool down. She had to get her phone and text Elsie. She'd know what to do. Maybe it was best to keep Mac here a bit longer, to make him think she was considering the play. That way, if Elsie had any questions, she could try to find out the answers.

The idea of playing spy made her heart beat faster. Where was her phone, anyway? In the bedroom?

Shasa made it back to the kitchen, and found Mac sitting back, thumbing his phone.

"I think I heard Lilla, I'm just going to check on her, okay?" She rushed out again, leaving him with his mouth ajar.

He had such a gorgeous face, dark eyes, a sculpted jaw and a delicious mouth perfectly framed by dark stubble. He dressed for success, all tidy and above board, but looked as dangerous as he likely was. A shark. Someone who'd eat her alive and spit out the bones.

Shasa shivered as she snuck into the bedroom, taking in the view of her sleeping daughter sprawled across the bed. Why did toddlers insist on sleeping sideways?

Shasa picked up her phone from the nightstand and sent a group text to Elsie and Marnie: *Mac's here, wants me to audition for a play with him (weird, right?). What do I do???!!*

She stood for a moment, waiting for a reply. Could she risk

bringing the phone with her? On silent, she'd feel the buzz if she had it in her pocket. If she had pockets. Her harem pants didn't come with those. Shasa scanned her wardrobe for options and landed on a pair of grey slacks that could hide the phone. She left her mustard top on, but wrapped herself in a long, white cardigan to hide her cleavage. A double win. She looked like she was ready for bed and could keep her phone discreetly hidden under the layers.

Shasa checked herself in the mirror, brushing her hair with her fingers. Part of her wanted to dab on perfume, but she stopped herself. Ridiculous! He'd think she was hot for him, like every other female in town. Mac was the kind of man she'd been trained to hate – a self-entitled jackass. Years of discussion on the widening wealth gap, white privilege and the mad, unfair ruthlessness of the property market flooded her brain, carrying fragments of truths, statements and sad stories. Shasa rubbed her forehead, trying to push aside the voices. Ollie's voice, the loudest of them all, called for justice, for revolution, for redistribution of wealth. Why was she even entertaining the idea of spending time with Mac? Why did seeing him have such an effect on her?

Shasa stopped at the kitchen doorway and studied his profile, his lips moving slightly as he read something on his phone screen. She wanted to kiss him again, feel that mouth on hers and the hot, white heat between them. Her lady parts agreed, waking up with a powerful jolt. If he knew what was going on in her mind, he'd think her absolutely mad. Well, he probably already thought that.

It's just a physical reaction, she told herself, taking a few unsteady steps towards him.

"Is she okay?" he asked, looking up from the phone.

"Yeah, fast asleep … now."

It was true, technically. She found it hard to lie to him, especially when he looked at her with such concern. It was fake, obviously. He was just a good actor. How could she ever match his skill on stage? It wasn't the same as doing improv. She'd have to remember her lines. And be good enough for a proper paying audience.

"Can you tell me more about the play?" she asked, more to win time than anything else.

His face lit up. "Look who's coming around! I don't actually know too much about the play, but if you're interested, we could meet up with Gareth and he can explain it better. Although he said we should watch the film first, because he'll be referencing that…"

"Whoa, hold on! I didn't say I'd do it. I was just asking…"

"I'm not saying you have to decide now. We could watch the film, meet with Gareth and then decide?"

The phone buzzed in Shasa's pocket. She drained her tea and got up to rinse her cup. As she stepped behind the corner separating the kitchen from the dining area, she fished the phone from her pocket. There were two messages.

Marnie's text began with a row of surprised emojis, like a tiny choir of yellow faces singing: *Oohh, he's snooping! You should do the same! Just be friendly, get him to talk. Find out how much he offered for the section!*

Elsie didn't do emojis. *Or find out his budget. Ask about the number of apartments, who the buyers are. That information would be valuable.*

Shasa replied with a 'thumbs up' emoji and hid the phone in her pocket. Elsie and Marnie were right, but how could she pull this off? Her nerves vibrating, Shasa placed her teacup in the sink and returned to the table, feeling like a dirty double agent. But her friends trusted her. They were investing in her project, and that's where her allegiance had to lie.

"Okay," she said, looking him square in the eye. "Let's watch that film."

She refused to flinch or to look away. He met her stare with such excitement she had to swallow a hot ball of guilt. I'm not lying, she reminded herself. Part of her longed to curl up on a couch next to him and inhale his scent, with his hand roaming under her skirt ... Okay, she didn't actually care about the film part. She was just lonely and horny.

"Tomorrow night?" Mac asked.

"Sure."

"Is it easier for you if we watch it here, after Lilla goes to bed?"

Shasa blushed. "I don't have a TV."

He looked around the room like he didn't believe her. The corner of his mouth tugged upwards. "Sorry. That's okay. I can bring my laptop?"

Shasa's fingers brushed against her pocket, feeling the outline of her phone. If he invited her into his house, she had a much better chance of snooping around. "I can get a sitter. Marnie's usually happy. She just brings her iPad and writes here instead of at home." She kept her expression neutral, like she didn't mind either way.

"Great. You can come to my place then. I'll download the film."

"Sounds good."

A faint cry from the bedroom told Shasa her daughter had woken up, this time for real.

She cast an apologetic look at Mac. "That's my cue. Seriously. You should go before she really gets going. Save yourself." She headed to the bedroom, leaving Mac to find his own way out.

At the bedroom doorway, she noticed him right at her heels. Lilla sat up on the bed, wide awake. Seeing both of them, she whipped her head from side to side, stunned silent.

Mac took a step closer, and she recognised him.

"Mac!" Lilla lifted her hands for him to pick her up.

Mac looked at Shasa. "May I?"

She shrugged. "Sure."

He wasn't a stranger anymore, and her daughter didn't seem scared. If anything, she was delighted to find him in her room and wrapped her hands around his neck as he held her. She was already too heavy for Shasa to hold for a long time. She usually lowered her back down as soon as possible or lay down on the bed next to her. But Mac stood and held her like she was still a baby.

Lilla relaxed her head against his shoulder and her eyelids dipped. In a couple of minutes, she was asleep. Shasa stared at the absolute miracle unfolding before her eyes. It must have been beginner's luck, if that was a thing with children.

"Should I put her back down?" Mac whispered.

"You can try. It doesn't always—"

He was already doing it. She hurried to catch the girl, in case she woke up and started thrashing around, but Lilla was gone, happily snuggling under the blanket.

They tiptoed out of the bedroom to the front door.

Mac reached for the doorknob, then turned back. "I'm sorry. I'm not sure if I should've done that. I just thought you might need a break, that's all. It can't be easy."

"Thanks. It's not."

"She's cute. Looks a lot like you." His gaze lingered on her face, making her tingle all over.

She feigned a yawn which quickly turned real.

Mac took the hint and opened the door. "I'll let you get some sleep."

She stepped back to keep a safe distance. This movie-watching was really going to test her self-control.

"Thank you for considering the audition," he said as he stepped out on the deck.

A gust of cool night air hit her face. "No worries."

"I'll see you tomorrow, then?"

He pulled a wallet out of his jacket pocket and unearthed a business card. The same blue one he'd given her earlier. "There's my phone number, in case you've ... misplaced the last one. Text me, and I'll text you the address."

"What time?"

"Any time that works for you. I don't have a kid, so..."

"It'll be closer to eight."

"Perfect. Look, I really appreciate this. Good night!" He took a step closer and reached out his hand, like he was un-sure of how to say goodbye.

Startled by what she thought was an incoming hug, Shasa raised her hand to his shoulder. His stubble brushed against her cheek as he kissed the air, then retreated down the steps. His warm breath lingered in her ear as she watched him dis-appear into the darkness. She'd been so close to sliding her fingers through his thick mane and pulling him in for a kiss. Dangerously close.

Chapter 18

Shasa inched forward in the ice cream queue, holding Lilla's hand as she swung in the air between her and Marnie. They were at Hamilton Gardens, along with hundreds of people who'd come to see a new themed garden. The midday sun was still scorching hot.

"You have a date tonight?" Marnie asked, casting her a meaningful look.

"No! Not a date," Shasa protested. "Just research for the play."

"But you're going to his place?"

"I thought that'd be good if I'm supposed to snoop around. Not sure I'll find anything, though. He knows we're after the same section. He'll be careful."

"You never know what might be useful."

"How was writing group? I mean, how was the new guy?"

Shasa asked.

Marnie sighed. "He didn't show up. I think he got weirded out by all the meddling. The ladies are a bit intense."

Shasa sighed. "Is there a scenario where you actually approach someone, or make yourself available? I wouldn't leave it to those old ladies."

Marnie shook her head, smiling. "I'm not impulsive like you."

Shasa cocked her head. "You write stories with perfect, chiselled guys … but you won't actually date one in real life?"

Marnie urged them ahead in the ice cream line, placing Lilla's sunhat back on her head. "In real life, no one's perfect. If they seem that way, it's more suspicious than if they had blatant flaws."

Shasa laughed. "I love your logic!"

Marnie dipped her head, hiding behind a cloud of curls. "Also, when I write, I pair those guys with gorgeous women, not someone like me."

"You are beautiful, you know that, right?" Shasa let go of Lilla's hand and hugged her friend.

Lilla joined in, hugging her legs. Marnie wasn't big, but she was touchy about her weight, something her ex-husband had teased her about. Shasa was jealous of her curves.

"Thanks," Marnie whispered, wiping her eyes. "I needed that."

"Promise me you'll at least be open to the possibility of someone liking you?"

She nodded against her shoulder.

"I ... will," she whispered, unconvincingly.

With Lilla and Marnie working on their ice creams, they wandered through the gates, towards the new Surrealist Garden, their agreed meeting spot with Elsie.

The gardens were Hamilton's pride and joy, built over what used to be the town's rubbish dump. Before Lilla was born, Shasa had loved coming in late at night and sitting in the Renaissance garden. When Ollie had dreamed of saving whales in the Pacific Ocean, she'd dreamed of climbing narrow cobblestone streets in Tuscany. She hadn't shared those dreams with Ollie. Tourist trips burdened the planet with a massive carbon footprint.

Lilla spotted Elsie's old dachshund and ran to give her a hug. Elsie waved at them, looking impossibly stylish in her wrinkle-free linen and wide-brimmed hat. They exchanged hellos and took a quick tour of the new garden. Apart from a couple of oversized items, it held nothing of interest. They tracked back towards the tropical garden.

"I received early drawings from the architect. I'll send them your way," Elsie said, "We're working hard to stay under budget, but it's important that you're happy with it."

Marnie waved her hand. "I'm not fussy as long as the roof doesn't leak. All those new builds look the same to me, to be honest."

"That's so true!" Shasa echoed. "They must order all the kitchens from the same manufacturer or something. White cabinets and that grey lino with fake wood grain. I'm fine with it, though."

"Me, too," Marnie confirmed.

Elsie gave them an odd look. "White and grey is the standard palette for rentals, but there are other options out there. Would you like me to find out what we can afford?"

Shasa looked at her like a fairy godmother. "Yes, please!"

They made it to the round atrium with a water fountain.

Shasa pointed at the long, hedge lined walkway. "Can we go to the Renaissance one, please?"

At the vine-covered doorway, Elsie suddenly stopped in her tracks. "Oh, no," she whispered.

***

Elsie took a deep breath to compose herself. Jeffrey stood under a pergola maybe ten steps away, surrounded by a group of well-dressed Asians. Elsie knew he occasionally entertained overseas investors. Taking them around the gardens was part of the package, but why did he have to be here right now?

She cast an apologetic look at Shasa and Marnie. "Can we please go somewhere else?"

The girls were about to respond, but it was too late. Jeff turned around and spotted her, raising his hand in greeting. Straightening her back, Elsie crossed the cobblestone path and stopped a few feet away from her ex-husband.

Jeff ran his fingers through his thick, silver hair. "Elsie! Good to see you."

"You too, Jeff." She glanced at his companions, waiting for the introductions.

"This is Elsie ... Joyce, my old business partner," he told the Asians, who smiled and did slight bows. "Mr Chu and his associates just arrived from Beijing. I'm showing them around Hamilton."

Elsie greeted the group with a friendly nod and ushered Shasa and Marnie to her side. "Meet Marnie, Shasa, and Lilla," she said. "They're working on a cohousing community I'm advising on."

Jeff's face looked blank. "A what?"

"A cohousing community," Marnie repeated louder, like Jeff was hard of hearing.

Elsie suppressed a smile.

Jeff recovered from his surprise and greeted the girls. "G'day. I'm Jeffrey Alders."

Elsie caught the flash of recognition on Shasa's face as she shook his hand. "We're so lucky to have Elsie onboard, she has a wealth of knowledge."

Elsie shuffled her feet, eager to move on. She wished she and the girls had a secret signal for this kind of emergency. Talking to this man was a very bad idea.

Jeff tilted his head, a smug smile on his face. "Cohousing? Like a commune? Yurts? Sounds ... exciting."

Shasa wrinkled her brow. "No, it's just an apartment

building with shared gardens."

Mr Chu and his associates wandered towards the balcony, cameras pointed at the fountain. Lilla ran after them, disappearing down the stairs to the orange grove. Shasa was about to chase after her, but Marnie signalled her to stay and ran to fetch the girl.

Elsie had noticed Marnie jumping in to look after the little girl every time they were together. They must be very good friends. She hoped Jeff would also move on, but it seemed her unorthodox companions had piqued his curiosity.

He folded his arms, studying her. "I see you've found a nice charity project. You should have done that years ago."

Elsie tried to match his stare. "Instead of butting into your business?"

Shasa shifted an inch closer, straightening her back. Elsie hoped the girl didn't feel like she needed to defend her.

Jeff huffed, a smug smile on his face. He didn't bother denying it. He'd always wanted Elsie to keep busy with the other wives and stay out of the big decisions. But Jeff hadn't given her a family, so she hadn't been busy like the mothers, she'd been an outsider. Was it any wonder she'd put her energy into their business?

"For twenty years, you complained about being lonely and disconnected. Still, you wouldn't get involved with anything. I had to drag you to every charity event and fundraiser." His scoff sent a cold shiver down Elsie's spine. How could he air their dirty laundry in front of a stranger?

She looked him straight in the eye. "This isn't a charity, just a fun project with ... new friends." Her word choice surprised her. Did she think of Shasa and Marnie as friends?

Jeff's eyebrows sailed up. "So, you're not funding this ... comm ... housing?"

Elsie rubbed her neck. What could she say? She'd promised to invest. Jeff's gaze flicked between her and Shasa, trying to make sense of it all. Elsie knew they didn't make sense – she and this girl in yellow harem pants and a headscarf.

Shasa beamed at Jeff, her eyes lit with pride. "Elsie is investing! We're very grateful. We couldn't do this without her!"

Jeff's eyebrows inched even higher. "Investing? Is that right? That's very nice of you, Elsie. You're right, it's nothing like those charity projects. What was it you said about buying your way into those circles? It's nice to see that you're cultivating *real* friendships now." He slipped out the word 'friendships' like it was a chicken bone he'd sucked dry.

Elsie shuddered. She had to shut this down right now. "G'day, Jeffrey." She motioned to Shasa, and they strode to the balcony, past the Chu group, and down to the orange grove, joining Marnie and Lilla at the far exit.

As they stepped through a small archway, past a small amphitheatre and up a leafy path, Elsie tried to slow down her breathing. Slowly, her upset over Jeffrey turned into a gnawing realisation. He was right. She'd jumped into this project, offering her time and significant resources. Was she trying to buy her way into Shasa and Marnie's inner circle? Was she really that pathetic?

***

Shasa struggled to keep up with Elsie. Why was the woman running out of the gardens, practically pushing people out of the way? She suspected it had something to do with the silver fox they'd run into. He'd introduced himself as a business partner, but she hadn't missed his name, or the way Elsie tensed next to him. He must have been *the* Jeffrey, the ex-husband. She felt sorry for Elsie; strolling around the gardens was supposed to be a relaxing experience.

She followed Elsie back to the courtyard and out the main gate. In front of the gift shop, they finally stopped.

Elsie's mouth set in a straight line. "I'm sorry you had to see that."

Shasa offered a sympathetic smile. "Are you okay?" Worry churned in Shasa's stomach. She could feel their dream slipping away, along with this woman. Was there anything she could do?

"I'm fine." Elsie clamped her lips in a way that suggested she didn't want to elaborate.

Marnie caught up with them and picked up a panting Lilla. Before Shasa could catch her friend's eye, Marnie launched into an excited babble. "I love the idea of those materials and other options you talked about! Can you email us something? Like links to the manufacturer's sites. I'd love to take a look."

Elsie's tone was cold. "I'll see what I can do."

Marnie's face fell. "I didn't mean to push you, no hurry or anything. And we can do our own research, too. I just thought since you have so much experience and Shasa was telling me how beautiful your own house is—"

"I'll see what I can do," Elsie repeated, turned on her heels and headed towards the carpark.

Marnie was about to go after her, but Shasa grabbed her arm. "Let her go. I think ... we need to give her some space."

"What's going on?"

"Her ex-husband got to her."

"Got to her? How?"

"I'm worried she's going to rethink her involvement in our project." Shasa's breath caught in her throat.

Marnie's eyes widened. "Are you sure? Maybe she's just reeling from the encounter and needs some time to cool off? Ex-husbands can really push your buttons."

Shasa shook her head and her face turned hot. "That jerk ... he was looking at her like 'oh, you've found yourself a new charity project' or something, and she looked mortified. She was embarrassed of us."

Marnie secured Lilla on her hip and used her free hand to rub Shasa's shoulder. "I think you're reading too much into this."

"But it's true!" Shasa insisted, fighting tears. "We need her, but she doesn't need us. It's not a collaboration, it's charity!"

"So what? There's nothing wrong with charity."

"She's not into charity projects, her ex-husband said that. So, if she realises that's what this is, she'll drop us. We'll be finished."

Marnie looked into the distance, biting her bottom lip. "Money's not the only thing we need from each other."

Shasa nodded. "I should probably cancel the movie night."

Marnie shot her a furious look. "No! You need to do everything you can to find out about this guy! The more we know, the better chance we have of beating him, and for this to be a good investment for Elsie. She told us your street is one of the best in town. Good investments aren't charity. I know it looks bad right now, but Elsie hasn't told us she's out. Until then, we'll keep going, right? Let's not self-sabotage, life's hard enough as it is."

Shasa took a deep breath and smiled, her eyes welling up. "You're wise beyond your years, you know that?"

Marnie lifted her chin, adopting a look of exaggerated graciousness. "I know."

They strolled towards the carpark, letting Lilla dart around the path before them.

Marnie linked arms with Shasa. "We'll sort this out, I promise. Just focus on your date tonight. Be charming. Don't … you know … channel Ollie, okay?"

"Channel Ollie?" Shasa rounded her eyes in mock horror.

"You know what I mean. Don't get judgmental. You need

this guy to let his guard down and trust you. He's clearly into you, so that's a good start."

Shasa sighed. There were several inaccuracies that she should have corrected. It wasn't a date. Mac wasn't into her. She'd initiated the stage kiss. She had wobbly knees around him. It scared her. To get him to let his guard down, she'd have to lower hers, and she was already in the danger zone. Shasa leaned on Marnie's shoulder, inhaling the familiar scent of mango body butter, taking comfort in the steadiness of her gait. She had to keep her eyes on the prize. Her own home. No more landlords. No more uncertainty. It was worth it.

Chapter 19

At seven p.m. that night, Lilla worked on a bowl of Weet-Bix, her pyjama sleeve soaking in the milk. Shasa rummaged through her pantry for snacks and tea. Her fingers fumbled from nerves.

Marnie placed her iPad on the table and sat down. "Stop. I can find my own snacks. I know where you keep stuff."

Shasa glanced at her daughter. "Just put her to bed when she starts nodding, okay?"

"All good. Go get ready."

Marnie waved her away and Shasa rushed out to take a shower. Ten minutes later, she stood in the bedroom in her underwear, staring into the mirror. She had no idea how to dress. It wasn't a date, but was she supposed to look nice? The address Mac had texted her was in the wealthy part of town. In her usual clothes, she'd stick out like a sore thumb.

It didn't bother her, but would it bother him? Would it affect her chances of connecting with him, spying on him or whatever she was meant to be doing?

The questions were pointless given the limited choice in her wardrobe. After some deliberation, she decided on a pair of tights and a casual cotton wrap dress with pockets, which highlighted her small waist and showed off her breasts. Not something she should have been concerned about, but hey, it was just a happy accident, right? She went light on jewellery and exchanged her ensemble of colourful bracelets for two simple ones.

Lilla let her go with minimal drama. She was getting used to Marnie as a babysitter. A huge relief. Marnie sometimes sat for her during the day to let her go to shopping or just take a break, but Shasa hadn't been out at night in two years. Not since Ollie had left.

A few minutes later, Shasa was on the road, trying to calm down by listening to mindless chatter on the local radio. Driving by herself at night brought on a strange feeling, like she'd just run away from her daughter. The sun was setting and the horizon glowed a hazy peach.

As Shasa turned onto Mac's street, she took in the enormous houses. Each design was more complicated than the last, featuring angled windows and multi-faceted roofs. They sprawled across small sections, leaving hardly any space in-between. Mac's house was the third on the left, a tall, dark and handsome specimen of stone and cedar panelling. Shasa parked in the empty driveway, wondering if Mac was home. Hopefully, he was just one of those odd individuals who used their garage for parking their car, not to store junk.

The yard was lit by several spotlights, revealing a landscaped garden of tiles, pebbles and tufts of yellow weave flax that looked almost too neat to be real. The pebbles were perfectly round, and the black tiles glinted in the evening light.

Shasa didn't have a proper handbag and decided to leave her canvas bag in the car. She slipped her phone into her dress pocket in case Marnie called, or she found something she needed to photograph. The thought terrified her. She approached the door, her nerves vibrating.

Before she could choose between knocking and ringing, Mac opened the door. Barefoot, in a pair of worn jeans and a T-shirt, he looked too informal for the setting. He seemed to have two wardrobe choices – the million-dollar suit or the overly casual tees and jeans, the kind she imagined celebrities wearing when they didn't want to be recognised by paparazzi. She preferred him in the casual outfit. It made him less intimidating and she found it easier to forget their differences and focus on other things – like the contour of his chest under the thin fabric.

Nope. Don't go there.

Shasa raised her gaze to his face. "I like your house."

His mouth twitched. "No, you don't."

"No, but I do appreciate its … um … curb appeal? It must have been very expensive."

Mac chuckled and led her across the marbled floor, past a high-tech kitchen of charcoal and cherry wood, to a toddler-death-trap staircase leading to the second floor.

He paused at the foot of the stairs. "TV's upstairs, but would you like a drink first? Coffee? Should we grab some snacks?"

Shasa shrugged, looking at the spotless kitchen. She couldn't see any traces of food or even a fridge. It must have been disguised as one of the cabinets. "I don't know. What-ever you're having is fine with me. Except alcohol, since I'm driving."

Mac circled the huge kitchen island and pulled open a drawer. "I have tea. Regular, or ... irregular?" He beckoned her closer.

Shasa joined him, peeking into the drawer to see a selec-tion of about fifteen tea packets, all wrapped in plastic. "You don't drink tea, do you?"

A faint pink appeared on Mac's cheeks. "No, but I thought you might."

Shasa stared at the selection. It was enough tea to last her half a year. "You went shopping for me? I mean ... you bought these for me?"

Mac flicked a switch to boil the jug. "What's the big deal? I knew you were coming over, and I thought you might not like coffee or beer."

Shasa thumbed through the packets. "And how many years did you think I'd stay over?"

Mac handed her an empty teacup. "Ha ha. I just wanted to give you a choice. I didn't know what you liked."

Shasa shook her head, dumbfounded. "Would you expect me to get every brand of coffee and beer for you, just in case?"

"No. I expect you to pick a tea you like and put the bag in your cup."

Shasa pulled out a packet of something called 'Relax' – appropriate, she needed to chill. It came in a triangular tea bag that held entire leaves and flowers, like pot-pourri.

They waited for the jug to boil, a heavy silence hanging between them. For lack of anything else to do, Shasa strolled around the kitchen island, surveying the shiny finish on every surface. There were no fingerprints.

"Do you wear gloves?" she asked.

"What?"

"It's so shiny."

Mac laughed. "I moved in two months ago. I don't use this kitchen a lot."

"Why? What do you use?"

"I eat out or ... I used to hang out at my girlfriend's place, but not anymore." He turned his back to her while he filled the teacups.

Shasa wondered if she could pry him about the breakup, if there'd been one. Maybe the girlfriend's place was unavailable for another reason, like a renovation. "We got a lot of takeout before Christmas, too," she confessed. "Things were so busy. I always felt bad, it's so unhealthy."

Mac looked up, his eyebrows arching in surprise. "Unhealthy? What about Japanese, or the vegan place downtown? It's full of veggies."

Shasa's eyes widened. What world did this guy live in? "Um ... those meals are pretty pricey. The only Asian we do is the chicken fried rice from the corner shop. It's under ten dollars and there're enough leftovers for the next day."

Mac tried to hide his disgust. "That's a very good deal."

Shasa looked around the kitchen and sighed. What a waste to have a kitchen like this when you didn't even cook at home.

Mac followed her gaze. "I know, I hardly need a kitchen like this, but it's hard to sell a house without one, so I told the builders to install it, anyway."

Shasa curled her lip at the joke. She was jealous – not just of his amazing kitchen, but of the way he was making fun of it. She could joke about her lack of money with her friends, but not here, surrounded by all this marble. It would sound pity-partyish and probably make him uncomfortable. She had to find some common ground, stop channelling Ollie as Marnie would say.

Mac handed her a steaming cup of tea. She inhaled the rich aroma, hoping the relaxing qualities transferred with the smell. Waiting for Mac to pour himself a glass of beer, she wandered over to the lounge which sprawled into another sitting area. How many living areas did one guy need? The house was furnished, but it didn't feel lived in. It looked like it had been staged for sale. Shasa glanced over her shoulder, unsure whether Mac was okay with her exploring.

"Go ahead!" He grinned at her. "There are more rooms I don't use in that direction."

He gestured through an arched doorway and Shasa stepped ahead, intrigued. Having a tour of the house with his permission probably didn't qualify as spying, but she couldn't help her curiosity. She'd never seen anyone her age living like this. Some of her friends had newer rentals with basic white walls and chrome appliances. Compared to her house, they looked fancy in a sterile cookie cutter way. Mac's house was something different altogether. Every detail was an upgrade from the standard rental look, from the complicated trims to soft oatmeal walls and feature lights that hung at just the right height. It didn't have the artistic flair of Elsie's house, but it looked similarly expensive, like an upmarket hotel. Shasa groaned at the thought of their first encounter, Mac witnessing her pigsty of a home. Even on a good day, her house didn't measure up. Had he been disgusted? Did he pity her?

Shasa stepped into a third living area with quadruple doors opening to the back garden and a large deck outside.

Mac joined her, holding a tall glass of beer. "It looks better in daylight. I haven't had a chance to install the outdoor lights yet."

"But you do have lights." Shasa pointed at the two spotlights illuminating the deck.

"I mean garden lights."

"Why? Do you garden at night?"

He laughed. "No. It's just looks better with lights. More ... festive."

"Doesn't it use a lot electricity?"

"You can get pretty powerful solar ones these days. They have batteries, so they charge during the day and then burn all night."

"Wow. Those must be expensive?"

"No, I reckon I can get the whole lot done for a couple of grand."

Shasa held her breath. That was more than she'd spent on her car. She stared into the black garden. "But you'll be asleep."

Mac shrugged. "Before I go to sleep, I might have people over and we might be sitting outside on the deck."

"And you need to see the garden?"

He knitted his brow. "Why is this such an issue for you?"

Why, indeed? Heat rose up Shasa's neck, burning her cheeks. "I don't know. I suppose it's the idea of someone spending thousands on lighting up their garden, when there are people living in garages who can't afford heating or shoes for their kids."

Shasa sighed in exasperation. Everywhere she looked, she saw more evidence of the giant chasm between them. How was she supposed to get closer to him, to build trust? They didn't even speak the same language. With every word, she dug a deeper hole for herself.

"You know what?" Mac's sharp tone gave her a start. His eyes bore into hers with a fierceness that made her shiver. "You've seen my parents' house. I didn't grow up rich, but I got tired of being poor. I got tired of the attitude, this idea that I was meant to give it all away as soon as something landed on my lap. That I was wasn't allowed to hold on to wealth, whatever that means. I wasn't allowed to invest. That's how my parents stayed poor, and that's why they struggle to feed all those kids every week. They give everything away, so now they have nothing left to give."

"It's not nothing. They feed the kids!"

"It's nothing compared to building houses for the homeless."

"Who's building houses for the homeless?"

Mac clamped his mouth shut, looking out the window.

What was he on about? Shasa sensed he'd said more than he'd intended, but she couldn't let it go. "Are *you* building houses for the homeless?"

Mac glanced at her, his jaw twitching. "That's the plan. Well, not exactly homeless, but I want to help people on low income into home ownership. I just need to build capital first. If I give everything away too early, it won't be enough to make a difference. It's not something I advertise, but I've set up a trust and I'm working on it."

Shasa stared at her bare toes, shocked by his admission.

Bloody Ollie. He'd poisoned her against everyone who didn't represent his own brand of charity and goodwill.

"I'm sorry," she whispered. "I thought you were just in it for yourself."

"Yeah, well. Looks can be deceiving." Mac studied her, his expression serious, voice barely audible. "But you're right. I have nothing to show for myself, yet. Sometimes, I worry I won't have the strength to carry out the plan, that I get greedy and decide to keep it all."

Seeing the pain behind his eyes made Shasa's chest squeeze. She shifted closer. "You've told me now. I'll hold you accountable."

"Good." He held her gaze for a moment.

Shasa caught a whiff of his scent and it sent her heart racing. She turned to look out the glass doors. "I'm sure the lights will look great."

"It's a good investment."

She smiled. "Like the huge kitchen that you don't use?"

"Yeah." His playful smirk both relaxed her and made her giddy.

She sensed the chasm between them closing, which scared her more than any argument.

"Should we start the film?" he asked.

She followed him through the house and up the floating staircase, leaving a good distance between them. The upstairs space was cosier, with a fluffy rug and two over-stuffed couches facing the largest TV Shasa had ever seen. "And I was worried you didn't have a TV big enough to do justice to fifties black and white film!"

He rolled his eyes. "Very funny."

Shasa sat down on the couch directly facing the TV, placing her teacup on the coffee table.

Mac remained standing, holding his half-finished beer. "Do you want popcorn? I forgot to bring it."

Shasa shrugged. Eating popcorn in a room this tidy felt sacrilegious. Mac hurried back downstairs.

Shasa took several seconds to recognise the opportunity. He'd left her unsupervised. She was here to spy, right? But his earlier admission had thrown her off. She frowned. So what if he was planning on doing something good with his money? It didn't mean they couldn't pursue the cohousing community. Mac could make his money a thousand different ways. They only had this one shot. Shasa took a breath, trying to focus. She couldn't afford to be derailed.

There was only one door leading away from the room. Through the half-open door, she saw a sliver of a perfectly made bed with a textured sheet. This guy really liked charcoal. The fabric looked like linen, softly wrinkled by design, not from haphazard folding and cramming into a tiny linen closet like her sheets.

Soft on her feet, Shasa moved across the luxurious thick carpet – also charcoal – into the bedroom. The bed looked like a king, or a super king, ridiculously big for one person. Maybe he had regular visitors. Part of her wished he did.

Knowing someone had a girlfriend or casual relationships was always a turnoff, and she really needed something to turn off her inappropriate thoughts.

The sound of the water running downstairs told her he was still in the kitchen. Shasa tiptoed across the room to the only island of disarray she could see, a pile of papers on his dresser. To her disappointment, it was a play. Not *Roman Holiday*, but *Closer*. She remembered the film. Was it based on a play, or the other way around? Why did he have it in his bedroom? She flicked through the pages and found a scene covered in yellow highlighter. He must have been practicing lines.

She didn't hear him enter the room and jumped when he said, "Please, check out my bedroom. Would you like to peruse my sock drawer as well?"

Shasa took a deep breath, waiting for her heart rate to settle. Thankfully, she could hear a smile in his voice.

She tried to match it, turning to him with a cheeky grin. "Well, you did check out my dirty laundry, so…"

Mac marched past her and pulled open a drawer full of balled up pairs of socks.

"Where are the odd ones?" she asked.

He stared at her like she had a screw loose. "Why would I keep the odd ones?"

"In case they get separated in the wash and the lost one turns up later. Then he'll be like 'where's my mate?'"

"Then I'll just throw out another sock. What's the big

deal?"

"You'll end up with a pair of perfectly good socks in your rubbish bin!"

Mac cocked his head, a cheeky smile tugging at the corner of his mouth. "What do you do with the odd ones?"

"You can make sock puppets, pin cushions, stress balls... Almost everything we throw out can be recycled into something useful."

Shasa blushed. Her odd sock collection was much larger than the one in her actual sock drawer – dozens of socks forever waiting for their mate, or a new life as something else. Would she ever have time to craft stress balls? The task itself felt so stressful that it almost defeated the purpose.

She lifted up the script to change the subject. "Are you doing another play?"

"That's just for my scene group. We practise scenes from movies and act them out."

"How many acting groups are you in?"

Mac smiled. "Just those two, at the moment."

Shasa turned the script in her hands and noticed some handwritten notes on the other side. Before she had a chance to read a word, Mac grabbed it from her and slid it in the top drawer. It landed on a pile of other papers. Why hadn't she looked in the drawer? If she'd gone straight to it, she might have been able to check if there was anything relevant in there. Feigning disinterest, Shasa turned to the bedroom window. The street sloped towards the town. Hamilton was

largely flat, so even the slightest hill offered sweeping views.
The endless carpet of domestic, suburban lights looked cosy,
like a scene from a picture book.

"I like this view."

Mac joined her at the window. "Me too. That's why I
bought the section."

"You built this house?"

"I designed it. Builders built it."

"You know what I mean."

Mac straightened his face. "This was my first one with the
builders I now work with. I thought, if they got this right, I
could trust them with the bigger developments."

Shasa couldn't fault the builders. Everything screamed
quality.

"Shall we?" he asked.

She followed him back into the lounge and sat next to him
on the couch. Maybe she should have taken the other couch,
but this one had a better view of the TV.

Mac didn't seem to mind. He edged closer and showed her
his phone screen. "I downloaded this file. I'll just cast it on
the TV screen. Let's hope it works."

Shasa wasn't sure why she had to see the file name in his
download folder, but she edged closer, inhaling his freshly
showered scent. Mac tapped on his phone, and the opening
credits rolled on the TV, grainy on the massive screen. Shasa
couldn't remember the last time she'd watched an old film.
She didn't really have time for movies, other than Frozen

and Frozen II. Days were long and exhausting. By the time Lilla fell asleep, she hardly wanted to stay up for another two hours.

Tonight, she wasn't sleepy. Every fibre of her body stood to attention, whirring from her proximity to Mac. He'd brought up a bowl of popcorn, cheese and crackers and two bottles of beer. Shasa wanted to eat, but she was too highly strung to digest food. She hugged herself, hoping for her insides to settle. Thank goodness the film was easy to follow. With her brain processing a flurry of conflicting emotions, it was hard to focus.

A few minutes into the movie, Mac sprawled back on the couch. Shasa leant forward, creating just enough distance between them that she could finally concentrate. Despite the slow fifties style filmmaking, she found herself drawn into the story of Princess Anya craving the anonymity of a commoner, touring Rome and falling in love with a reporter called Joe.

"Did they use the phrase 'regular Joe' in the fifties?" she asked. "Is that why the character's name is Joe?"

She turned to Mac, who jerked like he'd just woken up. "Huh?"

"I mean, she's a princess, and he's the regular Joe. It seems deliberate."

Mac shrugged. "Sure, why not?"

She narrowed her eyes. "Were you asleep?"

A hint of a smile played on his lips. "No." He reached for

his phone and paused the film. "I may have lost my concentration for a bit. Can you fill me in?"

"Seriously? The beginning was slow, but it was just starting to get good."

He twisted his mouth. "Sorry. I'm not usually this distracted."

She could swear the air was vibrating between them. Barely breathing, she risked a glance at his crotch. His jeans weren't that tight, but she could see his hard-on, tightly lodged in the left leg. So, she wasn't the only one. It was almost a relief, especially after she'd forgotten his closeness for a moment.

Well, any equilibrium she'd achieved was good and gone. Within seconds, her body was back in business, sending signals from one erogenous zone to the other, like a game of inner laser tag. Shasa focused her eyes on the screen, heat sweeping up her neck, burning her ears. The film was paused on a close-up of Audrey Hepburn, her giant eyes looking up at Joe. So innocent.

Mac's voice was gruff. "Okay. Full disclosure. I'm distracted by you."

"Me?" She looked over her shoulder, and her insides melted.

His eyes were dark and hungry. "I'm sorry," he whispered. "I just can't stop … thinking about you." He sat up, closing the distance between them.

His words fired up her body. She inhaled a lungful of his

scent and held her breath. His gaze dipped to her lips, full of aching need. Her body responded before her brain could catch up and she threw her leg over his lap to straddle him. For a split second, she feared he would push her away, but his arms locked around her, strong and solid, inescapable, and his mouth crashed on hers like she'd offered oxygen to a drowning man. Tasting him brought back the memory of their stage kiss, the one that wasn't supposed to be real. This one was. She felt him hard against her crotch, further melting whatever was left of her resolve, or better judgment. She explored his mouth like she'd paid a thousand dollars for a dessert. The price was too high, but it was better than anything she'd ever had.

Mac slid his hands down to her lower back, his tongue connecting with hers, sending a powerful surge through her body. She gripped a fistful of his T-shirt, her other hand tracing the sixpack underneath. Every inch of him felt hot and hard. Her undies were soaked, probably staining his jeans. Why hadn't she worn jeans, too? It was like she'd planned this – arriving here alone at night, in a dress that opened up like a bathrobe. Which he'd already figured out, pulling on the string that held it together, exposing her purple bra. This was further than she'd planned, even in the far corners of her mind. The bra was discoloured and had a noticeable rip. Intense embarrassment cut through her arousal. She wedged one hand between them and used the other to wrap the dress back in place, gasping for breath.

Mac released her, his eyes like two wildly clanging warning bells. "Wow."

"Yeah. Wow." Shasa used the brief moment of clarity to
roll away from his lap, back on the couch, back to safety. "I'm
sorry," she panted. "I don't know why, but being around you
just ... I don't know. I'm so, so stupid."

"No, I'm stupid." His voice was thick.

She exhaled like a deflating balloon, closing her eyes. "I
should probably go."

"Why?" He rubbed his forehead with his fingertips like the
whole situation was giving him a migraine.

"Are you okay?" Shasa asked.

Her throbbing arousal was turning into a dull ache as she
thought of the implications of this colossal mistake. It must
have been even more difficult for him, with the rock-hard
erection she'd felt against her thigh. No. Don't think about
that. She slapped herself on the cheek to wake up.

"That's a good idea," he said, slapping his own cheek. "I
might also need a cold shower." He flashed her a pained
smile. "Honestly, I don't behave this way. I never do this."

"You never kiss willing girls who climb into your lap?"

"I mean, I don't invite friends over under some pretence
of watching a movie for research, and, you know..."

"Me, neither! I never do this, period. I mean, any of this.
Not since Ollie left. And that was two years ago." That was
far more information than she'd intended to divulge, and
her stomach sank at the thought of it. He already thought

she was weird.

"Two years? Seriously?" He looked stunned, but not in a mocking way.

"I mean, I didn't know he wasn't coming back, until recently. I had my suspicions, but..."

Shut up, woman. What was wrong with her? She was here on espionage, not to pour out her sad life story to this guy who was out to destroy her dreams and rip out her blueberry bushes.

"I'm sorry. Two years is a long time." His voice was soft. Something about his eyes tugged at her heart, and it frightened her more than anything else that was happening.

"Yeah. I guess it explains me ... jumping you." She tried to laugh, but it sounded more like a cry.

Mac shifted, rubbing his chin. "That's not the whole truth." He turned towards her and waited for her to look him in the eye. "Look. There's something between us. Whatever it is ... it's physical. Maybe we just emit the right pheromones or something. I feel it when I get close to you. And it seems that you ... feel it, too?"

She nodded. "It's like my body has a mind of its own. It's scary."

He looked away, deep in thought. "Maybe that's why we have great chemistry on stage."

It made sense. Like a magic ingredient. "So, what do we do?" Shasa asked, her voice faltering.

Mac straightened his spine. "We'll use it."

"Use it?"

Shasa swallowed. The primal part of her hoped he meant for him taking her right here on this couch. But of course, it didn't. It couldn't. It definitely shouldn't.

"It's going to take a lot of willpower, but we need to just keep our hands off each other, except when acting. Use the heat between us for the performance."

Shasa gave him a slow nod. "Because if we do something..."

"We lose the tension," he finished for her. "And things will get complicated."

Shasa sighed. Complicated was an understatement. She had to agree, even as her lady parts protested, carrying angry signs and megaphones.

"Good plan," she said, trying to lubricate her throat with a bit of saliva. There wasn't any. All the moisture in her body had moved south a long time ago. "So we finish the movie?"

"Sitting on separate couches."

"Yes."

"And you cover that dress with ... um ... I'll bring you something."

"Then you have to cover..." She looked at him, letting out an exasperated sigh. "Everything. Including your eyes."

"My eyes? I don't know if I can do that." He flashed that gorgeous smile.

"And change your voice to something grating and high-pitched, please. Or do you have one of those vocoder thin-gies that you press against your throat and it makes you sound like a machine? That'd be good."

He chuckled. "So, you like my voice?"

Shasa blushed, realising what she'd just confessed to. Oh, well. She couldn't really pretend she wasn't turned on by him. As much as she also hated him, because she did. It was too confusing to think about. One thing she knew for sure was that she'd regret sleeping with him. And now she knew she had to work a lot harder to avoid that mistake. Being honest with what was going on with her stubborn, sex-depraved body was probably a good starting point.

"Yes, I like your voice. And your jaw, and your eyes. And your forearms, and that muscle above your collarbone. Cover it up, please."

Mac got up. "I'll just change and come out wearing a sack of some sort. I'll see what I can find."

The bedroom door clicked as he closed it behind him. Shasa crossed the room and pressed her forehead against the cool window. The view from the lounge was even more impressive than the one from the bedroom, stretching out further. Hamilton had never looked so big.

She focussed on the house she could have, the blueberry bushes, the safe playground for Lilla. Their plan was bigger than her and her sex-crazed thoughts. But what if Elsie pulled out? She had to find out what was going on, to fix it. If she couldn't get Elsie back on track, their project was already dead. In that case, why wasn't she in the bedroom with Mac? She could hardly stop thinking about that kiss.

She may have initiated it, again, but this time he'd responded in a way that left no room for ambiguity. He liked her.
No, he was physically attracted to her. She would do well to
remember the difference.

What a night. Shasa threw herself back on the couch and
sighed.

A few minutes later, Mac returned in his pyjamas. They
were bright red and had emojis all over them. Smiley faces,
thumbs up ... even the poop.

"Where did you get those?" she asked, doubling over with
laughter.

"My brother. He thinks it's funny."

"No shit!"

"Shit, indeed."

He held a rolled-up blanket under his arm. "Here's your
new dress." He threw it to her and cranked up the air-con.

As Shasa covered herself with the soft, charcoal throw, he
took the other couch, turned on the movie and opened one
of the beers. She stared at the other one. Maybe she could
have half of it and drive, but she couldn't risk it further lowering her inhibitions. Still, his drinking reminded her how
thirsty she was.

"Can you just pause for a minute? I'll get a glass of water."

She peeled off the blanket and turned to the stairs, but
he pointed at the two empty glasses on the coffee table.
"There's a tap in the master bath." He nodded at the direction of his bedroom.

Shasa took the glass and stepped in. It was only when she passed the dresser that she remembered the papers in the top drawer. She couldn't linger, but maybe, if she was really fast ... The drawer was smooth and quiet. The script was on top. She turned it over and scanned the page. The handwriting was messy, but she could tell it had nothing to do with the section. No numbers or property notes. It looked like a pitch for a movie. She caught words 'one-eyed girl', 'circus' and 'murder'. Shasa slid the papers back in the drawer and hurried to fill her water glass.

When she stepped back into the lounge, she found Mac watching rugby, the TV on mute. He must have been listening in on her.

"Sorry, just checking the score."

She sat down. "That's okay."

"So, did you snoop around my dresser?" he asked, his tone even, eyes firmly on the game.

"Yeah." If she lied, he wouldn't believe her, anyway. "One-eyed girl?"

"It was just a movie idea. A stupid idea."

"How do you know?"

"Most ideas are. It doesn't matter. You can't even copyright an idea. Execution's the hard part."

Shasa curled up on the couch. She was starting to feel comfortable. "Then you should write it, see if it works."

"My brother's the filmmaker, not me. He's obsessed with that stuff. Every time I'm with him, I start jotting down stupid ideas. Like it's contagious."

"That sounds like fun."

"Yeah, he's pretty entertaining. And he never has money. You'd like him." His eyes sparkled with mischief.

Shasa shifted under the blanket. "I don't glorify poverty. I don't wish it for anyone. It doesn't make you a better person or anything. In fact, it makes you worse. Just like extreme wealth."

"Extreme?"

"I'm not talking about you!"

"Good. Because I think if you ever visit the royal palace, or some sheik's summer cottage, you'll run out of words."

Shasa's scoff turned into a chuckle. "I get it. Your house is totally average. Which makes my house a dump."

Mac didn't laugh. "No argument. I don't know how you do it."

"Do what?"

"How you live in that house all year round, with a child. It breaks my heart." Mac looked at her with such concern her insides twisted.

"I don't let her get cold! I just heat up one room at a time and that's where we live."

"Like the lounge?"

"No, the lounge is too big to heat. Bedroom's better."

"You eat in the bedroom?"

"Only for those couple of months when it gets really cold." She looked away, suddenly sick with embarrassment. What she'd thought of as normal was shocking to him. Was she endangering her child? "I make sure she's warm!" she insisted. "She always has her beanie on, even in bed. I know it's not ideal, but I'm doing the best I can." Her voice faltered.

Mac sat up in his chair. "Please don't think I'm judging you. I'm really not. I just have my pet peeves ... these disgusting things that are normalised in New Zealand. My parents wash black mould off the ceiling every spring like it's no big deal. It shouldn't grow there in the first place!"

She heard the passion in his voice, and it surged through her. "So, you want to demolish their house?"

"Can't wait to!"

"And where are they going to live?"

"I can put them up in one of my rentals for a few months and then they can move into one of the new townhouses."

Shasa nodded. He had a plan. She had a plan. They weren't compatible. Was there any way they could build the cohousing community on another section, somewhere else? Maybe in time they could, even without Elsie. She could keep saving and hope for the best.

"So, you have rentals?" she asked, slowly tasting the words.

She'd brushed off his offer before, but if Elsie was out, she couldn't be too proud to ask for help. With the cohousing plans in motion, she hadn't done any house hunting. She hadn't submitted a single application. How stupid of her.

Mac's gaze lingered on her, the concern still clouding his eyes. "I have a couple of apartments vacating in town. Nothing with a backyard, unfortunately. But I'll ask around, see if anyone knows anything. It'll be a bit more than you pay now, though."

"I know." She'd never find another deal like that. They'd have to skimp even more, skip any longer car trips and stop buying takeaway altogether. Beans on toast was always cheaper.

"Should we finish this?" Mac nodded at the TV, which was displaying game scores.

He turned the movie back on, and they sank into their respective couches. Shasa was happy to focus on something outside her own reality. Going back to the fifties was perfect. The movie was full of royal references, from fancy mouldings to protocols. It had nothing to do with them, yet she couldn't help seeing parallels. They were just like Anya and Joe, only reversed. Mac was the princess, and she was the regular Joe.

With 'The End' hovering on the screen, Mac turned to her. "What do you think?"

"It's old but fun. Feels timeless."

"I think Gareth's planning to modernise it a bit."

Shasa hoped he wouldn't modernise the physical side of things. The old film was very mild on touching. Still, they'd have to close the distance in the rehearsals, and it worried her. They probably couldn't play their parts dressed in blankets and pyjamas.

Best not to think about it, Shasa decided, stretching her arms. "Thank you for a ... lovely evening. I better get home."

She got up and folded the throw on the couch. Without it,

she felt exposed, so she hurried down the stairs.

She heard Mac's footsteps behind her but didn't turn to face him until she was safely outside the front door. The night had cooled down, making her shiver. Next time, she'd go for jeans and the ugliest cardigan known to mankind. If there was going to be a next time. If there was, it couldn't be like this – the two of them alone in his house.

Shasa allowed herself one last look at the man who made her so wobbly. What was it about him? And what was he thinking?

"I'm sorry," she whispered. "I behaved horribly."

"No, you didn't."

"I did," Shasa insisted. "Not just, you know, but also before. I don't have any friends who live like this, I don't know how to be around you. It's Ollie. He blames the rich for everything and we used to talk about it so much that my mind just goes there. I'm sorry."

Mac lifted his brow. "Rich? I have some assets, but I also have a lot of debt. Can we blame the actual billionaires? The one percent, or the point one percent?"

Shasa laughed. "That's fair."

Mac took a step closer. "Now that the apologies are taken care of, I just wanted to say I really enjoyed hanging out with you."

"Really?"

"Really." His eyes glistened as he stepped closer. He whispered, "I know we decided it was a bad idea, but I'm going to kiss you goodbye..."

Shasa shivered, both from the cold and the sensation of his fingers tracing her cheeks, curling behind her ears, holding her captive. His hot breath mixed with hers. She couldn't fight it. She didn't even want to. The kiss was so hungry and passionate she nearly lost her balance. He tasted of beer and all the seductive things she shouldn't have been tasting. His hands travelled down her shoulders and traced her breasts, like he was trying to both sculpt her and keep her warm. She never wanted it to end, but it had to.

He pulled back to stare into her eyes, his gaze full of mischief. "There. Just a wee peck on the cheek."

"Totally."

He smiled and closed his mouth on hers again, firing up her body before she'd had a chance to cool down. Encouraged by his eagerness, she traced her fingers over his flat chest, all the way down to the waistband of his pyjama pants. He was so solid. So hot.

Finally, he let her go and flashed a sheepish smile. "I think I missed your cheek again."

"I may have turned my head the wrong way." Her voice was shamelessly breathy. "Sorry about that."

"No problem."

She took a step back, like getting away from a cliff before she'd fall. "Bye, Mac!"

She waved her hand and ran to her car. Oh, God. What had she got herself into?

Chapter 20

On a windy Sunday afternoon, Elsie took her usual table at Gotherburg, one of the nicer restaurants on the riverbank. The familiarity of the setting usually soothed her, but this afternoon it couldn't settle the nerves buzzing around her stomach. She'd asked Marnie to meet her here, without Shasa. Marnie was the easier option, the one without childcare issues, the older of the two who dressed more conservatively. They wouldn't look so mismatched sitting at the same table. Not something Elsie should have worried about, but a lot of her old friends frequented the restaurant.

She had to start with easy and work her way to difficult. This was uncharted territory.

Running into Jeff had raised difficult questions. Was she capable of building real friendships? What did Shasa and Marnie think of her? Was she a patron, an investor, or an acquaintance? She was too old to ignore these things; it was time to get answers and shape the life she wanted to live.

Last night, sitting on her balcony, drinking another solitary glass of wine, Elsie had decided she wasn't happy with the status quo. The divorce had left her with an empty life, but she didn't have to accept it. Come to think of it, she didn't have to accept any of Jeff's values or opinions. If Jeff thought she had nothing in common with Shasa and Marnie, she didn't have to agree with him. Her relationship with other people was up to her. The more she'd thought about it, the clearer it had become. By the time she'd dropped her head on the pillow, she'd made the decision to start with Marnie, and see if she could make a friend. How did single people make friends at her age?

Elsie watched as the waiter filled her water glass. She could have picked a different meeting place, but it was hard to break habits. She'd spent years avoiding the less affluent parts of the town and never ate at malls.

The lush greenery behind the ceiling-height windows shook in the wind, creating a tropical vibe. Elsie had always loved this spot, right by the sturdy glass that shielded her from the elements but allowed her to see everything, like being outside without any of the discomforts. Behind the branches, she caught a glimpse of Waikato river, brown and fast flowing. She couldn't believe people swam in it.

"Hi!" Marnie's chirpy voice gave Elsie a start.

"Hello! Please have a seat."

Marnie wrapped a light cardigan around her ample bust and sat down. "It's chilly in here!"

"They have very good air conditioning. Would you like to order?" Elsie slid the leather-covered menu across the table.

Marnie took it and perused it with a slight frown.

"It's on me, obviously," Elsie added.

"Oh, it's okay. I'm not that hungry."

"Try the scones."

Marnie tilted her head. Her curls bounced and earrings jiggled. Elsie experienced a pang of jealousy at her youthful, smooth skin hiding behind her conservative, unflattering clothes. Elsie was over twenty years older. What was she looking for? A mother-daughter relationship?

Marnie shrugged, closing the menu. "Tea and scones sound great."

Elsie beckoned the waiter and ordered for them.

As he left, Marnie broke into an anxious smile. "I'm so glad you called. Shasa told me about the encounter with your ex-husband. It must have been awful. I haven't seen mine in months, and I really prefer it that way. I'm over him, but every time ... he just knows how to push my buttons, you know? Time goes by and I start thinking that I've changed, I'm a new me, he doesn't know the new me, right? Wrong! He finds my one weak spot in two minutes."

Elsie sighed. "Sounds familiar. I thought Jeff was extraordinary in that way."

Marnie shook her head with a pained smile. "No, it's standard ex-husband stuff. Still sucks though."

Elsie returned the smile. She'd have never worded it quite like that, but she wholeheartedly agreed. Maybe it was best to be frank. It seemed to be Marnie's MO.

"I called you because it got me thinking and I ... I want us to be friends."

Marnie's mouth hung open.

"I know it takes time to build real friendships, and I'm sure this is very out of the blue for you, but I'm old. I'm divorced. I'm tired of playing games. I'm tired of the social climbing and using relationships for whatever gain. I know I got onboard with your cohousing project as an advisor, and I'm happy to advise. I'm even happy to invest. But I'd rather be friends." Elsie's heart pounded against her chest. Was she going to give herself a heart attack? She'd never been this forward in her life.

She studied Marnie's face, which slowly split into a wide smile.

The waiter arrived with their tea and scones, taking a while to arrange everything. Elsie wished he'd go. The smile gave her hope, but she needed to hear actual words.

Finally, the waiter left with the menus, and Marnie said, "I like that! I like not playing games. And you'll get no social climbing with me, I guarantee it. Knowing me won't open any doors."

"Good."

Marnie's expression shifted. "So, you want to be friends

with me, or both Shasa and me?"

"Both of you, of course! I just thought I'd start with you, with Shasa being busy with her daughter and Mac..." She paused, looking for clues about what Marnie thought of the developer.

"I know. She's been quite busy lately. I almost wonder..." Marnie stopped and focussed on splitting and buttering her scone.

"What?"

Marnie swallowed a piece of scone and washed it down with tea. Her gaze went out the window, like there was something out there, in the distance. "Shasa's been alone for so long, waiting for that useless man, Ollie. I think she's quite lonely. I know I am. Being alone does things to you. You might find yourself attracted to someone even if it's against your best interest."

"I was wondering about the same thing," Elsie confessed. "I'd hate for her to get hurt."

Marnie turned back to her, eyes blazing. "Oh, my God. Same! That's why I've been so worried. I know we told her to snoop on him, but what if?"

"If she's under his influence, she might accidentally reveal something to him, rather than the other way around. Especially if that's his end game."

Marnie's eyes widened with concern. "He's a bit of a player, isn't he?"

Elsie fiddled with her serviette. "From what I hear."

"Okay. Look. I agree with you, there's a risk. But I don't want to tell her to not date him or whatever, if that's what she wants to do. I don't believe it ever works. Some mistakes we just have to make. And maybe that guy's like a palate cleanser. He's so different to Ollie."

"A palate cleanser? I've never heard that before." Elsie suppressed a smile. She should use these terms with her old Zumba buddies to see if they knew them. She'd clearly been living under a rock.

Marnie took a long sip of her tea, rolling her eyes from behind the cup's golden rim. "Nothing wrong with cleansing Ollie out of her life, though. Anyone who puts the planet before his own child gets a pass in my books."

Elsie gave her a measured look. "If you're worried about Shasa accidentally revealing something, there's an easy solution."

"What?"

"Well, how much does she need to know about the build, the numbers? I mean, eventually she's going to have to sign the purchase agreement and get a mortgage, but we could keep the details vague while we're formalising the plan. I get the idea she's not into budgeting, anyway."

"You're right! She's not a numbers person. She hates doing the community house accounts so much that she volunteered to clean the gutters to get out of it. She signs anything I put in front of her."

"That's not very wise."

"She trusts me."

"We don't want to abuse her trust."

Marnie shook her head. "No, but like you said, we don't want her to get hurt. And if this guy's playing her, then he's playing us. If he succeeds, we all lose out, including Shasa."

Elsie took a breath and gave a firm nod. The sun had broken out from behind the clouds and cast its warm glow on the opposite side of the river, the perfect afternoon tea moment.

She dropped her butter knife on the plate and cast a meaningful look at her new friend. "We'll make sure that doesn't happen."

Chapter 21

Thursday afternoon, Shasa dropped her bursting canvas bag on the floor and joined her friend at a table in the Grey Gardens Cafe. Marnie had left work early to visit their mortgage advisor and had invited Shasa and Elsie for a 'cohousing catchup' in Hamilton East afterwards.

The tiny café, Shasa's favorite, was full of recycled items, including sixties style school desks for tables. Best of all, it had a playroom that kept Lilla happy. Oh, the bliss of child-free teatime.

It had been nearly a week since her movie night with Mac. The following day, he'd sent a text confirming their next rehearsal on Thursday night. Reading those few words had made her wobbly all over again, but since then, she hadn't heard a word. With each day that passed without seeing him or hearing from him, she found it easier to function. Drawing from Marnie's enthusiasm, she found herself enthusiastic about the cohousing project again.

"Hi there," Marnie chirped, pulling a stack of papers from her handbag. "Good news! According to the mortgage advisors, it looks like we can make this work with four investors – me, you, and the mystery person we haven't found yet – as long as Elsie covers the remaining deposit."

Shasa nodded, excitement coursing through her. Marnie had filled her in on her meeting with Elsie and assured her they were forging ahead. She reached for the papers, but Marnie tucked them inside a black folder.

"Don't worry. We're getting a good deal."

"I just want to see the total."

Marnie's grin was cheeky as she slipped the folder into her bag. "Why? So you can choke on your tea? Relax. It's Thursday, the week's almost over!"

Shasa took a long sip of her tea as soon as it arrived, wincing as it burned her throat. Tonight, she'd see him again. The thought turned her insides to jelly.

"Besides, I have something you'll find far more interesting..." Marnie winked as she laid a stack of paint samples on the table.

"Paint samples!" Shasa grabbed the pile and flipped through it.

She'd spent far too many nights on Pinterest, saving ideas for her dream home. It wasn't the healthiest activity for someone on a tight budget, but it was the only way she could avoid thinking about Mac. If she kept her eyes on the prize, she could have a forever home for her and her daughter. It was worth every sacrifice. Even better, she was doing it with a friend – or as Marnie now insisted – friends.

The door rattled, and their new friend Elsie walked in. Shasa lifted her hand in greeting and smiled. She couldn't quite understand why the fancy lady wanted to befriend them, or even what she meant by it. Shasa couldn't imagine the three of them hanging out, watching a movie and eating pizza or painting toenails. Still, she was grateful Elsie hadn't pulled the plug on their project. If the lady needed a friend, she'd be one.

Elsie sat down at the tiny school desk acting as a table, her eyes wide. "Interesting ... um, cafe."

They followed her gaze, which landed on a retro electric whisk that hung on the wall.

Shasa gestured at the counter. "The scones are amazing."

Marnie got up. "I'll order for you."

Elsie waved her to sit back down. "I can see there's no table service. That's fine." She got up and went to place an order.

Shasa was grateful the line was short; she had a feeling Elsie wasn't used to standing in one.

When Elsie returned to the table, Shasa and Marnie had narrowed down the selection of paint swatches by half.

"We figure these are too bright or too boring. What do you think?" Shasa handed the 'no' pile to Elsie, who flipped through them.

Elsie pulled out a sheet of greys. "I wouldn't discard this. I've used some of these with great success. This one with a blue hue is very calming, perfect for the bedroom."

Shasa placed the sheet back in the 'yes' pile.

"But I didn't come here to look at paint samples. I'm sure you're capable of picking colours you like. If something doesn't work, you can always repaint."

Shasa nodded, knowing she couldn't afford to repaint in years.

A young waiter in a bushy hipster beard and a beanie approached them with a scone. Elsie did a double take but moved her iPhone to make room for the plate.

Once the waiter was gone, Elsie scooted closer and dropped her volume. "Your landlord approached me today. He's ready to hear our offer. I assured him he'd have it by the end of the week, and that it would be worth his while. If we can't find out what Mac's offering, we'll just have to take a guess. An educated guess."

"So, he's happy to wait?" Shasa asked, amazed.

Elsie brushed invisible crumbs off her silky blouse. "I introduced myself earlier, he'd have googled me by now."

Shasa and Marnie exchanged a knowing look. They'd googled her and could imagine the effect. Elsie had a high profile, her name popping up in various articles about property business and new developments. It was mostly in connection with her ex-husband, even her divorce settlement had made local news. Shasa couldn't imagine what it was like to live under such spotlight.

"Well … I'm meeting Mac again tonight," Shasa said, her face burning. "Maybe I can find out something."

Marnie's eyebrows shot up. "Tonight? Is it getting serious?"

Elsie frowned, confused. "Are you two … dating?"

"No, no!" Shasa's heart pounded in her chest. "I'm absolutely not dating him! I told you about the play. I agreed to audition, and now we have a rehearsal with the director."

Elsie nodded, studying her thoughtfully. "Be careful. He's a very clever man. You might think you're spying on him, but he could be playing the same game."

"I know." Shasa hid behind her teacup. Could they tell what had already happened? She was sure her ears were bright red. They felt hot.

Marnie turned to Elsie. "I emailed you the loan documents. Did you have a chance to take a look?"

Elsie buttered her scone. "I had a quick look. It's a decent offer, considering we're doing something a bit unorthodox. You know what the banks are like."

Shasa peered into the playroom to check on Lilla. The girl was filling a miniature oven with stuffed animals, talking to herself.

Shasa turned back to Elsie and Marnie. "How much can we offer for the section?"

Marnie and Elsie exchange a look.

"What?" Shasa demanded. Why did they look like they

were breaking up with her?

After a dreadfully long moment, Marnie spoke. "Maybe you shouldn't look at the numbers just yet. You're hanging out with this guy who's trying to find out our plans. I trust you, but I know how easy it is to let something slip. So I thought, if you don't know the details, you can't possibly reveal anything. Even if the dude drugged you, and..."

"He's not going to drug me!" Shasa buried her burning face in her hands. This was humiliating, but her friend had a point. She didn't trust herself around Mac. She was under some horrible spell and would take her friends down with her.

"That's a good idea," she said in a small voice. "I'm terrible with numbers anyway, I shouldn't be discussing them with anyone."

"How's it going with Mac?" Elsie asked softly, sipping her coffee. "Are you gaining his trust?"

Shasa stirred her tea. "I'm ... getting to know him." Worried about her face giving her away, Shasa got up to check on Lilla.

She found the girl standing on the toy oven, throwing building blocks on the floor. Shasa helped her put the toys away, a task her daughter embraced for ten-seconds before getting distracted by a stuffed parrot.

When she returned to the table with her girl in tow, Shasa found Elsie talking to the guy in the beanie, trying to find out how they made the best scones she'd ever tasted. "Could you just give me a hint?"

"Sorry, it's a trade secret." The waiter winked and left with their empty plates.

Shasa sat down with Lilla in her lap and gave her the remains of her scone. She tackled it with enthusiasm.

Elsie smiled at them, eyes sparkling. "It's good, isn't it? Thank you, girls! Without you, I'd have never discovered this place! Now, if we're done with the cohousing items for now, I could use some advice."

"From *us*?" Shasa blurted.

"What kind of advice?" Marnie asked, far more appropriately.

"Shasa, you may remember a gentleman caller I had the other night?"

"The council guy! Earl?"

"Yes, Earl."

Shasa noticed Elsie's cheek twitch, like a wayward smile trying to break through. Elsie liked Earl! With everything else going on, Shasa had forgotten all about her visit to Elsie's house.

Elsie recounted the night's events for Marnie's benefit, her cheeks getting rosier as she spoke. She sighed. "Now I don't know what to do. I don't like how things ended, but how do I fix it? The only idea I've had so far is to make a similar surprise visit to his house. I've had his address for years, since I always send a Christmas card…"

Shasa and Marnie shook heads in unison.

"Don't just turn up," Marnie said. "You said he works at

the council. How do you think he lives?"

Elsie shrugged. "I don't know. But he invited himself over, so I thought if I do the same, make a fool of myself, that'll balance things between us."

Shasa grimaced. "When your house isn't that nice, surprise visits can be humiliating. At least call ahead and give him time to get ready. Better yet, offer to meet somewhere else, like a restaurant."

Elsie raised her brow. "I hadn't thought of that. You're right. I'll call and ask him out for dinner."

"Or coffee?" Marnie added. "That way he doesn't have to dress up."

"Right." Elsie slid her fingers under her gold necklace like it was strangling her. "This is really not my area. I haven't been out on a date in decades."

"Don't think of it as a date," Marnie suggested. "Just two friends catching up."

Elsie stared out the window, deep in thoughts. "Okay. I can do that."

Shasa could barely imagine what it was like to be single at Elsie's age. She'd been out of the game for five years, two of them in this limbo of long-distance abstinence. If she had to get back out there, she'd be just as lost. She wanted to share these feelings, but how could she talk to them about Mac?

Lilla fidgeted in her lap. Noticing the restless girl, Marnie gathered the paint samples. "Good meeting, girls! So, Shasa will spy on Mac, Elsie will patch things up with Earl, and I—

"Babysit Lilla?" Shasa cast her a pleading look. "Remember, I need a babysitter tonight, for the rehearsal?"

Marnie's hand flew over her mouth. "Oh, no! I can't! I know I said I'm free all week, but Tom called yesterday. He's coming home and wants to take me to this gallery that's showing one of his paintings. I'm so sorry!" Marnie's firstborn had started college and was rarely home.

Shasa's heart fell. "No, I'm sorry. I should have double checked. Seeing your son is way more important!" She'd have to cancel on Mac. Her whole body ached at the thought, even if part of her was relieved.

Marnie squeezed her arm. "Could you get a babysitter through an agency?"

Shasa hugged Lilla, who'd coated herself in scone crumbs and was trying to climb on the table. She'd never used a babysitting service. How would her daughter react to a random stranger?

"I'll take her," Elsie said. "Just bring her over with some extra clothes and whatever she needs."

Shasa's mouth dropped open. "Are you sure?" Was she just being polite? Lilla could be a lot to handle. What if Elsie decided she didn't want anything to do with them after the babysitting gig?

Elsie offered her a reassuring smile. "I'm sure."

Questions running through her mind, Shasa turned to Lilla. "Would you like to play with the doggy tonight?"

"Yesss!"

"Sold." Shasa turned to Elsie and lowered her voice. "Can you please put any priceless artwork and stuff like that behind locked doors? I won't be able to cover the cost should anything happen."

Elsie's hand did a dismissive wave. "I have great insurance."

After they'd settled on the details, Elsie got up, waved them all goodbye and disappeared out the door.

Marnie got up and scooped Lilla in her arms. "Are you sure about this?" she asked Shasa.

"She'll be fine, I think. She loves the dog."

"How about you?"

Shasa took a deep breath, trying to erase the image of Mac her brain offered up in vivid detail. Was she going to be okay?

Chapter 22

Elsie took another look at her living room, trying to see it through a child's eyes. Was there anything interesting? She had no toys. All she had was an old, tired dog, napping on the couch. Why had she signed up for this? She had no experience with children, at least no recent experience. She'd looked after her sister's child a few times before his untimely death over twenty years ago. After that, Bridie had left her husband, the unwitting driver of the car, and moved overseas. These days, she was happily settled in Sydney with a long-term partner and a cat. There were no other kids in Elsie's immediate family, so it had been easy to keep little people at arm's length.

Elsie strolled into the kitchen and lined up the age-appropriate snacks she'd bought on her way home. She heard the doorbell and quickly closed her laptop. Shasa didn't need to see her searching 'foods three-year-olds like' on Google.

Shasa stood at the door holding Lilla's hand, using her other one to manoeuvre a huge rectangular pack Elsie guessed was the travel cot.

Elsie held open the door, hoping her smile was relaxed. "Come on in."

"Where's doggy?" Lilla asked, looking up at her.

Elsie pointed to the living room, and the girl sprinted away, her socks slipping and sliding on the polished wooden floor. An adorable unicorn backpack hung off her shoulders, stuffed so full that the unicorn looked bloated.

"Don't run, walk!" Shasa called after her.

Elsie noted that Shasa wasn't wearing her usual ensemble of ethnic fabric and excessive jewellery. Her outfit was rather revealing – denim shorts and a light knit over a tank top. Elsie understood the shorts – the night was exceptionally balmy for early March – but she wondered if Shasa was changing her style for Mac. She didn't want to ask, since the girl had been so touchy about it in the cafe. Developing feelings for someone you shouldn't was confusing and embarrassing. Elsie could certainly see why women fell for Mac. He wasn't Shasa's type, but he possessed charisma similar to movie stars. No wonder he was acting in this play.

"Would you like a cup of tea before you go?"

Shasa shook her head. "No, sorry, I'm running a bit late, and I don't want to draw out the goodbyes. It's easier with Lilla if I just go."

She heaved the travel cot inside and carried it to the living room. To Elsie's relief, she set it up in the corner. One less thing for her to worry about.

Lilla had found her spot on the couch next to the dog. Poor Stina already had three pink hair clips hanging off her fur and a little girl with a hairbrush working on her tail. Thank goodness the dog was mellow.

After everything was set up, Elsie saw Shasa back to the door. The girl seemed on edge, like she was expecting the sky to fall at any moment.

"We'll be fine," Elsie reassured, as much for herself as for Shasa.

As soon as the door clicked, Lilla appeared by her side, panic in her eyes. "Where's Mummy?"

"She'll be back soon. Let's go back to doggy."

"Mummy!" Lilla reached for the doorknob, desperately trying to turn it.

Elsie moved in to stop her from actually getting out, the terrifying screams sending shrills down her spine. Two-seconds in, and this was already a disaster. At least Shasa wouldn't hear anything through her solid, custom made door. She was probably already at her car.

The girl hung off the doorknob, tears running down her face. Elsie needed help, but who could she call?

Earl! He had children and grandchildren. He'd know what to do. Before she could talk herself out of it, Elsie ran to grab her phone off the kitchen counter and dialled.

While she waited for Earl to pick up, Lilla opened the front door. Elsie ran ahead of her to check the front gate was closed. All good. Having made it out of the house, the girl seemed calmer, her sobs subsiding as she explored the garden. It was still light, but the low sun cast long shadows across the lawn.

Earl's 'hello' sounded like a question.

"Hi, Earl," Elsie said. "I'm so sorry to call you like this, but I could really use your help. I'm looking after Shasa's little one. She's three, and she got very upset when her mum left. I honestly don't know why I said I could do this. I don't have kids in my family, and I'm completely out of my depth."

She was cut off by Lilla's harrowing scream. It seemed the girl had figured out her mum wasn't hiding in the garden.

Elsie raised her voice to compete with the cries. "So, if you have any tips on how to settle her, what to do ... I'd be very grateful!"

"She sounds quite upset. How about I come over with some toys, and we tackle this together? I keep some things in my house for the grandkids."

"That would be wonderful!"

They ended the call with Earl promising to get to her as soon as possible.

Elsie slipped the phone in her pocket and looked for Lilla. It was suddenly quiet. The girl had vanished. After double checking the garden, Elsie returned to the house, her heart pounding. The front door was still open. Had the girl gone back inside?

Elsie hurried to the living room and there she was, back on the couch, hugging the dog like nothing had happened.

Lilla cast her a measured look. "Mummy's gone."

"Yes, she's gone. She'll be back later. We can play with the dog. And have snacks."

By the time Earl arrived, Elsie had managed to give Lilla one grape.

"She won't accept any food," Elsie said, grateful for Earl's presence.

He gave her a comforting smile. "Maybe she's not hungry?" The plastic crate under his arm looked heavy, full of worn out, mismatched toys. "Trust me, this stuff is kryptonite," he said, dropping it on the living room floor.

"Lilla?" he called the girl. "Would you like to have a look at these toys?"

Lilla glance up from the couch, her eyes still wet with tears.

"It's okay if you don't. I know another girl who might like them, I'll just take them to her instead."

Lilla perked up and slid herself off the couch. "I can take the toys."

"Good girl. I'll leave them here, then."

She started digging through the box like her life depended on it, pulling out one-legged barbies and other unidentifiable objects.

Earl joined Elsie on the couch. "She'll calm down soon."

"Thank you so much!"

Earl seemed less nervous than the last time he'd been in her house. He sat back on the couch and sighed. "Kids are pretty straight-forward. Their brains get stuck on something and you have to get them to switch gears. Most of the time you can simply distract them."

Lilla held up a stuffed unicorn and smiled. "I found unicorn!"

Elsie stared at Earl, full of newfound appreciation. "I can't believe how quickly you calmed her down!"

She'd always liked Earl. He'd been nice, helpful, and loyal. But she'd never thought of him as someone who came to her rescue, someone who took charge of the situation.

"Let's all get something to eat," she suggested, getting to her feet.

Lilla followed them into the dining room, probably out of curiosity. Elsie set all the snacks she'd bought on the table and made a cup of tea for herself and Earl. When she returned from the kitchen with the cups, she found Lilla at the table, helping herself to a handful of grapes.

The corner of Earl's mouth tugged upwards. "I think she's hungry now."

Elsie joined them at the table, dipping a rice cracker in hummus. She knew Lilla had eaten an early dinner, so she'd filled bowls with strawberries, grapes, crackers, cheese, bread and various dips. After getting home, she'd stared at the selection in despair, wondering if any of it was child friendly.

"She's eating!" Elsie marvelled. "I thought I got it all wrong. I should've bought those kiddy biscuits, or yogurt, or cereal."

Earl laughed. "You're overthinking this." He had a nice laugh, one that beckoned her to join in.

"How many grandkids do you have?" To her surprise, she sounded relaxed in her own ears. The topic of children had been off the table for such a long time, she'd assumed herself incapable of discussing it without a cloud of pain.

"Four," Earl answered, popping a grape in his mouth. "The youngest was only just born. Little Ayla."

"Congratulations! What a lovely name!"

He nodded. "You have to be grateful these days if it's a proper name, don't you? Not a colour, or a food, or something else they thought to repurpose."

"Oh my God, you're right! Like Blue, or Cinnamon, or ... Princess."

Earl smiled along, his gaze lingering on her face like waiting for the right moment. "I was wondering," he said, shifting in his seat. "Could you tell me more about the cohousing community? Is it all sold out?"

Elsie raised her brow in surprise. "Are you interested?"

"I just sold my unit in Whitiora, close to all those motels. It was handy for work, but it got a bit too restless there for my liking."

Elsie shuddered, thinking of the area. "Yes, two out of four units are still available. And Marama Street is lovely. Very close to here."

If Earl bought into the community, he'd be on the opposite side of the small lake. She hoped he was interested in the connection, rather than just a place to live. A strange buzz vibrated in her stomach, like butterflies waking up after thirty years of hibernation. She couldn't remember the last time she'd felt this way, sitting next to a man.

Earl's voice was serious. "I understand it's not a regular housing development. I looked up some links about cohousing. I rather like the basic principles, such as sharing the outdoor areas."

"It's very good for grandkids!" Elsie agreed. "And this is a small-scale community with no frills. We're not building a common house or anything like that, just four units. The girls would be delighted to have you."

"I'd love to talk to them about it in better circumstances." Earl cleared his throat. "Last time, I left quite abruptly. I'm sorry about that. It was..."

Elsie could see him struggling for words and jumped in. "It's all good. A misunderstanding. I'm sorry, too. I was quite tone deaf myself. I haven't really ... um ... dated in decades, to be honest. It's been very quiet since the divorce." She let out a sigh, relieved to be speaking honestly. All the politeness was getting on her nerves.

Lilla reached for the last grape in the bowl, her eyes searching for the next best thing on offer. Strawberries.

Earl turned his chair to face Elsie. "I find that hard to

believe. You're absolutely gorgeous." Earl's face turned red with the bold statement, but he didn't turn away. He held his head up high, the light in his eyes burning more brightly than before.

Elsie experienced a sudden jolt. Maybe he wasn't such a teddy bear. Maybe she'd misjudged him. A man didn't need to be a self-important jerk to have presence, or courage.

As if reading her mind, Earl planted a light kiss on her cheek. It was forward, yet reserved, like a formal invitation.

She smiled and kissed him back, this time on the mouth. It was hardly more than a friendly peck, but she'd never done anything so playful. Elsie pulled back, and a giggle escaped her lips. She hardly recognised the sound as coming from own mouth.

"Yuck!" Lilla yelled, smiling with a mouth full of strawberry, bright red juice running down her chin.

"Right back at you, buddy," Earl chuckled, handing her a napkin. "I like Auntie Elsie, I hope you're okay with that?"

Lilla shrugged. "I guess."

Elsie couldn't help laughing at her suspicious, wide-eyed expression. For the first time in twenty years, she felt lucky to be Auntie Elsie. Maybe there was hope for her yet.

Chapter 23

The single spotlight cast a perfect, bright circle on the stage floor. Mac did some deep breathing, trying to prepare himself for the rehearsal. Last weekend's events played in his mind like a film reel, an R-rated film. He couldn't believe he was so out of sorts over someone like Shasa. Not that she wasn't sexy. She was probably every Greenpeace volunteer's wet dream. But not his.

They were night and day, so horribly wrong for each other that the following morning, he'd called Rick and pleaded for him to set him up with a date. He'd clearly been alone for too long and needed to focus his sexual energy on someone else. Anyone. Anyone who wasn't trying to sabotage his most important business deal yet. That was a large enough scope, surely. There must be a woman out there who could take his mind off Shasa.

Shasa. Gareth had gone out to make a phone call, which left him alone with Shasa when she arrived. A dangerous move. She was wearing a tank top and denim shorts. Bloody woman. Bloody never-ending summer season.

He shook his head, waving his finger at her outfit. "What the hell is this? We agreed on sacks, remember?"

She pulled her adorable face. "It's one hundred degrees out there! And Gareth said we should wear something we're comfortable to move in. Sacks are really cumbersome. I tried." She took a step closer, imitating his finger-waving. "Besides, you're not doing your part." Her waving finger landed on his T-shirt-covered chest, waking up his body like she'd hit a big red button.

He steadied his feet, willing for Gareth's phone call to end. "I don't have anything else. It's T-shirts and jeans, or a suit."

"If you truly cared, you'd wear those pyjamas."

"In public?"

"It's Hamilton! Go shopping in Nawton, you'll see pyjamas in public every night!"

"I don't go shopping in Nawton."

"Of course, you don't. That's why I said 'go'." She flashed a cheeky grin, and her gaze dipped to his lips.

"You need to take a step back," he whispered, inhaling her, wrapping his arms around her waist. She was so delicate, yet wild and foreign, someone he'd never truly understand but still wanted.

He stood for a moment, breathing in the darkness that

allowed them to misbehave, waiting for a cue, something to stop him. Could he risk a taste of her?

Gareth would be here any second, he'd force them to rein it in. She was so close. He could almost taste her, taste the willingness that had burned in her eyes on Saturday night, evidenced by the stain on his jeans she'd left behind. Her scent had lingered in the air, intoxicating. He'd met willing women before, plenty of them, but no one had ever climbed on him like that, with such fierceness. Getting involved with Shasa was probably a bad idea, a story without a happy ending, but he'd keep the memory of that moment. A perfect movie scene he'd watch over and over.

As if reading his mind, Shasa moved sideways, brushing her leg over the bulge in his jeans. She whispered, "It's good we're not alone tonight. I couldn't trust myself."

"Me neither," he rasped, closing the distance, his mouth landing on her parted lips with force he could barely contain, muffling the soft moan that escaped her.

Fireworks, as soon as their tongues collided. And at that moment, the door opened.

***

"Evening," Gareth bellowed, bursting into the room.

Shasa launched herself off Mac at the exact moment he let go of her, resulting in an uncoupling that was far too theatrical, even in a theatre. But it was dark, and they were far from the spotlight. Their feet clattered on the hardwood floor. Shasa's brain scrambled for a way out, a way to undo everything.

Before she could form a coherent thought, Mac grabbed her hand and spun her around on the floor like they were dancing.

"What are you doing?" Gareth asked.

Mac let go of Shasa, smiling. "We were just acting out that scene where they go to the stairs, holding hands, and Audrey walks past. He spins her around and guides her up. We were trying to figure out if there's a way to do that without stairs on stage. Probably not, but it's such good comedy."

Gareth nodded. "I see you watched the film then? Great! I'm not sure we'll have stairs. If we can figure out a way to use them for more than one joke, maybe it's feasible."

"That makes sense."

Shasa stared at Mac, astonished at how effortlessly he could think on his feet. He didn't even sound nervous. Gareth's gaze shifted from Mac to her. She smiled, not trusting herself to speak. She'd never be able to match Mac's breezy tone.

If Gareth suspected anything, he didn't show it. He asked them to join him on the stage and kicked off a series of warm-up exercises. All the jumping, flexing and stretching made Shasa feel like she was at the gym, something that hadn't happened in years. It was more fun than a workout though. Moving her body in a dimly lit space felt liberating, like swimming in the night.

"Theatre is physical," Gareth explained. "You need stamina, flexibility, endurance."

Shasa flinched. Trying to focus on stretching her mouth open like a lion then squinting like a mouse, her facial muscles ached. She walked everywhere and sometimes took part in exercise classes at the community house, but she didn't train every muscle group. She survived.

After a couple of minutes of trying to touch their noses with their tongues, Gareth stopped them. "Okay, that's enough warm-up for now."

"Thank God!" Shasa gasped, erupting in giggles. Watching Mac stretch his tongue, she couldn't concentrate on anything else.

Gareth handed them two scripts. They flipped to a scene further on in the story.

"I have one highlighter. Did either of you bring a pen? Let's do a cold read and you can mark your own lines any way you want. This is the scene we decided to use for the auditions. Not the whole scene, just the first two pages."

Shasa began reading, casting her mind back to the princess waking up in Joe's bed, not remembering how she got there.

Gareth rustled his copy of the script. "I love this scene. Joe now knows she's a princess. The stakes are higher. She wakes up slowly. In her half-asleep state, she reveals how much she enjoyed her nightly escapade, thinking it was a dream. Then, she fully wakes up and tries to process what happened, but she doesn't react like a commoner. She's trained to act gracefully in any situation."

Shasa swallowed, thinking of how she'd acted in Mac's house.

Gareth turned to Mac. "Joe's put everything on the line here. He's gambled his money, his career. It all hinges on her. He needs a story from the princess. He needs to keep her in his apartment, to stay with her long enough to get the photographer there to take pictures. But he's also enamoured by her sweet innocence and beauty. He's never met anyone like Anya before."

Shasa glanced at Mac. He stared at the script, frozen and glassy-eyed. She could tell he wasn't reading it.

Gareth went on, his deep voice making her feel like she was listening to radio. "What's important here is that they're both deceiving each other. Joe conceals the fact that he's a reporter. Princess Ann introduces herself as Anya, thinking she can hide her identity from him. Each of them thinks they're fooling the other, and that's where the tension arises."

Shasa's body heat rose, steaming out of her like she was on a stove. It was the after effect of the exercises, nothing to do with her and Mac, she told herself. This movie, or play, wasn't about them. For starters, she wasn't a princess. Marnie had told her that in her short hairdo, she looked a lot like Audrey Hepburn, a lovely compliment. Maybe that was why

Gareth wanted her to audition. but that's where the similarities ended.

Prompted by Gareth, they read through the scene, trying to memorise the lines. The stage adaptation was a bit different to the movie, but the beats were essentially the same.

Next, they moved on to acting out the scene. Shasa dutifully laid herself down on the stage, relishing the sensations of the cold the floor against her back. It grounded her. Acting in itself was an escape – being someone else, someone without the internal conflict that made her a wobbly mess, especially around Mac. She'd kissed him again, knowing Gareth was about to step in any moment. She was getting reckless, hormones running rampant in her veins.

Gareth poked her with a rolled-up yoga mat. "Put that under you, it'll be more comfortable."

She did, laying down on the slightly sticky mat. Mac hovered at the edge of the spotlight, giving her a bit of space.

"Now, allow yourself to go into the story. You're a real princess. The real deal. That's all you've ever known."

Shasa nodded, her eyes closed. Whatever she thought about the monarchy, whatever Ollie thought about it, there was no way of doing this without going all in. She drew from her own experience, waking up, remembering something tantalising had happened the night before, enjoying the memory before her conscious brain kicked in.

"I'll feed you the lines this time," Gareth said. "Let's just run through it once."

They did. Shasa was surprised how easy it was to stay in character, even with someone speaking words in her ear, words she had to first process, then repeat as her own. Mac didn't seem to need the script or a stage whisperer. He played off her reactions, radiating a mixture of fascination and nerves that perfectly fit the scene. He wasn't doing Gregory Peck. There was more angst, a different masculine energy that reminded her of James Franco. Unpredictable, cheeky, dangerous.

They ran the scene twice.

"Let's go through it once more," Gareth suggested. "Try something different, whatever you want. Forget the lines, use your own words. Have fun."

Shasa laid back on the mat, her nerves sizzling in the most delicious way. She'd just follow Mac's lead; he was so much better at this. Clearing her head of further thoughts, she stretched her arms over her head, imagining herself waking up after that Saturday night, reliving the craziest thing she'd ever done.

"I had the craziest dream." She sighed. "A gorgeous, hot guy took me into his house. I was someone else, someone fearless ... I didn't act ... proper. I was a naughty girl..."

She cracked her eyelids and peered through her lashes at the blurry darkness. Mac was right there, hovering above her like he was about to eat her, but somehow held himself back.

"Is that right?" he asked, his voice low and gravelly. "Tell me, what did you do?"

That woke her up. Her mouth dropped open, and she scrambled up, hugging herself.

"What did I do?" she asked, her heart pounding. "What happened?"

He sat back, his eyes soft. "Nothing to be ashamed of. And something I'll always remember." His voice was achingly wistful, making her chest squeeze.

It was just a scene. Make believe. But his words soothed her like balm, like he was trying to talk to her through this alternate reality. She tried to compose herself. Be a royal. But she'd played the role differently, her words lacked grace, they dripped with real worry and regret, her voice catching in her throat. "Thank you for saying that, but I must forget. I don't know how, but I must."

"Thank you," Gareth said quietly. "I think I need to rewrite this scene."

Cold sweat prickled on Shasa's neck. "Did we ... do it wrong?"

Gareth broke into a smile. "No! No! You guys are fantastic. You brought so much more to it that it made me think. We can do more with the emotions at play here. Less cute, more real. The shame, the arousal ... the regret. It's not the fifties anymore, we can take this story to the next level. Joe's character could be a bit more dangerous, less of a gentleman."

The spotlight glinted off Mac's eyes. "I'm okay with that."

Oh, no!

"And Shasa, your character could have more pent-up desire, ferocity. She's been in a prison of sorts and hasn't been able to live life on her terms. Now, she's going after what she wants."

More ferocity? Shasa was already scared of what welled under the surface. She was out of her depth, yet part of her wanted to drown.

She weaved her hands together to stop them from shaking. "Sure." Standing up, she rolled up the yoga mat and returned it to Gareth.

They made plans to meet up in three days at Mac's, since the theatre was booked.

Gareth rubbed his hands together. "Thank you, guys! You've given me a lot to work with. I'll bring the updated script, so don't worry about learning the lines for now. Just work on your intentions, inner dialogue, all that. In fact, maybe go out tonight, grab some dinner, get to know each other. You have to be able to trust each other implicitly, since you may be asked to do a bit of improv, too."

"Will you come with us?" Shasa asked, her heart thumping in her chest.

"I would, but I need to get home. We have a babysitter booked and we're going to see a cabaret."

They hopped off the stage and headed towards the front doors.

Mac turned to Shasa. "That's a good idea. Let's grab some dinner?"

As they reached the door, Gareth stopped at the alarm

control panel on the wall. He punched in a code. "Just be careful not to get involved." He focussed on the digital screen flashing the words 'ALARM ON'. His voice was matter-of-fact, like he'd told them to avoid carbs late at night.

"Involved?" Shasa repeated, her breath shallow.

Mac shot her a warning look and turned to Gareth with a level expression. "Of course not." His voice was relaxed, like he was also talking about carbs and the night bloats. How could they discuss something so flammable in such a prosaic way?

Together, they stepped on the street. Gareth locked the doors, said his goodbyes and hurried towards the carpark. The sun hung low, casting its last rays on the riverside trees.

"Where's your car?" Mac asked Shasa.

She shook her head like her hair was on fire. "Oh, no. We're not going out."

"Why not? Do you have to go home? Who's babysitting? Marnie?"

"No, Elsie. It's not that. We just can't."

Thinking of Lilla and Elsie, she pulled out her phone to check her messages. Elsie had sent a photo of her daughter, asleep in a travel cot, with a caption. 'Happy and asleep. Stay as long as you want.' She showed it to Mac.

"Elsie Alders is looking after your daughter," he said, staring the screen in amazement. "Whad'ya know."

"Yeah, she's great."

"So, you have no excuse." He smiled his permafrost-melting smile, grabbed her hand and placed it on his chest. "Feel me. I'm solid. I won't try anything. Let me just buy you dinner, as a friend. I haven't spoken to you for like two weeks, you've no idea how hard it was, but I kept our agreement."

Shasa's heart did a back flip. She'd thought about calling him, texting him, shadowing him … it had taken all her willpower to not make contact. Knowing it wasn't just her made her both hot and cold. She allowed herself to look into his eyes, to drink in the long shadows his lashes cast across each iris. The chocolate brown glinted with a hint of amber in the evening light.

Shasa licked her bottom lip. "It's been six days and I think we both broke the agreement about an hour ago."

Following her gaze, Mac glanced over his shoulder at the theatre. "Oh, that. It doesn't count. Anything that happens in the theatre is make believe. Didn't you know that?"

Shasa rolled her eyes so theatrically it hurt. Mac squeezed her hand, still placed on his chest, and her lungs vibrated.

"Come on! Just a simple dinner between friends. Then we each go to our respective homes and sleep like logs."

Oh, how she wished it were that easy.

Mac carried on. "We'll be in a restaurant. A public place. It's not like I'm taking you to a secluded spot by the river."

Shasa glanced in the direction of the river. It would have taken them five minutes to cross the street and descend the steps. Nobody would be around. The short stretch of sand would still be warm from the long day in the sun.

Mac's breath tickled her face. "What do you say?"

She exhaled, turned around, and headed towards town. Getting away from the bridge, the river and the warm sand would be job number one.

"I get to choose the restaurant!" she called over her shoulder.

Chapter 24

Shasa took in the visual overload of the Mexican restaurant she'd led them to. She'd counted on it being busy and not too intimate, with shared tables and zero privacy. But seeing there were only two of them, the waiter showed them to a private corner table.

At least there weren't any candles, or a particularly romantic soundtrack. Although she wasn't sure romance was the problem. There was nothing romantic going on between her and Mac. It was primal. Once she got hold of her inappropriate urges, there'd probably be nothing left. If she were lucky, she'd get there without having sex in a public bathroom. Shasa shuddered. She found it reassuring how off-putting the idea sounded. Much worse than the riverside, or his couch. Maybe she was safe here. As long as she didn't order a mojito.

"So, what did you want to chat about?" she asked, trying to keep her voice business-like.

"Can we order first? I'm starving."

"Sure." Shasa shrugged. She was hungry, too. They ordered fajitas and ginger beer, so he wasn't drinking either. Good.

When the drinks arrived, Shasa tried again. "What do you think of *Roman Holiday*? The film? And the play? Honestly."

Mac sat back in his chair, looking out the window. "It's a fairy-tale, but there's something real at the heart of it."

"I know. The secrets they're keeping, how they're both playing a game, and both think they're winning."

"I think he wants to save her." Mac's brown eyes glistened like chocolate lakes she wanted to dive into.

"I thought he wanted to make money out of her, sell her … story?"

"It starts that way. Then he falls for her and it changes. But it's not just about winning her over. If it were, it'd be a happy ending of sorts. She kisses him, so there's your happily ever after. I mean, it's the fifties, they're not going to give you a night of passion. But that's not what he wants. He wants to save her. And he doesn't get to."

"So, it's an unhappy ending?" she asked.

"I suppose."

"You think if the film were made in this decade, they'd spend a night together?"

"Totally. That kiss in the taxi, at the end. It's like a metaphor."

Shasa gave him a slow nod. "A metaphor for sex?"

"Yeah. The director originally wanted to show Gregory Peck pounding Audrey Hepburn against some royal carving somewhere, but they had to downgrade it to that godawful snog in the taxi."

She laughed. "It was an awful kiss! It looked like mouth-to-mouth."

"Back then, they had a three-second rule for kisses on film. Anything longer would've been indecent."

She furrowed her brow. "Are you sure? I think I've seen kisses longer than that in old films."

"You need proof?" He picked up his phone, ready to google it.

She waved her hand. "No. But if that's the rule, we may have broken it a couple of times."

"What? No! With those couple of pecks on the cheek?"

They locked eyes for a moment. Shasa sucked in her bottom lip, thinking of the kiss. She was teasing him, testing his resolve. It was mean, since she hardly had any herself.

Mac took another gulp of his ginger beer and got up. "Excuse me."

She watched him disappear through the bathroom door. Shasa pressed the cold ginger beer bottle against her blazing hot cheek, trying not to think about what it would be like to follow him in there. What was happening to her? Every moment with Mac was another giant step down a slippery slope.

Warm, tingly and distracted, Shasa nearly missed her opportunity. Mac's phone. He'd left it on the table. Could she? Shasa slid her hand across the table and picked it up, trying to act natural. Her forefinger touched the screen, and it came to life. No passcode? He must have bypassed it with his thumb when he'd picked it up a moment ago.

Her heart beating like mad, Shasa opened Mac's email inbox, searching for something related to the section. Within a few seconds, she spotted her landlord's name and opened an email exchange, jumping to the very beginning. Bingo. There it was. No attachment or legal papers. He'd typed his offer for the section in the body of the email. In the next email, her landlord accepted it. Just like that. Cold sweat prickled on Shasa's back. She picked up her own phone, took a photo of the email on Mac's screen, and sent it to her group chat with Marnie and Elsie.

She wanted to keep reading, to see what the latest message was about, but she couldn't risk Mac catching her. She hit the home button and placed the phone back to exactly where it had been, hoping Mac would stay away long enough for the screensaver to activate. Was there a way to turn it on manually? Shasa drank her ginger beer, watching the phone like she was expecting it to catch on fire.

Mac stayed away.

The fajitas arrived, the approaching waiter making her jump. Past the steaming tray he set on the table, she saw that the phone lock screen had finally turned on.

Okay. She was in the clear. The biggest giveaway of her

transgression would now be her face. If she really had any natural acting talent, she needed it now. All of it.

The bathroom door opened, and Mac joined her at the table, hungrily eyeing the food. "This looks good!"

He offered her half of everything, far more than she could handle.

Rather than think about what she'd just done, she reminded herself he wasn't a nice guy. To get to where he'd got in life, he must have taken every opportunity, every advantage he could get. There was no reason to feel sorry for him. He had several houses. Losing this one deal would only hurt his pride.

Shasa tried to focus on her plate. She had to relax her body enough to accept food. As she took a sip of her ginger beer, she noticed Mac's eyes on her.

"Okay, I'm just going ask. You don't have to say anything if you don't want to, but what happened with Lilla's father? Is he around?"

The question took Shasa by surprise, like someone had dunked her head in the river. She hadn't thought about Ollie in days. Was that right? She could hardly believe it. After all the heartbreak she'd wasted obsessing over him and whatever was happening on that ship, she'd turned a corner in the most unexpected, albeit unhealthy way. Like a drug user replacing one substance with another. Mac was her new obsession, one that kept her company late at night, and during quiet moments at work.

"He's not around," she said, poking her fajitas with a fork. It smelled so good, but her intestines were closed for business. Only nerves were at work, misfiring on all cylinders. "He's been away for two years now and just decided to extend his contract on the ship."

"Ship? Is he in the navy?"

Shasa burst out in laughter. Ollie, the life-time pacifist, who couldn't wear leather shoes. "No. He works for Greenpeace. Saving whales, working on oil spills, that kind of thing."

Mac smiled. "That makes more sense."

"When I found out he's wasn't coming home, I cut off my dreadlocks. That's why my hair's like this. The hairdresser tried to fix it, but it was a bit too much of a challenge. I have to wait until it grows out." She pointed at her uneven pixie cut, her hand shaky.

"I like your hair," he said. "You look just like Audrey Hepburn. Except hotter."

Shasa nearly choked on the tiny piece of chicken she'd managed to put in her mouth. She smiled, trying to shrug off the compliment.

Mac shook his head. "What doesn't make sense is why he'd choose to stay away from you and his own daughter?" His voice was thick with compassion.

Shasa shivered. She wasn't ready for this. She could make it through the waves of physical desire, like waves of nausea. You only had to stop and wait, get some fresh air. But she couldn't have him say those things, scrape through the scales over her heart. She had to shut this down.

"It's his dream. He's saving the planet. In the grand scheme of things..." The words got stuck in her throat, unable to get past the fresh lump.

No. No. NO. She was not going to cry. Not here. Not over Ollie. Shasa took a deep breath and counted to five. It almost worked. She was nearly over the hump when he rested his hand on hers, releasing a gush of warmth that shot straight into her heart.

His voice was heavy and solid. "There is no grand scheme of things that matters more than you. Not in this context."

Nothing could stop the tears from falling.

"Let's go." He placed a hundred-dollar note on the table and helped her up from her chair.

She grabbed her handbag and let him guide her out the door, into the cool night air. His arm around her, she felt safe. If only she could stay there forever. If only they were two different people, in a different town, at a different time, they could be happy together. So happy, like Audrey Hepburn had said at the end of the film. So happy. Was there a way, somehow, for this to work?

They walked quietly down the road, back towards the theatre. He didn't take his arm off her shoulder, and she didn't want him to. Maybe this night was all they'd ever get. She wanted to soak it all in, to never forget what it felt to be this desired. To be this heard. She smiled up at him, her lashes heavy like pine needles after rain.

"So happy," she said.

"So happy," he said.

Part of her wanted to leave everything behind, take him by the hand and flee. If they could shed all the baggage. Her job, her plans, his business...

"Let's go to the river," she said, half expecting him to say no.

"Okay."

They strolled down the road onto a side street leading down to the river. Without streetlamps, they had to feel for the footpath, the leaves rustling against their clothes as they descended through the bush onto the sand. In the dark, the water looked solid, a piece of black marble. The sand still held warmth, and the beach was deserted, just like Shasa had imagined. Dangerously deserted.

"What's your favourite place in Hamilton?" she asked as he sat down next to her.

He slid his arm on her shoulder. "Here, with you."

Shasa laughed. She should have wiggled away from under that arm, but she didn't want to. They were in the dark, like in the theatre. It didn't count. "No, seriously, what's your favourite?"

Mac sighed. "Maybe the gardens late at night or early morning when there're no tourists."

"Which one?"

"The Italian one, no contest."

Shasa drew in a sharp breath, her heart beating faster. "No contest. In springtime, at dusk."

Maybe they'd crossed paths in the Renaissance garden in the past without noticing. Shasa shook her head at the thought. This evening, she'd sensed his presence from across the theatre floor before she could even see him.

"It's only physical, right? Pheromones?" she asked, her voice shaky with nerves.

Heavy silence fell between them, filled by a soft woosh of wind that carried the smell of wet earth.

Mac drew his arm off her shoulder, his voice rough. "Honestly ... I don't think sleeping with you would get you out of my system."

Shasa's breath caught in her throat. "Me, neither. I could never have sex with no strings attached. Not without getting hurt. I'm not Teflon."

"If you want to be a good actor, you can't be. You have to be vulnerable."

"Are you?"

She could hardly see him but felt his body shift against her as his voice dropped. "What makes you think I'm not?"

She shrugged. "Money. Power."

His voice was like gravel in her ear. "Shasa. I'm falling in love with you. You'd hurt me by walking away."

Shasa's head swam. She wanted to stay there forever, staring at the black river, talking to him, breathing his scent. But his words carried more weight than she could handle. Was that why he'd left his phone on the table? Because he trusted her, loved her? What had she done?

"I should go," she said, getting up. "I have to pick up Lilla."

He followed her up the path, along the side street, towards the city lights. When they reached the theatre, she turned towards the parking lot. Her car was there, next to his huge, shiny pickup truck. What did he need a pickup truck for? She heard the sound of his keys, and the double beep as he unlocked the doors.

Time to go. His hand was still on her shoulder, the only thing that kept her from falling. Yet she knew she'd already fallen.

"I don't want you to go," she whispered. "I know we're wrong for each other, two people in the wrong place, at the wrong time. It's all wrong, but..."

"I know. Me too."

"I—"

He took her face into his hands and kissed her so deeply and tenderly she couldn't feel the ground under her feet. His hands travelled down, embracing her waist. She pressed herself against him, desperate to close the distance, to keep him there. They broke the three-second rule, ten-second-rule, and probably some modern rules on Netflix, until he finally pulled away.

Mac's voice was gruff. "I know what I promised, and I know this is too little too late, but I'll stop here and let you go. Good night!"

Shasa felt a sharp twist in her gut. After what she'd done with his phone, she needed him to fuck her against that shiny truck, to use her, slap her. Anything. He was supposed to be the bad guy, not her.

Mac brushed the side of her face, his touch unbearably gentle. Then he got into his car and drove away.

Shasa stood in the empty parking lot, letting the warmth of his hands, his mouth and the rest of him fade off her skin, until the last trace of it was replaced by the cool night air.

Her phone pinged, and she opened it to find two enthusiastic messages from Marnie and Elsie. Exclamation marks and party emojis. What a success! The price was lower than Elsie had expected. They could easily outbid him.

It's go time!!! Marnie's text shouted on her screen.

Her eyes blurred by fresh tears, Shasa typed a reply, informing Elsie she'd pick up her daughter in ten minutes. Then she dropped her phone into her bag and sank into her car. If tonight was such a success, why did she feel like she'd just lost everything?

community.

Chapter 25

Shasa parked in front of Elsie's house, tears pooling in her
eyes. She sat in the car and breathed deeply until she felt a
bit better, then got up and approached the door.

Instead of Elsie, the door was opened by Earl. Shasa took
a step back.

"Hi Shasa," he said. "Didn't mean to scare you. Elsie asked
me to help with babysitting."

"Oh. Was Lilla a lot of trouble?"

Elsie appeared by his side. "No, absolutely not."

They seemed cosy together, her friend's eyes shimmering
with joy. Shasa smiled back, trying to push her own mood
aside. She was happy for them. Earl was good for Elsie.

"Earl's also interested in the cohousing community, so he
came over to discuss that."

"I need to discuss it with you and Marnie, obviously," Earl

injected. "But the timing is perfect for me. I've been saving
to buy another place and rent out my old apartment."

Shasa swallowed. "That's wonderful."

It was. If she didn't focus on Mac, it was great news. This
was exactly what they wanted – lovely people joining their
community.

Elsie pulled her inside the house, ushering her towards
the kitchen like the mother hen. "It's quite late and Lilla's
fast asleep. Would you like to have a cup of tea, and spend
the night in the guest room? It might be easier than trying
to transport the poor wee girl? We already moved her cot in
the guest room, so it'll be right by your bed."

Shasa nodded, feeling numb. "That sounds perfect," she
rasped.

Earl picked up his jacket off one of the chairs. "I'll leave
you to it, then. Good night!" He looked like was about to kiss
Elsie but ended up just waving his hand.

Elsie blushed, rushing after him to the front door.

Their sweet, burgeoning relationship made Shasa smile.
She sat down at the dining table, glancing at a display of
half empty snack bowls. She hadn't managed to eat much
tonight. They'd left behind half the meal Mac had overpaid
for. What a waste. With her stomach gradually settling, she
noticed her hunger and cleaned out the remaining crackers
and hummus. Elsie stayed away, probably talking to Earl at
the door, like two teenagers unable to say goodbye. It was so
sweet and good. Not all tangled and wrong like her and Mac.

Shasa got up and tiptoed around the house to find the guest room where her daughter was sleeping. It turned out to be a huge room in its own wing, with its own lounge and an ensuite. Lilla slept peacefully in her cot, her cheeks rosy under the night light's soft glow. It was cosy and inviting, like a country inn. Exhaustion taking over, Shasa lay on the bed, letting her body sink into the plush quilt. She wanted a new home. A safe and comfortable home. But she wanted Mac, too. One way or another, her heart would be broken.

Chapter 26

Mac pulled into his driveway, his heart beating like a drum. He'd turned on the radio and listened to dreadful elevator music the whole way home, but nothing calmed him down. He knew what was happening. He was falling for this girl. It wasn't just physical. He'd known it the moment he wrapped his arm around her, out on the street, in public. He wasn't ashamed to be seen with her. And it wasn't because she was wearing mainstream clothes for once. He wouldn't have cared if she'd been in a rainbow-coloured tribal dress. She was amazing. Brave, selfless, and fierce. He couldn't have cared less about her clothes or political views. He cared too much about her.

Mac got out of his car and looked around. The street was deserted, like it always was – an expensive ghost town. He looked at the house, trying to see it through Shasa's eyes.

What had she thought of it, of him? He knew he could turn her on, and it gave him immense pleasure, but could he offer her more? A life together? Could she be happy with him? Would her child be happy with him around?

Mac approached his house, his head hurting from the unanswered questions. Before he reached the door, his phone rang.

"You're going to love me," Rick said. "I have a date for you next Saturday and she's hot!" Loud dance music nearly drowned out his voice. He must have been at a club.

"Geez, thanks. You shouldn't have."

"Shut up. You were practically begging me. I'll send you the details via text. And another thing..."

"What?" All Mac wanted was to end the phone call and throw himself in bed.

"The Marama Street seller. Is he still onboard? He said he was expecting another offer. Has he got it? We need to be more proactive here. Offer more. Now."

"He said he'd let me know when he gets another offer, and we can negotiate."

"No! If the other offer's a lot higher, he'll think you won't be able to match it and he'll sign the papers. We already told him we were giving him our best price. He doesn't know we're lowballing. He's not that bright."

Rick was right. Mac hung his head, angry with himself. He'd been distracted and complacent, thinking Shasa's group would never get their ducks in a row to compete with him.

They were just poking him with a stick to annoy him, show him he wasn't untouchable. Which he definitely wasn't. He was an idiot.

Rick's voice blasted through his phone, agreeing with his inner dialogue. "Don't be an idiot! The other section needs to be in the bag, too. Get your parents to sign on the dotted line, okay?"

"Okay."

He'd go over this weekend for Sunday lunch and sort it out. Since Shasa's house was right next door, he could pop in to see her as well. He needed to talk to her, pour out his heart and see if it was possible. There was no other way. All this other crap standing between them, like ... a couple of million dollars' worth of real estate ... there had to be a way to work that out. Even if it meant he should lose. Even if he had to sell half his portfolio. Mac swallowed, realising what he was suggesting to himself. He'd be finished in this town. He'd have to move somewhere else, start over. Was he ready to gamble everything he had?

Chapter 27

Lilla woke early on Saturday morning. Shasa got up and gave her a banana, hoping to postpone breakfast. She'd slept poorly. Again. Ever since Thursday night, her mind was scrambled. On Friday, she'd waited all day to hear from Mac. Instead, she'd received a Skype call from Ollie. She'd fetched Lilla for him but had stayed out of the room and ended the call when he'd tried to talk to her. Whatever it was, she didn't have the mental capacity to take it in.

She couldn't stop thinking about Mac's arm around her, the words he'd dropped in her lap like hot coals. Why had she picked up his phone and read his email? Did she really want the new house so badly? Was it worth it? If only she could return to that moment in the restaurant ... but it was too late. She'd made her choice.

Elsie had contacted her landlord straight away, but they

hadn't yet heard back. Shasa wondered if her friends would keep her in the loop. Surely, she'd proven her trustworthiness. Would someone who was falling in love with Mac act the way she had?

Shasa lowered herself on the couch, watching Lilla dance around the lounge with her banana. No more sleep, then.

"Pancakes?" she asked her daughter without even lifting her head.

Lilla nodded vigorously. She stuffed the rest of the banana in her mouth and reached out a sticky hand to pull Shasa up.

Shasa resisted, collapsing back on the couch. She'd just relax for one more snooze.

A knock on the door a jolted her, forcing her upright. Who was bothering them at this ungodly hour? It was only six in the morning.

She staggered to open the door.

Mac's eyes burned bright and warm in the early morning sun. "I'm sorry, I tried, but I couldn't stay away," he said, taking a step closer.

The way he looked at her made Shasa ache. Unable to handle his gaze, she stared down at her striped night socks. She hadn't even brushed her teeth yet, but her whole body fought her brain, desperate to dive inside his arms.

"I didn't want you to stay away," she whispered, letting him pull her against his chest.

Here, she was safe. She was okay.

But she had to tell him. "We're making an offer on this section. I'm sorry."

She expected him to pull away, but he didn't.

"That's okay. It's just an offer. Can we put that aside for this morning? I have something I want to show you. You and Lilla."

Shasa shivered. He didn't know what she'd done. He didn't know their offer was higher, perfectly calculated to beat his.

Shasa lifted her chin and met his gaze. "But what if we get it?"

His expression was dark. "If we get into a bidding war, and you win ... I don't know. To tell you the truth, I've got a lot riding on this. If you win, I'll have to sell up."

"Sell up? Everything?"

"I'm in a bit of tight spot. The banks are tightening their lending criteria. They've started liquidating high risk assets. Mine are right up there so ... so, I don't know."

Shasa took a step back, her mouth hanging open. "But ... you have so many houses! You're rich."

"I've had some setbacks, so I really need this one to work out. Otherwise, I wouldn't get in the way of your cohousing project. I really like that idea." He paused for a moment, his eyes searching for hers. "And I like you."

Shasa couldn't swallow. With the cantaloupe-sized lump in her throat, she could hardly breathe. She felt Lilla's arms around her legs, then Mac's hands around her face, guiding her to make eye contact.

"I'm so sorry about the cohousing thing. I'll help you guys

find another piece of land, I promise. Can we please put that aside for now? I have a surprise for you..."

"Surprise?" Lilla chirped.

Mac turned to pick her up, his voice rising an octave. "Yes! A big surprise, you'll love it! Let's get you dressed and in the car. Have you eaten? We can pick up some breakfast on the way."

Shasa followed them in the house. Lilla showed Mac into their bedroom and began pulling clothing options from her dresser. Mac examined the selection of unicorn shirts and skirts. Together, they landed on a light yellow one, paired with a pink ballerina skirt and green tights.

Mac nodded appreciatively as Lilla laid the outfit down on the floor. "Gorgeous."

Her head spinning, Shasa stepped in to help Lilla change into her outfit. She needed to get out of her own pyjama shorts and the T-shirt she'd slept in. Maybe it was best to just focus on the next three minutes and not think about the rest of her life.

Mac stepped out of the bedroom to let them get changed.

"I have water bottles in the car," he called from the hallway, "so you don't have to pack anything. But take a jumper, okay?"

A jumper? Where were they going?

Once dressed, they followed Mac to his car parked in their driveway. She'd never seen it there, right behind her own. It didn't look like it fit, but it made her feel safe. She wanted his car, him, everything about him in her life. And she'd already blown it.

Put it aside. That's what he'd asked her to do. Shasa looked into her daughter's eyes, sparkling like it was Christmas morning. She couldn't take this away from her.

Shasa grabbed Lilla's booster seat from her own car and slid into the backseat of Mac's truck to buckle up her daughter. "I'll ride here with her if that's okay."

Mac met her eyes in the rear-view mirror. "All good."

He reversed on the street and drove north through town.

After a few minutes, he stopped at a roadside cafe and turned to them. "Wait here. I'll get us coffee and maybe a couple of pastries. What do you want?"

"Sounds good. Flat white, please."

Shasa rarely drank coffee, but this morning was not business as usual. She rummaged through her bag and pulled out a reusable cup. "It's a bit dirty, but you can ask them to give it a rinse," she said, reaching across the car to hand it to Mac.

He stared at it. "You brought your own cup?"

"I always carry it with me."

Mac looked like he was about to say something but changed his mind. He turned to Lilla. "And for you, Miss?"

"Lollies!" Lilla ordered.

Shasa shook her head. "Bring her a muffin or something."

Mac gave a brief nod and disappeared inside the building. The giant backboard outside the door advertised a coffee and muffin combo deal. Shasa hoped Mac would ask for that. He'd save at least two dollars.

A few minutes later, Mac returned with several brown paper bags and two coffees, one in a takeaway cup, the other in Shasa's green ceramic one. The silicone lid was a bit wonky, and she secured it with both hands to avoid spilling her drink.

"Here you go, Miss." Mac handed Lilla one of the paper bags.

Shasa tried to grab the bag. "Not in the car. She'll make a mess."

"Then I'll get it cleaned. Chill. It's not like she's eating radioactive paint."

"If that's what she's eating, car cleaning is probably least of our worries."

"Exactly."

Mac steered back on the road. Shasa wondered if they were going to his house, but he drove past his own suburb and turned onto a country road.

Five minutes later, they arrived at a sprawling lifestyle property. And there it was – a hot-air balloon, tethered to the front lawn. Lilla squealed, clambered out of the car and ran towards it. Shasa followed at her heels. The balloon had a classic lightbulb shape with pink and white stripes like a piece of candy.

She turned to beaming Mac. "Where are we? Whose is it?"

He gestured at an old man who appeared from behind the basket and climbed in. "This is Hank, the pilot. The house belongs to my friend Rick. He sponsors the balloon festival."

Hank waved to them. "Morning, Mac!"

Mac introduced Shasa and Lilla.

Hank held his hand up to the burner above his head, letting out a towering flame into the balloon. "The weather's perfect and we're ready to go. Just waiting for Felicity. The kiddos are up and she's dealing with them."

Shasa looked around. "Ready to go where?"

Mac pointed at the sky. "For a balloon ride. If you're okay with that. Lilla's a bit too young, but we'll do a tethered ride with the kids first."

"It means we lift off to about fifty metres up and then come back down," Hank explained. "After that, she can ride in the chase vehicle with Felicity. Kids love that."

Shasa looked at Mac. "So, you and I go up without the strings, just up in the air?"

"Only if you want to?" He searched her face for an answer.

Before she could form one, a lithe blonde woman approached them with two kids in tow. The girl was maybe a year older than Lilla, the boy a bit younger.

She grinned. "Mac! I've never seen you up this early! Rick's still out like a light. He just turned over in bed and mumbled something."

Mac laughed. "I promised we wouldn't wake him!"

Shasa noticed Lilla approaching the other kids, reserved but drawn in by curiosity.

Felicity stepped closer to Shasa, exuding relaxed confidence. "She'll love chasing the balloon. My kids think that's the best part. They can't see much when they're in the basket, anyway."

"Right." Shasa tried to relax. Mac had organised this amazing experience. Whatever was going on with her, or between them, she couldn't ruin this for Lilla, who appeared by her side and hung her entire weight off her arm.

"Can we go up in the balloon, Mum? Please?"

Mac appeared on her other side. "Are you okay? I know I sprung this on you."

"I'm fine," she lied. "I'm sure Lilla will love the ride, even with the strings attached."

Mac pulled Shasa in for side hug and placed a light kiss on her hair. "Some things are better with strings attached," he whispered.

Shasa squeezed her eyes shut for a second and filed away his words, too heavy with meaning. She could cry over them later.

Mac gave a signal to Hank, who gathered the kids and helped them into the basket. After double checking the strings, he hopped onboard with them, explaining something about aerodynamics, which surely went over the heads of his young passengers.

"Mummy!" Lilla called from the basket.

"Mummy can get in, too," Hank hollered. "There's room for one more adult."

Shasa cast a questioning look at Mac.

"Go!" he urged. "She'll enjoy it more if you're with her."

It was almost a relief to get away from Mac. He was too sweet to her, too lovely, too serious about them. He didn't know she's already destroyed everything. Climbing into the basket, Shasa wondered if there was any way she could get her friends to pull the offer and reconsider where they were building. They'd think she was nuts, but that was a small price to pay.

Anxiety turned her stomach. She couldn't do anything about it right now. Her phone was in the car, and she was about to go up in the air with three excitable kids.

"I actually needed another adult here," Hank confessed, "to keep the kids from climbing."

"Feet flat on the floor, Ryan!" He told the blond boy, who tried to pull himself up the side of the basket. "Use the peeping hole."

Shasa followed his pointing finger. Close to the floor, the wicker basket really had a peeping hole. The kids took turns looking through it as Hank turned on the propane burners, and with a loud whoosh, they lifted off the ground.

"Mac is tiny!" Lilla exclaimed, peering through the hole. "House is tiny."

From high up in the air, everything looked small. For a brief moment, Shasa felt weightless, like she could see her tangled, complicated life from a God perspective. So small and inconsequential. The green fields spread out as far as the eye could see, dotted by occasional houses. So many lives, so many dwellings. Her life couldn't be tied up to one building project.

She had to get hold of Marnie and beg her friend to change their plans. At least, she had to try. Tiny Mac on the ground waved at her, and she waved back. He was good to her. He was good to her daughter. She looked at the cables tethering the balloon to the ground. Was there anything like that between them? As much as she craved them, she could see no strings, nothing to stop them from floating apart.

Hank explained to the kids what would happen next, how they'd return to the ground and then follow the balloon with a car as it flew across the sky with Shasa and Mac. His reassuring voice calmed Shasa. Everything would be okay. She wasn't scared of heights or flying, but the thought of spending an hour in the basket with Mac made her hands shake. Thank goodness Hank would be with them. The silver-haired pilot carefully guided the balloon down on the ground and helped the children out, staying in the basket with her.

Felicity gathered the kids, handing each a helium balloon.

"Okay, it's time!" she announced.

Her blondies immediately let go of their balloons, watching them float up in the sky.

"What are they doing?" Shasa asked.

Felicity smiled. "Prepping you for the flight. This way you see the wind direction. Better than the weather forecast. Plus, it's fun for the kids."

The two released balloons rose high in the sky, but Lilla held onto hers.

"Let it go, Lil. You get to see where the wind takes it," Shasa coached her, trying to reach her daughter over the side of the basket.

The girl was too far and too stubborn, locking the string in her white-knuckled grip. She'd never had a helium balloon.

Mac approached Felicity. "Let her keep it. Two in the sky is enough for us."

Felicity turned to the kids and pointed at a huge black people mover parked in front of the house.

"Are you ready to chase the balloon?"

Lilla shouted 'yes' with the others.

Shasa sighed from relief and waved. "Mummy will see you a bit later!"

Lilla waved back. "Don't worry Mummy, we're going to catch you!"

As Felicity steered the kids towards the car, she called over her shoulder to Shasa, "I have an extra booster seat for your girl!"

Next thing she knew, Hank hopped out of the basket and Mac climbed in, grasping the lever Hank had been holding above their heads.

"Where's Hank going?"

"To drive my car, to pick up the balloon. It doesn't fit into the other car with all the kids."

"What? We can't ride without a pilot!"

Mac chuckled. "There's a pilot right behind you."

"You? You know how to drive this thing? Seriously?"

"Would you like to see my licence? Hank trained me."

Shasa turned to see where Hank had gone, and found him standing outside of the basket, a couple of steps away.

He smiled. "It's true. He's qualified. Not as good as me, but qualified."

Mac glared at him, then turned to Shasa. "I'm just as good. My ego's just less inflated."

Hank rolled his eyes. "You're good to go here," he said, unhooking the last tether from the basket's side.

He hurried to Mac's car and Mac pulled the handle on the burner. Shasa was expecting the sound this time, but it still startled her. They lifted off the ground, higher and higher. In a few minutes, the ground turned into a quilt of green fields, sprinkled with roofs. The sun still lay low on the horizon, giving the landscape a golden glow.

Shasa held her breath, drinking in the scenery. She'd never seen anything like it. Unlike the view from a plane window, this felt closer, more real, as if she could almost touch the tops of the trees.

Mac pulled the lever again and the whooshing flame lifted them higher. He wrapped his free hand around her waist, pulling her closer.

"Shasa," he whispered.

She shivered despite the hoodie he'd made her wear. "Shouldn't you keep steering, or driving, or whatever you're doing."

"The wind's driving us at the moment. We're good." He stroked her back, and she burrowed her head into his jacket, breathing in the scent of soap and coffee.

"Why do you even like me?" she asked, her voice wavering.

"Who says I like you?"

"You did, like half an hour ago."

"Right. I guess the cat's out of the bag, then." She could hear the smile in his voice, along with the gravity.

She wrapped her hands around his waist and held still, waiting to feel grounded again. Not that it was going to happen. They were literally floating in the air.

"What if it's not enough?" she whispered, turning to face him. "What if all this stuff between us..."

Mac's fingers landed on her mouth. "Let's not talk about that stuff right now. We agreed to put it aside, remember? Besides, we don't know what will happen with the section. It's all up in the air."

"Up in the air," Shasa giggled, scanning their surroundings. "Ha ha."

She was grateful for the stupid pun that stopped her from hurtling further into desperate thoughts. "Okay. Tell me something else. Distract me."

Mac peered into the horizon. "It looks like the weather's holding. We are right on course. If we're lucky, we won't accidentally land on someone's backyard."

"Has that happened to you?"

"Once."

She peeked over the basket's edge. They were close enough to see kids moving in one of the backyards, jumping into a pool. That would be an unfortunate landing spot.

"How did you become a balloon pilot?"

Mac smiled. "It was Rick, actually. He wanted to sponsor the festival, and I thought it was cooler to fly the balloons, not just pay for them. He had a better idea of what was actually involved, so he told me if I got a license, he'd sponsor me. I don't think he expected me to follow through. It took way more work than I'd thought, hours of flying and pretty expensive."

"So, you did it on a dare?"

"Makes me sound very mature, doesn't it? Honestly, once I did my first flight, I fell in love with it. I'd have kept going either way."

The green fields bathed in the early morning sun, every tree and house casting a long, sweeping shadow like a scattering of tiny sun dials.

"I can see why," Shasa said, peering at the landscape. "It's amazing."

Mac kept his hand on the lever and his eyes on the horizon. Despite his relaxed tone, she suspected piloting the balloon was a full-time job – one she didn't want to distract him from. Part of her desperately wanted to kiss him, but the buzz of adrenaline in her veins kept her in check, her arms locked around his waist. She rested her head on his chest, enjoying the feel of his jacket against her cheek, rough and waxy.

They travelled in silence, watching the sun climb higher in the sky, warming their skin. Heading out of town, the houses became few and far between, with endless fields and occasional forests stretching ahead of them.

"Thank you for bringing me here." Shasa exhaled. "I'll never forget this."

His arm slipped around her waist again. God, she would miss his touch. Was there any way she wouldn't lose him? Any way she could get Marnie and Elsie to back out from the deal and not bankrupt this man? Her phone was still in the car. She hadn't even thought about getting it during the brief landing. There was nothing she could do, nothing but enjoy being with him, even if it was for the last time.

Shasa slid her hands under his open jacket. She noticed her anxiety had settled. Maybe she could trust the balloon, trusted him. "If I kiss you, will you crash the balloon?"

"Let's find out."

His playful tone relaxed her, and she melted into the kiss, his mouth hot in the cool breeze. His tongue invaded her, sending a wave of fire through her body, like the propane burner right above them. His hands gripped her waist, then slid onto her bottom, pulling her against him. She felt him through the layers of denim and light cotton, rock hard. She was ready for him. Not that it made any difference. They were floating across the sky, with nothing but a bag of hot air keeping them from crashing down. 'Horny idiots killed in a balloon crash' the headline would read.

Shasa pulled away, breathless and frustrated. Her body craved more, but this way she'd only end up with that terrible, hollow ache.

"You couldn't have another hobby to share with me? Like testing hotel beds?" she asked, trying to laugh.

He winced, adjusting the crotch of his jeans. "I'm seriously reconsidering every life choice that led to this moment."

"I have no idea why I'm so hot for you, Mac. I wish I wasn't. If there was a way to turn it off..."

"I know. Although, I'm beyond even wanting to. I'd rather..." He paused, searching her face.

Her heart skipped a beat. "What?"

"I'd rather just go for it. I haven't felt this way about anyone in a long time. Maybe ever. And I don't mean just wanting you, you know ... I mean, wanting to be with you. I don't want to question it anymore. I want to dive in and give it a go. If you're in?"

As he said it, he glanced over his shoulder and grasped the lever, pulling hard. They were suddenly a lot closer to the ground, floating towards the treetops.

Shasa hung onto Mac's jacket. She was the world's biggest idiot, kissing him like that. "Are we going to crash?" she yelped, her heart jumping into her throat.

"No. We just need to get over this hill and land on the other side."

She left him to work on the equipment. To her relief, they rose above the trees. She could see a large, level field in the distance. As they got closer, Mac let out air to lower them down. It seemed the wind was taking them too far to the left.

"Are we going to miss it?" she asked.

They were close to the treetops again. Strangely, being this close to the ground was scarier than floating far above.

"We won't hit the middle, but if we go down fast enough, we should be in."

"And if not?"

Mac looked down in deep concentration. "We'll make it. It might be a bumpy landing, though. Hold onto the basket."

Shivering, Shasa grasped the edge of the wicker basket. It felt too light and hollow, something that shouldn't have been able to hold them in the first place. She didn't want to ask what happened if they hit the trees.

Mac's question lingered in the air, but she couldn't focus on it. At least not enough to give him an answer. Was she in? Her whole body screamed 'yes'. Her heart shouted 'yes'. But her conscience told her 'no'. She'd betrayed him, and she'd been too chicken shit to admit it.

She'd fix it. She'd find a way to fix it.

The ground got closer and closer, the solid green of the field turning into a detailed image featuring tufts of long grass and occasional rocks. Just before the edge of the forest, they touched the ground, bumping against it twice before the landing for good. The basket fell on its side, piling Shasa on top of Mac. For a moment, they remained in place, panting, then simultaneously they burst into laughter.

Shasa lifted her head off Mac's chest. "We made it!"

"You sound surprised."

"I am!"

She climbed out of the basket and stood in the field. The balloon had flattened along the grass. Looking at the pile of nylon fabric, it was hard to believe it had held them in the air just moments ago. There was nobody else around.

"The chasers aren't here yet," she said, gesturing the landscape.

Mac joined her side. "Does that mean we have time to test some hotel beds?"

Shasa laughed, looking around. "I must have missed the hotel."

An engine roar penetrated her naughty thoughts. The black people mover appeared from the other side of the field, driving along a rudimentary country road. Mac's car appeared right behind it.

Shasa ran towards them, waving her arms. Mac followed a few steps behind. Felicity parked a few metres from the balloon and the kids poured out, their eyes shining with excitement.

"I saw you the whole time, Mummy! We never lost you!" Lilla yelled, wrapping her arms around Shasa's legs.

Shasa lifted her up on her hip. "Good chasing!"

"Excellent chasing," agreed Mac, offering Lilla a high-five.

Felicity appeared next to them, beaming. "We had a lot of fun, didn't we?"

Hank parked behind the people mover and joined them. He nodded at the balloon basket. "Bumpy landing?"

"Smooth as," Mac insisted indignantly.

Hank looked at Shasa for confirmation. She shook her head and he laughed. "I knew it!" He handed Shasa her handbag. "Your bag was ringing, so I thought I'd bring it to you."

As she took the bag, Hank tossed Mac his car keys. "Thanks for lending me your car. You're right, it drives well. I have to consider that one."

Shasa fished her phone from underneath snacks, hairpins and supermarket receipts. It showed three missed calls – two from Marnie, one from Elsie. There was also a message.

Her heart thumping in her chest, Shasa brought up the text. It was from Marnie.

You're going to love me! The seller has accepted our offer!!! Just doing the paperwork with Elsie. Call me as soon as you can! Xox

Overcome by nausea, Shasa accepted Felicity's offer of a ride and immediately piled into the backseat of the people mover, squished between the kids, her head bumping against Lilla's helium balloon. She couldn't look Mac in the eye. It was easier to focus on the kids as they chattered about their balloon experiences.

Fortunately, Mac was busy with Hank, loading the balloon on his pickup truck.

As Felicity drove away, Shasa caught a glimpse of Mac. She doubted he could see her through the tinted window. The longing in his eyes made her insides hurt. He was all in, and she hadn't given him an answer.

Chapter 28

The next day, Shasa watched Marnie pour champagne into the crystal flutes Elsie had supplied. They stood in the middle of Shasa's backyard, eating blueberries straight off the bush. The weather had been ideal, ripening the berries in record time.

"These are delicious," Elsie said, popping another one in her mouth.

Earl joined her, asking them something about gooseberries. Shasa tried to smile, half listening. She liked these people, and this was an opportunity of a lifetime. If it weren't for Mac, she'd have been jumping for joy. They'd won. She could hardly believe it.

She couldn't let her personal heartache ruin everyone else's celebration, so she lifted her glass. "To our community!"

Everyone echoed. This many people really felt like a community. Marnie had brought her teen daughter, who was pushing Lilla on the swing. Elsie was accompanied by both Earl and her architect. The blueprints he'd provided were spread across Shasa's wobbly outdoor table – one of many things flagged for the skip as soon as they could organise one. The table was extra wobbly under the weight of all the party food they'd brought for the celebratory morning tea. Shasa was grateful Marnie had done most of the shopping. She'd struggled to sleep last night and had been fairly useless during party preparations, blaming a headache.

Marnie picked up a teaspoon and clinked on her glass. "Excuse me! I have an announcement to make."

Everyone turned to look, and she continued. "Elsie already knows, but I haven't told Shasa yet, because she's been so moody with her headache..." She paused to roll her eyes, and everyone laughed. "We've just sold the last apartment. We're officially sold out!"

Everyone cheered. Everyone, except Shasa. How could they sell the apartment without consulting her? Were they not in this together?

"Perfect timing!" Marnie shouted as Mac's parents appeared from around the corner. "I was just telling everybody that you're joining our community! Welcome!"

Shasa's mouth hung open as John and Sue introduced themselves, apologising for being late as they'd just come from church. They were just as lovely as she remembered, but the situation made her feel sick.

Shasa nudged closer to Marnie, lowering her voice. "What's happening?"

"We figured you'd be okay with them since they're your neighbours anyway."

"Yeah, they're great. But ... what did you do? How? Does Mac know about this?"

"I don't know. Not my job to tell him, he's their son. I just went to visit them and told them about our project. I took those slides you prepared and told them who's involved. They know you, and they like you. They got really excited, and said they'd take down the fence and join the two gardens together. Isn't that amazing?"

"Aren't they selling—"

She stopped talking as John raised his glass, along with his voice. "We're really excited about this community initiative. We've been looking for ways to help families on this street, and now it looks like we'll be able to do up our old house to rent out to someone in need. There's a family down the road sharing a three-bedroom house with another family. They could use some extra space. We don't need such a fancy house, or so many rooms. By downsizing, we can also make a big, safe yard for all the kids in the street. I know that's also very important to my wife, Sue." He nodded at Sue, who blushed.

"I'll drink to that!" shouted Marnie and waved her glass.

"Would you let me lead us into a short prayer?" John asked.

Marnie lowered her glass in embarrassment. Elsie and Earl bowed their heads.

Shasa couldn't stop staring at John. His strong jaw and cheekbones reminded her of Mac. The man she'd betrayed. The man she loved. Craved. Missed. But yes, loved. A tear fell out of her eye. Large and round like a glass bead, it landed in her champagne.

Shasa sniffed, trying to compose herself, but it was too late. She couldn't be part of this celebration. Her fake headache would have to progress to a fake migraine.

"Hey Marnie," she grabbed her friend's arm. "Do you mind if I lie down for bit? My head's killing me."

"Good idea. I need to you to be functional by 3pm for the reporter."

Shasa sighed. She couldn't even think about that yet.

***

Elsie edged closer to Marnie, her gaze following Shasa's retreating back. "Where's she going?"

Marnie furrowed her brow. "To lie down, she said. Headache."

"Not ... heartache?"

"Hope not. Why?"

Elsie drained her champagne. Shasa had jerked at the mention of Mac's name. She hadn't even tried to cover it up. For a moment, her face had given her away like a funeral guest in the middle of a wedding reception. "Talk to her. Find out what happened with Mac. She's out of sorts. And it's not just a headache."

Marnie nodded. "You might be right. She's been quite odd lately. I think she saw him yesterday, but she wouldn't talk about it."

"It's over. We got the section, so there's no need to worry about Mac anymore, no reason they can't be together."

Marnie's eyes widened. "I suppose. I mean, if he can handle the ... situation?"

Elsie sighed. Shasa and Mac faced a tricky romance. She quite enjoyed her drama-free relationship with Earl. They'd had a couple of lovely dinners – which he'd insisted on paying for – and had met once for a walk around the lake. She confessed to him her loneliness and shared her regrets. With each word, the cloud had lifted higher, until she barely noticed it. Talking to Earl worked better than therapy, restoring her faith in love and life, even in those moments they said nothing, strolling side by side in companionable silence. She was still building up the courage to ask him to spend the night, but it was only matter of time. Elsie smiled as giddiness bubbled up in her chest. She fought to straighten her face when she noticed Marnie's eyes clouded with worry.

"What's wrong?"

Marnie fiddled with her greenstone necklace. "Do you really think we can finish the build in four months? The timeframe feels..."

Elsie gestured at Earl. "It's ambitious, but we have everything lined up. Earl's rushing the council approval. And going with a modified prefab saves a lot of time, and money. A flat section, minimal site works."

Marnie's face split into a wide smile. "I can't believe how quickly it's moving!"

Elsie smiled at her enthusiasm. Marnie had sold her house and the settlement date was four months away. If the new build wasn't finished in time, she'd have nowhere to live. Elsie had offered her guest suite to Shasa and Lilla.

She patted Marnie's arm. "We'll get there."

"Thank you for everything." Marnie wrapped her in a tight hug. "You're the most amazing person."

Elsie froze for a split second, but quickly found her bearings and hugged her back, amazed at the ease of her affection. She'd do everything in her power to make sure the build was finished in time. She could only hope the new friendship continued beyond the house building, and that what she'd found was real.

Chapter 29

Mac knocked on the open door of his parents' house out of courtesy. He'd arrived early, hoping to catch his parents before the neighbourhood kids showed up. He placed a bouquet of purple daisies on the table and looked for his mum. The smell of a roast came from the oven, but the house was empty After a quick check, he returned outside.

Laughter and chatter came from behind the fence. Shasa's fence. Was there a party? Mac tracked softly along the fence until he got to the missing board Lilla had used as a doorway. He peered through the hole and saw his parents with Marnie, Elsie and an old guy who looked familiar. He heard Lilla's voice from the swings but couldn't see Shasa.

Okay, enough with the hiding. If his parents were there, he had enough reason to go over and ask what was going on.

As he entered the gate, Mum rushed to hug him. "Hi! Everyone, this is our son, Elijah!"

"Call me Mac," he corrected.

Lilla got off the swing and ran to him. He smiled at her, the only person who didn't judge, who accepted him for who he was. Mac picked her up and swirled her around the yard, then returned her to his hip.

"I want to go in the balloon again!" Her mouth spread into a wide smile.

"Do you?"

Lilla nodded three times. "Can I?"

Elsie stepped closer. "You'll see the balloons when the festival starts." She turned to Mac. "We talked about going next Saturday morning to see the balloons take off."

The start of the balloon festival was a nice excuse for a picnic. Mac suspected it wasn't an invitation for him, but he decided to humour Lilla. "I'd love to join you," he said with a wink. "You know, this year, they have a pink unicorn one?"

Lilla's eyes looked like they were about to pop out of her head. "A pink unicorn balloon?"

Mac nodded. "A friend told me."

Elsie studied them, then offered him a surprisingly gracious smile. "It's nice to see you're not a sore loser."

Loser?

She moved away, her champagne flute held high. A weight landed on Mac's chest, making it hard to breathe. Before he had a chance to ask, his mum squeezed his hand.

She spoke in a low voice, her smile unwavering and eyes

darting over the yard as if she didn't want it to look like they were having a conversation. "I wanted you to hear this from us first. Your father and I have decided to invest in this co-housing community. We'll move into one of the small flats and rent out our house, maybe to the Mills down the road. That way, we can help more people. I hope you understand. We don't want luxury apartments. It's just not us."

Nausea welled in Mac's stomach. This was insane. He knew he didn't always see eye to eye with his parents, but he hadn't imagined for a second that they'd go behind his back and line up behind the person who was out to destroy his business deal. Shasa. She'd well and truly bested him.

He'd asked Shasa if she could see herself and in a relationship with him, and she'd fled. Mac had told himself she'd been distracted by the balloon landing, but he hadn't missed the glimpse of regret in her eyes. She'd already known. She'd been saying goodbye.

"Mum, I'd have worked with you to build the kind of place you like. As small as you like. I can't believe..."

His mum squeezed his hand even harder. "I'm sorry. We thought about it, but we didn't want to become a problem for you, lower the value of your investment with our ideas. They're just not compatible. One day you'll understand."

"Mum, I don't care about the investment! I can make less money, we can change the drawings to fit in an extra apartment for the poor, whatever you want. I'll fund it myself. Just let me build it. If I lose this, I lose everything!"

Mum turned to him, misty-eyed. "I hate to disappoint you, but we already signed the contract."

With that, Mac turned around and left. It was over.

When he got to the gate, Lilla wrapped her skinny hands around his legs. He turned around, trying to rise above the pain in his chest.

The girl's eyes were huge, full of hope. "Can you take me to the unicorn balloon?"

"Maybe one day," he said with a sad smiled and snuck through the gate.

If his mum thought he couldn't be trusted to build something that fostered community, or wellbeing ... well, lying to little kids was just par for the course, right?

Chapter 30

"I'm not sure about this," Shasa said for the umpteenth time, pulling on another T-shirt.

Marnie gave her a weary look. "It's just the local paper. All you have to do is smile and talk about cohousing. You did those two presentations. You know your material."

Marnie had agreed to an interview with Barbara Bell, the woman who'd joined their first cohousing meeting. The whole point was good to get the word out there, Shasa reminded herself. She wanted more people to get excited about cohousing and more communities to appear around the city. If only she could get herself excited. At the moment, she wasn't a great advertisement for the concept.

"What if you do it? You'd be so much more ... happy, you know? Spunky?" She looked at Marnie, pleading for understanding.

Her friend stared back, a stern expression on her face. "Seriously. What is up with you? We're about to make history! Why aren't you excited?"

Shasa looked into her dressing mirror and caught sight of her own face, morose as a petulant teenager.

Marnie joined her, peering over her shoulder. "And what's up with your clothes? You've gone mainstream!"

It was true. She'd put on jeans and a simple tee. "I don't want people to judge cohousing as something 'alternative', you know? If I wear something ethnic or different, everyone will look at the photo and think I'm talking about a commune, an ashram, or something."

Marnie threw up her arms, smiling. "I'm not saying it looks bad. You're most welcome to join us T-shirt and hoodie minions, although, you're an actor now so you'll get to wear all kinds of costumes, right? That'll be fun!"

Shasa knew her friend was trying to cheer her up but thinking about acting brought up Mac. Their next rehearsal was supposed to be this week, on Wednesday night. Was it still happening? She'd had no word from Mac since the balloon ride. He must have heard about their victory. Shasa looked at her friend, who'd worked hard to achieve this goal. Marnie deserved to celebrate. Shasa dug deep and found a genuinely happy smile that lasted a few seconds. Satisfied, Marnie left her to finish dressing and went to put on the kettle.

At the knock on the door, Shasa glanced in the mirror. She was as ready as she'd ever be.

"I'll get it!" she yelled to Marnie.

She opened the door, ready to smile from the bottom of her heart. Instead, her heart fell to the bottom of her heels. Ollie stood there, all dreadlocks, hemp and golden tan, smiling like he'd won the lottery.

"God, I missed you!" he sighed, enveloping her in a hug that brought up a sense of familiarity, along with queasiness.

She scrambled free, stumbling over the threshold into the house.

Ollie followed her inside, flinging his rucksack on the floor. "It's so good to be home! Did I surprise you?"

Did he ever. "I ... wasn't expecting you." Shasa rubbed her forehead, like he was a hallucination she could will away.

Ollie took another look at her. "Wow, you've really gone mainstream, haven't you?"

He'd seen her new hair on Skype, but she'd disconnected the call before he could comment. Shasa looked away, her heart pounding. He had no right to judge her appearance. She owed him nothing.

Ollie softened his voice. "Don't worry, the hair will grow back."

"I don't want it back!" she yelled, her eyes stinging.

She didn't want any of it back, including him.

Ollie rolled his eyes, smiling. "Okay, chill. Where's the bean?"

"Backyard." Shasa pointed at the back door, hoping he'd go straight there and give her a moment to think.

Ollie jogged past her, calling for Lilla. She heard the girl's incredulous voice, "Daddy?" and imagined her running to his arms. Ollie should have done this long ago, but this was the worst timing she could have imagined.

Eyes blurred with tears, Shasa wandered into the lounge and dropped down, missing the couch by inches. She landed on the floor with a thud.

Marnie appeared in front of her. "Who was that? What's happening?"

"Ollie." Her voice sounded like it didn't belong to her.

"What the fuck? What's he doing here? Why now?"

Shasa shook her head in disbelief. "I wish I knew." A large part of her wanted to kick him out without further questions, but he was the father of her daughter. She had to hear him out.

Ollie returned from the backyard, carrying Lilla. The girl looked startled, like when she'd sat on Santa's lap at the mall.

Ollie lowered her onto the floor. "I brought you a present."

So he really was Santa. He opened a side pocket of his rucksack and pulled out a necklace made out of seashells and twine. Hundred percent natural, no doubt.

"Did you make that?" Shasa asked.

"Yes. I've been learning some new skills." His voice was soft.

He sat on the floor next to Shasa, leaning on the couch. Marnie took the hint and returned to the kitchen, pulling

Lilla with her.

"I'm sorry, Shasa. I've done a lot of thinking and I don't want to be that guy. The guy who chooses work over his family. No matter how important it is." The way he said the word important made her shiver. Slow and serious. Like it was something she'd never understand.

"What about the other woman?" she asked.

"What other woman?"

"Don't play dumb. It was right there in the subtext."

Ollie looked away, his face twitching, like he was deciding how much to reveal. "Fine, I'll be honest. There was some-one else, but I told her I'm going home, so ... it's over."

"But if you went back, you'd just pick up from where you left off?"

Ollie ignored her and stood up. "Are you saying you've been a nun this whole time?"

Shasa swallowed. "Pretty much."

If he'd been sleeping with someone on the side, she'd defi-nitely been a nun. A sexually frustrated one, but that was a given.

Another knock rapped on the door. Shasa's stomach lurched. The reporter. This couldn't be happening. Before she made it up from the floor, Ollie opened the door to Barbara Bell, who wore a bright red blazer and carried a big black bag.

"Hi there! I'm Barbara Bell. I'm here to interview Shasa Daniels about the cohousing community."

"Cohousing community," Ollie repeated, his voice raising in surprise.

"Yes," confirmed Marnie, appearing at the doorway next to him. She led the reporter inside and seated her on the couch.

Shasa finally made it up from the floor, and, directed by Marnie, sat next to Barbara.

Ollie took the old armchair, leaning in with curiosity. "You didn't tell me about this cohousing thing," he said pointedly, staring at Shasa.

"Ollie's been away at sea," Marnie told the reporter. "Don't mind him. He just turned up out of the blue."

Ollie raised his hands in surrender. "Sorry. I won't get in your way. You carry on. I'll go unpack and leave you to it. If you need more time after that, can I take Lilla to the park?"

Panic squeezed Shasa's throat. She couldn't let him unpack. He wasn't moving in with them, not like this. How could she get him out without creating a scene?

Marnie read her mind and jumped in. "Ollie, why don't you take Lilla out first? That'd really help us."

Ollie scooped up his daughter. "Okay. Should we go get vegan ice cream?"

"What's vegan?" Lilla asked.

Ollie shook his head. "I've been away too long, haven't I?"

As they approached the door, the reporter got up, pulling a camera out of her bag. "Wait. Before you go, can we take a couple of family pics, maybe out on the deck?"

Ollie gave the reporter a charming smile. "Absolutely."

Carrying Lilla, he stepped with Barbara onto the deck.

"Shasa, could you join us?" Barbara called from the door.

"No. No. No." Shasa whispered to Marnie, but her friend gave her a gentle shove.

"It's one pic in a community newspaper nobody reads. You can do this."

Shasa stepped outside like a lamb to the slaughter, taking her place next to Ollie and Lilla.

"Great. Now, smile!" commanded Barbara and clicked away.

Shasa wasn't sure whether she smiled or not. She wasn't quite in control of her face. Barbara, however, seemed happy, and let Ollie leave with their daughter.

Watching them disappear through the gate, Shasa felt ready to vomit. He couldn't just take her daughter away. But of course he could. He was the father.

They returned inside and Barbara began the interview, firing off question after question. Shasa made it through the session with Marnie's help.

At the end, Barbara took them to the back yard, and snapped several photos of the two of them and the section. She even spent time with the blueberry bushes, no doubt trying to frame an artistic shot with ripe berries in the foreground.

When Barbara had finished, she flashed them a professional smile. "It's been a pleasure. You can expect the story in the next issue."

She bagged her camera, waved and headed to the street.

Shasa caught her at the gate. "It's not going to be a ... big story, is it?"

Barbara looked puzzled. "That's up to the editor, but I don't think so. The balloon festival's always a big deal, that'll probably get the front-page. Sorry."

"No, that's good. Also, if you use that photo of me and Ollie, he's not my ... we're not together. He doesn't live here."

"Okay," Barbara nodded. "We'll caption accordingly."

Relieved, Shasa let her go and returned to the house. Now, she just had to make sure that what she'd said remained the status quo. Ollie had to go.

Chapter 31

Mac stepped out of the elevator into the SkyCity bowling alley and headed straight to the bar. He had to talk to his business partner, face-to-face. On Sunday nights, Rick often met up with his old buddies for drinks here. Mac had been invited to join them in the past but found their endless bragging tiresome.

He spotted the familiar group on the balcony – two real estate agents and Daryn, a property developer who worked with Rick. From their rolled-up shirt sleeves, he could tell they'd just finished work. The fourth guy looked like a newbie, shiny and smooth like a Ken doll.

Counting on Rick being late as usual, Mac bought himself a beer and stepped through the balcony doors into the crisp night air. City lights shone below. He suspected the guys liked the bar for its view. From a distance, the human lives faded away, turning property into a game, a Monopoly board of tradable assets that lit up the night.

"Mac! Haven't seen you in ages!" Daryn pulled out a chair for him. "You remember Dale and Nick? This is their rising star, Jaden. He sold his first house today."

Mac congratulated grinning Jaden, focusing all his energy into channelling confidence. He had to keep going, fake his way through the pain. Through the confusion gnawing his gut.

"Where's Rick?" he asked.

Daryn pointed at an empty chair. "He went to take a phone call."

Mac took a long sip of his beer and opened a shirt button, letting the night air cool his skin. His heart pounded. He couldn't shake the nausea that had dogged him ever since this morning, the feeling of impending doom. He'd lost, but the game wasn't over. There had to be a way to turn this around. He'd talk to Rick, do some damage control, offer an alternative plan. It all came down to mindset.

Daryn's eyes gleamed as he returned to the conversation Mac had interrupted. "We're talking about a struggling holiday park. No beach, no views, no playground. But it's on prime land in the boys' high zone, and you can fit at least twenty units on it. Hamilton East is da bomb, an easy sell. You guys know how to word that more eloquently on the listings, eh?" He winked at the agents and they laughed.

"Where in Ham East?" Mac asked. "Is Rick in on this?" He

drew a deep breath, his fingers tightening around the beer glass. A new development in the right school zone was a safe bet.

Daryn raised his brow. "Rick's driving this. He's looking for a couple more investors. I thought he'd talked to you already?"

"I haven't seen him for a bit. Too busy." Mac tried to keep his tone light.

This could get him back on his feet if only he could get the bank on board. He'd sell the city apartments, if necessary, and his Tauranga rental. That way, he could dive into pre-sales and make some quick gains. Without the lakeside condo deposits, he needed something else to generate cash flow. The leaky townhouse renovation was sucking him dry. If he had to sell it at a loss ... he didn't even want to think about it.

Preoccupied with calculations, Mac missed the figure approaching him from behind.

"Mac?" Rick radiated stony disappointment.

Mac turned to face him. Blood chilled in his veins. Rick knew. "You heard about...?"

"I heard."

"I need to talk to you." Grabbing his beer, Mac got up and pulled Rick away from the table. They stopped at the balustrade. Mac rested his weight on the steel railing for support.

"I know I messed up, but I have a new plan. I know how to fix this. There's another section on Alison Street—"

"Shitty school zones. Those buyers were after boys' high."

The chill travelled down Mac's spine. "You pitched them this Hamilton East one, didn't you? The holiday park?"

Rick cast an angry glance at the table. "Daryn told you?" He turned back to Mac, defiant. "It's a great opportunity. The buyers deserve to know about it."

Mac's throat tightened, panic squeezing his every muscle. "I deserve to know if you're leading our buyers to another property! We're partners."

"You deserve nothing! You fucked up a sure-fire deal! You lost us—"

"I'll make it back. Let me in on this Ham East deal. I'll work hard, I'll—"

Rick's tone was ice cold. "I called the vendor and he told me about the community housing, the tenant pulling together all these hippies to buy the section. Seriously, it's unbelievable. I tried to offer more, but the deal's done. He said you never even called."

Mac's insides clenched, a wave of pain radiating through him. "I'm sorry. I've been distracted ... but it won't happen again, I swear."

"Distracted with that bohemian chick you took for a balloon ride?"

"Yeah."

"I guess you want me to cancel that date since it sounds like ... Wait! This hippy chick, is she involved in that community housing thing? Sounds like the same crowd..." Mac watched in horror as Rick connected the dots. "She's the tenant, isn't she? She's the one who—"

"She's the one." Mac fixed his eyes on moon. Unbearable sadness pressed against his lungs, making his eyes ache like a rapidly expanding brain tumour. He hoped it'd kill him on the spot.

Rick shook his head, stunned. "I thought it was Elsie whatever née Alders who shafted us. But it was you. Hope she was worth it."

Mac's gaze dipped to the city lights across the dark river. Exhaustion swept over him. It was over. He couldn't fix it. This show had come to an end.

"She *is* worth it," he sighed. Rick would never understand.

Mac drained his beer and closed his eyes. The beer glass slipped out of his hand and smashed on the parking lot somewhere below.

Rick huffed. "Shit, mate! You're losing it over a tree-hugging hippy. I never thought—"

Mac's right hook landed square on Rick's nose. Rick staggered backwards, colliding with a nearby table.

Mac braced his fist as pain shot through it.

Two security guards scrambled through the doors to stop the fight, but not before Rick made it back to his feet and took a swing at Mac.

A red flash. A shock of pain around his eye. The hurt made him feel better, transferring some of his anguish onto his flesh, where it belonged.

Rick left with his posse, their over-the-shoulder looks

filled with contempt. The guards manhandled Mac into one of the chairs. Glancing around to check the situation was over, they left.

Remorse set in, as thick and overwhelming as the night around him. Mac hadn't lost it in years but seeing the pity and disgust in his friend's eyes had been too much. Nothing was left of their friendship or mentorship. He had only one thing left, one thing he cared about, and it wasn't on this balcony.

Chapter 32

Mac never visited his parents during the week, but this couldn't wait. After three gruelling days of phone calls with investors and the bank, interspersed by poorly slept nights, he was done. By some miracle, he hadn't lost everything, but it was close.

He'd put his apartments up for sale and agreed to sell his own house to fix cash flow issues. That way, he could keep one property. He was still technically on the property ladder and in due time, could start again.

After he found his will to live.

Mac had to see his mum. He had to know. Like witnessing a magic trick that left him dumbfounded, he had to know how it was done.

The door chimed as he stepped in.

Mum called from the kitchen, "Mac, is it you?" She was

cooking something that smelled like lentil soup. She rushed to hug him against his will. "I missed you! I really wanted to talk to you on Sunday, but you left."

"I couldn't stay."

Mum pulled back, taking in the bruise around his eye. "What happened?"

"Stupidity."

She shook her head, eyes wide with worry. "Dad said you're selling your house, that you're losing all these houses ... We didn't know. You never told us you were in such a bind! Otherwise, we'd never have signed up for this thing."

"But you love the cohousing idea."

Mum released him from the hug and gave a sheepish smile. "We do."

"Then you should do it," Mac said, his shoulders heavy as lead.

Mum knitted her brow. "But I never meant for you to lose out like that."

Mac sighed. He'd wanted to be the big shot, their clever firstborn who had his life together. Admitting he'd made bad investments and was trying to dig himself out of a hole didn't fit that narrative. He'd been too proud.

"It's just money." He knew that's what she wanted to hear – if he only blinked at losing millions, they'd succeeded as parents. Oh, high road, how he hated it.

Still, under all the disappointment and hurt, there was a tiny ray of relief. Lying awake in bed with his swollen eye, he'd considered his new reality. He'd been brought back down to earth, down to the level of most people. He had a house, but he wasn't the rising star anymore. He no longer lived in a different world to everyone in his improv group, to his brother, to Shasa ... The market was out of control. It wasn't right that he'd been able to make so much money while others couldn't get into their first home, no matter how hard they tried.

Mum gave him another hug he hadn't initiated. "We're so proud of you."

He sat at the dinner table and let his mum make him a cup of tea she insisted he needed. He didn't need tea, he needed answers.

"How did you find out about the cohousing?" he asked.

Mum peeked from the kitchen doorway. "Marnie came to see us. I know her from KidsCan and she thought we might be interested."

"Marnie?"

"We tried to call Shasa to ask her opinion, but she didn't pick up," Mum said, placing a steaming cup of tea in front of him.

"When was this?"

"Saturday morning."

Mac stared into his tea. Shasa had been with him. Had she known about Marnie visiting his parents? She must have known about the plan. That's why she'd been holding back.

Mum slid into a seat next to him and lowered her voice.

"Dad saw you leaving Shasa's house the other night. Quite late at night. Are you two...?"

Mac shook his head. "No, we're not."

"That's what I told John. She's a lovely girl, but you're very different."

Why was everyone so focused on their differences? "You mean we dress differently?"

"No, I mean she's a single mum and you're ... a bachelor."

Mac nodded. He couldn't contest that, but how could he tell his mum it didn't matter. Every cell in his body still called for her, even after everything he'd lost. It was only money. He'd said it before and he wanted to believe it, even if part of him felt like throwing up.

"Will you stay for dinner?" Mum asked. "It's only lentil soup, but you're welcome to join us."

"That sounds great, but I have to go."

He glanced at the door, but something on the dining table caught his attention – the local paper, opened on a story titled 'Hamilton's New Cohousing Community'. There were several photos of Shasa and Marnie. The main picture, however, was a family shot. Shasa next to a tall man with a head full of dreadlocks, holding Lilla on his arm. He smiled like he'd won a prize. Shasa smiled too, but in a more startled way.

Heart pounding in his chest, Mac read the caption: 'Marama Street cohousing project lead Shasa Daniels with her partner Ollie and daughter Lilla.'

Partner Ollie? Mac stared at the paper, willing the image to change before his eyes. Anything else. Local man eaten and digested by a deer. Zombies attacking Central Business District. No. The image stayed. The man smiled, his dreadlocks taunting him. 'I'm like her' they seemed to say. 'We're the same. You'll never understand.'

Mac dropped the paper and left, not responding to his mother who was saying something about the coming Sunday.

He climbed Shasa's steps two at a time and banged on the door. He had to see it for himself. Was it true?

The door opened and there he was – the dreadlock man in the flesh.

"Where's Shasa?" Mac asked without introducing himself.

Ollie leaned on the doorframe, scanning Mac's suit with a mixture of pity and disdain. So, a hemp shirt and cargo pants were the path to enlightenment? Good to know.

"And you are?" Ollie asked, narrowing his eyes.

"Mac. I'm a friend. We do theatre together."

"Theatre?" he raised his brow. "Shasa doesn't do theatre."

"How do you know? I haven't seen you around."

"I just got back. But she's never mentioned theatre."

"Well, we have a rehearsal tonight, so maybe she'll mention it then?"

"Maybe. She's still at work."

Mac looked at Shasa's car in the driveway.

Ollie noticed. "She walks to work. I thought you knew her?" There was a challenge in his voice.

"Sweet. I'll catch her later then." He raised his hand by way of a goodbye and descended the steps.

So Ollie was back. He was also a total douche, but that was neither here nor there. He needed to talk to Shasa, hear it from her. She owed him that much.

Ollie appeared between him and the gate. "Look, I don't know what was going on between you and her, but … I'm back. I know I was gone too long, but I'm here for good. We're a family. I hope you respect that." His earlier cockiness was gone, replaced by fear.

"So, you're back together? That article in the paper…"

"Oh, you saw that?" Ollie said, almost cheerfully.

Overwhelmed by the urge to punch the nose ring off his face, Mac buried his fists in his pockets and slipped through the gate. He had to get out of this town.

Chapter 33

Shasa browsed her kitchen for anything suitable she could pack for a picnic. If Lilla hadn't been so invested, she'd have skipped the whole thing. But since the balloon flight, the girl had been talking about hot air balloons for two weeks straight. Now the festival was here and they had to spend Saturday morning sitting on the lawn, watching the balloons ascend.

"Are peanut butter sandwiches okay?" Shasa asked, although she had no choice. It was the one thing she could throw together from the half-packed mess in her kitchen.

She'd spent the week sorting out her belongings, hoisting various useless items into the big rubbish bin that occupied her driveway. The house had to be empty by the end of the week to allow for the removal company to take it away. A storage container would be delivered later that day. Anything she wanted to keep for her new home would have to go in there. Everything except a couple of suitcases.

Shasa hadn't seen Mac all week or heard a word from him. He hadn't shown up for the last rehearsal. She'd stood there with Gareth, unsure what to do. Gareth had tried calling him but couldn't get through. They'd decided to keep trying and stay in touch. The audition was next week.

After the missed rehearsal, she'd driven home and spent the night with Marnie. Two glasses of wine later, Shasa had finally admitted to her obsession with Mac and what had happened between them. Marnie hadn't judged her. She'd just hugged her and listened to her snotty sobbing. Shasa wasn't sure what her friend really thought about Mac, or if she could understand her actions. That was okay. She could barely understand herself. Marnie kept saying she'd get over him, but what if she didn't want to?

It had taken three days and four night to get Ollie out of the house. She didn't want to throw him onto the street, so they had to find him somewhere to live. For three nights, he'd slept on the couch and complained about this back. On the fourth night, he'd climbed into bed with her and she'd climbed out, camping the rest of the night on the couch.

She couldn't let him get close. He'd suck her in once again, back into a relationship she'd worked so hard to leave behind. She didn't need him anymore. She didn't want him in her ear, constantly educating her on something else she should be enraged or shocked about. The lectures had already started, from the type of detergent she was using, to the tuna and eggs. Always the eggs. The chickens were never happy enough, free enough, pampered enough. A vegan diet was the only answer.

What about human suffering? They'd spent the last four years living in a draughty shit hole that leaked and creaked and smelled musty even on dry days. Now that she could see a way out, she'd begun to despise the house. She hoped it would accidentally split into fifteen pieces when they tried to move it.

With Ollie out of the house, it was a bit easier to breathe. The only thing she worried about was Lilla. Ollie was trying his best with his daughter, and after some initial weirdness, the girl had been excited to have him back. It broke Shasa's heart, but she couldn't let it go on. She didn't trust Ollie's change of heart. This time, Lilla was old enough to understand. This time, she'd really get hurt.

Ollie had already mentioned a friend working on another ship, how amazing they were to be confronting the fracking in the Pacific. Shasa knew it was a matter of time before the part of him that had responded to that siren call years ago took over. Whether it took a few months or years, eventually New Zealand would be too small, their life too boring.

Ollie could see his daughter, but they couldn't play happy family. It was better to pull the plug before Lilla grew too attached.

Shasa dropped her meagre picnic into a canvas bag and

took Lilla's hand. "Let's go!"

The balloon picnic was on the other side of the lake, but the distance didn't faze Lilla. She ran ahead of her mother, carrying her unicorn purse, which contained another stuffed unicorn.

From the distance, they could already see the balloons, most of them full of air, tethered to the ground. Sun streamed in from behind the hospital, casting its golden rays on the field. Mist still hovered from the morning dew. The grass had brown patches from the ongoing drought, but it was gorgeous. Shasa was so happy to live near the lake.

So happy. The words made her choke up. If she hadn't betrayed him, if Marnie hadn't gone to his parents, could they have made it work? She loved the idea of the cohousing community, but did she love it more than him? Did she really love him?

Tears blurring her vision, Shasa nearly missed Elsie and Earl, who were set up on a large picnic mat with a huge basket in front of them. Elsie looked relaxed in yoga pants and a jumper. Her smile was wide as she leaned on Earl's shoulder.

Lilla leapt to play with the dog and Shasa sat down with them. "Morning."

"Morning, Shasa! So good to see you! Big day today! Are you all packed? Do you need help?" Elsie asked.

"We're okay," Shasa assured her, discreetly dabbing her eyes on her sleeve.

Elsie opened her basket. She'd brought food for an army,

an army of foodies. Admiring the spread of strawberries, pâtés and cheeses, Shasa didn't feel like revealing her peanut butter sandwiches. She laid them on the side of the mat and grabbed a strawberry. This was one thing she could get used to. Elsie had a taste for good things in life, and her catering was next level. Soon, they were going to be surrounded by it.

"Have you heard from Marnie?" Shasa asked Elsie. "I thought she was coming, too."

"No."

"I'll check on her."

As Shasa picked up her phone, it beeped. It was a text from Ollie: *Where are you?*

Her heart sank. Lilla had told everyone about the balloons, including her father. So, he was here, worming his way back into their lives.

She texted back their coordinates. Maybe she had to accept her life as it was, stop fighting it.

"I'm sorry," Shasa said, turning to Elsie and Earl. "Lilla's father's here, and he wants to see her."

Elsie smiled. "That's perfectly fine. How are things with you two?"

A lump rose in Shasa's throat. "Not great."

Shasa had told Elsie that Ollie was back after a two-year absence, that he wasn't moving into the new apartment with them. Beyond that, Shasa found it hard to talk about Ollie. On most days, she worked actively to forget his existence and the fresh bag of complications his return had brought.

She hadn't told Elsie about Mac. Maybe in time she would, although there wasn't much to tell.

As the first balloons lifted off the ground, Ollie arrived. Relaxed and casual in T-shirt and worn-out shorts, he'd tied a scarf around his furry mane, revealing a deep tan on his neck and shoulders. She'd always loved his broad shoulders, sinewy arms and his cheeky grin. The attraction was all still there but looking at him no longer ignited any passion.

Ollie introduced himself and sat next to her on the blanket. Too close, like he was claiming her. She kept her gaze on the sky, watching the lifting balloons, hoping for an excuse to move away.

Her rescue came in the form of a phone call. Shasa didn't recognise the number. It took her a couple of seconds to recognise Gareth's voice.

"Look, I don't know who else to call. I just heard Mac's out of town. Sold his house, moved to Tauranga. He sent me this really short, bullshit message. Apologies, whatever. I don't know what's going on, but I feel like you do."

Mac had left town? Shasa's stomach tightened at the thought, the pain spreading from her chest all the way to her fingertips. She'd been agonising over her own betrayal, over how much he hated her right now. Still, a small part of her kept hoping she could somehow make it right. One day, she'd work up the courage to drive to his house and ring the bell. She got to her feet and hurried away from the picnic blanket, searching for privacy. There wasn't any, but a few steps away at least she was surrounded by strangers.

"Why do you think I know something? I didn't even know he moved." She tried to sound flippant but failed. He'd lost so much money he'd had to sell his own house. That beautiful house he'd designed himself.

Gareth's deep sigh crackled on the phone microphone. "Please don't bullshit me."

Shasa paused, staring at a red balloon as it lifted off the ground. She had no reason to lie to him. If Mac was gone, there was no audition. No more secrets. "I messed up one of his business deals, he lost a lot of money and I think he now hates me."

"Messed up a business deal? How?"

"I'm sorry," she whispered. "I know we weren't supposed to get involved. But we kind of were to begin with, through this property deal. And also..." She couldn't finish the thought. There was no relationship to speak of. She had no claim on Mac. He was free to sell his house and move town.

The line went quiet. Shasa wondered if Gareth had ended the call.

Finally, he spoke. "I didn't want to risk you guys breaking up in the middle of this, but it sounds like you already have. Look. Whatever's going on, the audition's booked for tomorrow. I'll be there, the producer will be there. I can't tell you what to do, but I'm going to send you the details and this address I got for Mac. Then it's up to you. If you hurt him, fix it. Apologise. Whatever you need to do. One thing I know about

Mac is that if he doesn't show up for this, he'll regret it."

Gareth ended the call.

Shasa lifted her gaze in the sky. The balloons were rising in the air all around her. Pink, yellow, blue, green, red. They floated up, getting smaller and smaller, crossing the lake, slowly disappearing on the horizon. She'd never be able to look at a balloon again without thinking of him.

With a heavy heart, Shasa returned to the picnic blanket. Acting. Mac was so passionate about acting. How could he throw it all away like that?

"Unicorn balloon!" Lilla screamed, appearing by her side. "Mac told me about it! He said we can go on the unicorn balloon." Shaking with excitement, she pointed up at the sky. There it was, a pink unicorn, floating across the lake.

Shasa blinked at her daughter. "Mac told you? When?" A pointless question. Three-year-olds had no concept of time. Either way, what was he doing making promises to her daughter?

She shook her head, trying to erase the image of Mac. No such luck. Her memory only became more vivid, lighting up every part of her body he'd ever touched, making her heart ache. Could she turn up in Tauranga and talk to him?

"What's wrong?" Elsie asked, her face wrinkled with concern.

Shasa must have sighed too loud. Ollie stared at her as well.

"Mac's sold his house and moved to Tauranga."

Elsie cocked her head. "Is that right? He must have taken a bigger hit than I thought."

"Mac?" Ollie asked, like tasting the sound of his name.

Something about his tone sent a cold shiver down Shasa's spine. "You know him?"

Ollie hesitated for a second, then nodded. "Someone by that name came to the door looking for you."

"When?"

Ollie shrugged. "I don't remember. When I was still there, before you kicked me out. You were at work, and this guy said you had a theatre rehearsal or something. He thought you must be home since your car was there. Like people couldn't get anywhere without a car." He rolled his eyes at the preposterous idea, but the snipe barely registered with Shasa.

Mac had come to see her. After everything that happened, he'd come to her door. And Ollie had no doubt chased him away.

Ollie smiled. "It's okay. It's been two years. You're allowed to have new friends. Even ones who wear shiny suits and resort to violence."

"Violence?"

Ollie's voice held an air of superiority. "He had a black eye."

Shasa shivered from fury. "Why didn't I get that message?"

"What message?"

"You just said Mac came to see me and you never said a

word!"

Ollie shrugged. "He came to tell you about the rehearsal. You went to that rehearsal. What's the problem?"

Shasa lowered her forehead on her hands, wanting to scream. Ollie was an ass, but it was nothing new. She didn't want to waste another second on him.

Where was her daughter? She found Lilla standing behind them, looking up at the sky. All the balloons were now up in the air, getting further and further away.

"Are you leaving already?" Elsie asked as Shasa stood up.

"We have to finish packing so we can get everything into the container when it arrives."

"We'll see you around midday," Earl said. He, Elsie, and Marnie were coming to help shift the large items and look after Lilla.

"Do you need help?" Ollie asked.

"No," Shasa snapped. "You've done enough."

She farewelled Elsie and Earl, grabbed Lilla by the hand and took the path leading to home. They had a lot to do. With all the idle moments she'd spent thinking of Mac in the last two weeks, this should have been the easy day, the one so busy she had no time for self-torture. The day she moved on, literally and figuratively.

Pulling her reluctant daughter in tow, Shasa ploughed up the hill, back to the house that was no longer a home.

Once they reached the porch, she dug up her phone and called Marnie.

"Hi! I was just about to call you," Marnie said. "Why aren't you here? I just arrived."

"Sorry." Shasa winced. "Ollie showed up and told me something ... I couldn't stay."

"Do you want to talk about it?"

"Later, okay? I have all this packing to do and I have to ask you for one more favour."

"Anything."

Shasa sniffed. She didn't deserve a friend like Marnie. "Could you watch Lilla tomorrow? I have to go to Tauranga."

Chapter 34

Before ten on Sunday morning, Shasa arrived in Papamoa Beach, one of Tauranga's premium suburbs. Church bells rang in the distance as she crept along the endless coastal street, looking for the address Gareth had given her. The 80-minute drive had felt long, with her small car struggling up the Kaimai ranges, windows rolled down for natural cooling. Her air con hadn't worked in years.

House number 76, the quintessential weatherboard rental with a decaying, uncovered deck, looked nothing like she'd expected. She was about to double check the address when she spotted Mac's car. Thank goodness he hadn't downgraded that. It shone as her only beacon.

Shasa approached the door with trepidation. She had no idea what to say or what to expect. It's not like they had a relationship. They'd only shared a collection of moments she'd stored in her heart and relived over and over. Shasa stopped at the door, hoping for the hot ball of despair to lift off her chest. It didn't. She was getting close and her body knew it. The glass door was shut, covered on the other side by thermal curtains which gave no way of peeking in.

She knocked on the sliding door and waited.

The curtain behind the window moved, and she saw him. In boxer shorts and a sleeveless tee, he looked like he'd just woken up. The black eye Ollie had mentioned had faded into yellow and light purple. He looked lost.

Mac unlocked the door and opened it a crack, staring at her. She couldn't figure out if he was angry, sad, or indifferent. Of all the things she'd imagined, she'd never expected this stony silence. He was waiting for her to make a move, but she couldn't speak. She stood at his doorstep, frozen like a statue, her heart punching the inside of her ribcage. Why had Gareth sent her here? This had been a horrible idea.

Gareth. Her brain landed on the one solid piece of information she had. "The audition's today."

Mac shifted his weight. "I know." His expression remained unreadable. Where was the flirty smile, the eyes that lit up and explored every inch of her?

Shasa took a deep breath, closing her eyes. "I'm sorry about everything, all the money you lost, what I did ... I didn't know you had so much to lose. If I'd known..."

"I don't care about that," Mac said quietly.

She opened her eyes. "You don't?"

"It sucks, but it's just money. I know you have me pegged as this heartless rich guy, but you're wrong, on both accounts."

Shasa drew a raggedy breath. "I know I can't fix anything, but can we just go to that audition, please? If we leave now, we'll make it before..."

"And what if we get the part? I live here now."

"No, you don't! You just fled here when things got tough!" Why was she yelling at him? This was the opposite of what she'd come here for.

"Yeah, things got tough. I had to sell my house. My tenants moved out of this one, so I moved here. I didn't have a lot of choice."

She could see it now, the hurt and regret in his eyes.

"I'm sorry," Shasa whispered. "I really am. It wasn't my idea to go to your parents. I didn't know about it. And ... I thought we had something. You asked me if I was all in, and I never replied."

He looked away. "You don't have to. You have a daughter with him. You're a family. Think whatever you want of me, but I'd never break up a family."

Shasa stared at him in disbelief. "My family was already broken! I don't know what Ollie told you, but he's not in the picture."

"I saw the picture of you in the paper."

That news story! Shasa rubbed her forehead, desperate to erase the image. When she saw the caption that identified them as a couple, she'd sent the paper flying across the room. That day, Ollie had finally moved out of the house.

"It's rubbish. I'm not back together with him."

Mac raised his brow. "Why? You guys are cut from the same cloth. It makes sense." He sounded resigned.

A fire lit up in Shasa's belly. She'd had it with these arbitrary differences. Her nostrils flared as she stared into his eyes. "Let's get rid of the cloth then."

Holding his gaze, she kicked off her jandals, peeled off her tank top and dropped it on the deck. Mac didn't blink, but his eyes dipped to take in her grey cotton bra. She hadn't dressed for this show, but it didn't matter. Shasa yanked off her two remaining bracelets, letting them clatter on the wooden floorboards. Then, she pulled off her harem pants, turning them into a pile of fiery red fabric at her feet.

The church bells were still ringing. The bright morning sun heated her back, yet she shivered in the late summer breeze as she searched his face, hoping to catch a hint of the man she loved.

She scanned his boxer shorts. "I suppose my underwear doesn't match yours, either—"

She was about to take off her bra when Mac grabbed her by the elbow and pulled her inside, manhandling her onto the couch.

"That's enough!" His voice was hard, his touch like an electric shock.

She burrowed into the couch, hugging her knees. The sparsely furnished room was small, nothing like his house in

Hamilton. Uncontrollable sobs escaped her throat, and she hid her face inside her arms, trying to hold herself together. She'd lost him. The hot ball of despair expanded in her chest, turning heavy like iron.

She had to get out of here, fall apart somewhere else.

She tried to get up, but his arm blocked her. "Where're you going?"

"Back," she gasped, paralysed by his hand on her arm.

"So, you come over to tell me about the audition, apologise for ruining a two-million-dollar business deal, and then you strip on my deck ... for the enjoyment of my elderly neighbours Patty and Neil who were on their way to church." There was a hint of lightness in his voice, an opening.

Shasa's heart jumped, and she lifted her chin to look at him. "There was nobody in the street," she argued, although she had no idea. She hadn't looked. It didn't matter. If Mac could forgive her, Patty and Neil were the least of her worries.

"Neil was quite excited. Patty had to grab his walker and roll him away."

Shasa dropped her head, unable to stop the laughter or the tears that immediately followed. Her words came out in a sputtering ramble. "I didn't know Marnie was going to your parents. I was about to call off the whole thing, but I didn't have my phone on me and then it was too late ... I didn't care about the house anymore, I still don't, not really..."

"I bought my underwear from Kmart." Mac leant forward, elbows over knees.

The cheeky, random comment cut through Shasa's inner turmoil. She wiped her eyes with the back of her hand. "Really?"

"I heard it's a good way to save money. Nobody's going to see them, anyway."

She glanced at his boxer shorts. "I see them."

He huffed, a smile playing on his lips. "Well, there are risks with any decision."

Shasa's heart fluttered. He gazed into her eyes, waiting for her. This was her chance. "I know you lost a lot, but you haven't lost me. Not unless you want to. I'm all in."

"You don't mind me being broke?"

"No!"

"Or living in a house like this?" Mac looked around the dim, boxy room.

"I mind you living this far away, but we can figure it out."

"Good. Because I've missed you so much..."

She caught the hungry intensity in his eyes, just before his mouth closed on hers. Every nerve in her body fired up, and she matched his fierceness, climbing onto his lap and pushing him against the couch. If she could have him, she'd never let him go. A warm flood of passion poured through her, relaxing every tense muscle, melting away the fear and pain.

"I want you, Mac," she whispered, looking at him through wet eyelashes.

Mac's hands slid lower on her hips, sending a delicious

sensation to her lady parts. His hard-on pushed against her thigh, straining against the boxers. She slid her hand on it, gasping from pleasure, and kissed him again. His body tensed, and his hand landed on her shoulder, pushing them apart.

His eyes were inky black as he brushed a strand of short hair from her eyes. "We do this, and you're mine. Do you understand?" His voice was gruff as he held away from her, waiting for an answer.

Shasa tried to speak, but her voice had disappeared somewhere down her throat. She nodded, her heart beating so fast she feared it would give out.

"I can't lose anything more, Shasa. I can't lose you." The pain in his voice made her shrink.

She tried to breathe, to regain her speech. "I'm crazy and stupid, but I'm all yours."

Mac relaxed his hand, letting their bodies mould together into another kiss that took her breath away. Finally, they ran out of air, hot and panting.

"Do you have a bed?" she whispered. "If not, I don't mind the couch. I don't mind the floor."

Mac pushed them upright, then pulled her to standing. The room was warm and stuffy, but she shivered against him, her arms locked around his waist.

"Do you mind the table?" he asked smiling, lifting her on the small dining table, standing between her spread legs.

His erection pressed against her, stretching the cheap

K-mart boxers out of shape. He unhooked her bra and dropped it on the floor, lowering his mouth to her breast, sucking each one in turn. A sweet sensation shot down her spine. His hand slid down, grazing her wet panties, then sliding inside to circle her. Oh, God. She'd been waiting for this for so long, but she was almost too far gone.

"Protection," she whispered. "Quick."

He left her on the wobbly table, aching and desperate and ran to fetch a condom. Scared that the furniture would give out, she hopped down and followed him into the bedroom. There was only a mattress on the floor, covered in balled up sheets and clothes.

He gestured at it, apologetic. "I'm sorry, it's not—"

"I don't care," she whispered, pushing him on the bed.

He kicked off his boxers and she helped him roll on the condom. It was last part of him she hadn't seen, and it was perfect.

She peeled off her undies. "Let me ride you."

They could experiment with unsteady dining tables later. Now, she needed a release.

Mac lay back on the bed. "Be my guest." His thick voice made her throb.

As she lowered herself on him, guiding him in, she searched for his eyes. Was he okay with her being this forward?

Mac's eyes locked on hers. Her own hunger reflected back from them, along with tenderness. He'd do anything for her. Her throat tightened at the thought. She wanted him so much it hurt. Her hips moved as if they had free will and he groaned, his hands gripping her buttocks, letting her set the pace. With the tidal wave of orgasm building, she forgot everything else, chasing her own pleasure. He matched her gasps with grunts, calling her name. It was too much. She wanted the moment to last forever, but she couldn't hold it any longer. A moan escaped her lips as she unravelled, gripping his chest. He twitched inside her, coming within seconds of her.

She laid her head on his chest, shivering. "We'll do the kitchen table next time, okay?"

He laughed. "I don't care about the table. I just didn't want to show you the mess in here."

Shasa looked at the open suitcase in the corner of the room, its contents spilling across the floor. She thought of the day they'd first met. "I think we're even now."

He laughed. "Nah, you won the race. But that's okay." Mac wrapped his arms around her. His chest rose as he inhaled deeply, then exhaled into her hair. "Next time, we'll take it slow, I promise. Like ... hours."

Would they ever have hours? What time was it, anyway? Shasa bent her arm to look at her wristwatch. Oh, no. "The audition!" she gasped. "We can make it, if we leave now and ... speed a little."

Mac groaned. "But I don't want to get up."

Shasa pushed herself up to sitting. "You want the part. I know you do. I can't let you..."

Mac took a deep breath and peeled himself off the mattress. "Okay. Put some clothes on!" he ordered, reaching for his own shirt.

Shasa ran to the front door and peeked out, checking the street for passers-by. They were probably all in church. Wincing at the thought of Patty and Neil, she reached for her pile of clothes on the deck and dressed quickly.

When she was slipping on her jandals, Mac appeared in shorts and a T-shirt, holding a hoodie. He led Shasa out the door and locked it behind them.

"We'll take my car," he said, unlocking it remotely. "It's faster and won't fall apart on the way."

Shasa stared at him in confusion. "I can't leave mine here. How will I get it back?"

Mac cast her an amused look. "We'll sort it out. Meanwhile, you have me and my car."

"We could just take both cars," she said, turning to look at her Toyota. It made sense, but suddenly, she didn't want to make sense. She wanted their lives together, tangled and inseparable.

Mac clasped her hand in his, pulling her toward his truck. "Come on. I don't want to drive by myself. I want to be with you."

He playfully shoved her onto the front seat, stealing a kiss. She loved him for taking charge. She didn't want to be without him, not even for one hour, regardless of practicalities. Sitting next to him in the car, her whole body fizzed with tension. She'd thought sleeping with him would bring her back to normal, but her mind kept replaying the previous moments, maintaining the high. Mac drove quickly, making every bend so tight that Shasa slid on her seat, the fabric of her pants catching under her, tightening against her crotch. Every move sent a delicious shock wave through her.

But as they passed the signs for Hamilton, she couldn't contain the thoughts that popped up. Real life, with all its complications, waited for them.

"We're moving house! Everything's in storage and the house removal company is coming late tonight. Marnie has Lilla, I have to pick her up after the audition and then we're moving into Elsie's guest room." Shasa's breath caught in her throat.

She couldn't bring Mac into Elsie's house, could she? She couldn't be with him. They didn't have hours, not even minutes. After the audition, they'd have to say goodbye.

Mac's hand squeezed her thigh. "Don't worry about it. I can crash somewhere else. Then we'll drive back here when you're free. We'll bring Lilla with us, go to the beach, make a road trip out of it. That house is basic, but the location's good."

He was making plans with her, with them. Hope flooded her heart. She leaned her cheek against Mac's shoulder, enjoying the low hum of the air con. His car was a lot more comfortable, but she wasn't with him for nice things. She'd happily live in his half-furnished Papamoa house if it were close enough to work.

On the motorway, Mac called Hank and confirmed that he could sleep in the balloon pilot's office, a freestanding cabin at the back of his house equipped with a sofa bed. Shasa's stomach tightened at the thought, but she couldn't suggest anything better. If he had to be careful with money, this was how it worked. The future opened up in front of them like a terrifying jigsaw puzzle.

They spent the rest of the ride rehearsing the play and listening to music on the radio. Shasa could feel her stomach bubbling as they approached Hamilton and the theatre. Mac went quiet.

Finally, he turned on the theatre parking lot. Shasa had texted Gareth from the road, confirming they were on their way.

At the door, Shasa froze, her heart pounding in her ears. She grabbed Mac's arm. "Are we ready? I mean, we slept together. Isn't that going to kill all the tension? Are we going to tank?"

Mac took her hand, a cheeky smile splitting his face. "I don't know about you, but I'm hotter for you than ever. We'll be fine."

He gave her a quick kiss and opened the door.

Gareth stood, talking to a woman. When they entered, he rushed to greet them. "You're here! Thank God. Nice special effects." Gareth pointed at Mac's bruised eye. "Was it you?" he asked Shasa.

Shasa let out a nervous laugh as Mac shook his head. "I accidentally punched myself."

Gareth introduced them to the producer, a middle-aged lady in blue-rimmed glasses called Iris. Without a hint of a smile, she gestured at the stage.

Something about the stage, now in bright daylight, called to Shasa. She longed to return to the world of make believe where she'd had the first taste of Mac, a safe space where real life couldn't reach them.

Shasa climbed on the black, wooden platform and lowered herself on the cool floor, allowing it to transport her away from here, into the story. She was the princess, waking up in the reporter's apartment in Rome, the dream of him still lingering in her mind. The dream. She stretched her arms over her head, waiting for the director's cue. She was ready.

As she opened her eyes, she saw him. The Mac she knew, the one she loved. Without the pain and hurt that had hovered between them. His eyes lit up, and he studied her with curiosity. They kept to their lines, with a good dose of innuendo. Mac was completely in character and she longed to match his commitment. The director and producer faded into the background. Only Mac existed, his brown eyes she wanted to drown in, the hands she longed to feel on her again. But she was a princess, she reminded herself. She belonged to another world – one where he couldn't follow.

The scene ended. Shasa peeled herself off the floor, blinking like she'd just woken up. Beside her, Mac shuffled his feet.

"Thank you," Iris said, her voice polite, emotionless.

Gareth thanked them with a quick smile. "I'll see you out."

Had they completely bombed?

Shasa forced her feet to move, to follow Mac and Gareth to the doors. She cared about the play, but she cared more about Mac. If this was important to him, she wanted it to work. And if it meant he had to move back to Hamilton, even better.

As they approached the front door, Shasa noticed a faint rumble. Rain. She couldn't remember the last time it had rained. Mac and Gareth stopped in their tracks and stepped back to stay under the small cover. Shasa joined them, hugging the wall. She could hardly see the other side of the street from the steaming waterfall.

Gareth's voice rose over the rumble. "Thanks for coming, guys. I appreciate it."

"I hope we did okay?" Shasa asked. She hated sounding so needy, but she had to know.

"You were fantastic. I'll have a chat with Iris and see what she thinks. Although, I don't know if we can risk casting someone who doesn't live locally?"

Mac met his gaze. "Why don't we cross that bridge when we get to it?"

"Very well. Thank you for coming. I'll be in touch." Gareth slapped them both on the back and retreated into the theatre.

Shasa's heart pounded in her ears. The audition had been such a thrill that she hardly wanted to return to real life, especially if Mac were heading somewhere else, to Hank's office, or back to Tauranga.

Mac wrapped his arms around her. "Thanks for dragging me here. I'm glad we did the audition, even if it doesn't work out."

"No problem."

The rain eased and Shasa looked up at the sky. "We should probably go."

"Where's Lilla? At Marnie's?"

"Yeah."

"I'll give you a ride." Mac gestured towards the carpark, but Shasa didn't move. She wasn't ready to let go. What if all they had disappeared as soon as they left this theatre? Elsie didn't even know about them. She'd told Marnie she was going over to apologise and fetch Mac for the audition. Her friend knew she was madly in love with him, but nobody seemed to believe they had a future.

"I'm scared," she whispered. "How do we make this work? What do we tell everyone?"

Mac pulled her into a tight embrace. She caught a whiff of his deodorant, mixed with the dampness of the rain.

"We'll make it work. I'll sell the Papamoa house and move here. And I don't know about you, but I'll tell everyone I'm in love with you and want to spend every waking moment with you. Every sleeping moment, too."

He slid his arms around her waist and lifted her off the ground like a feather. His hot mouth landed on her neck, ear, cheek and eventually, her mouth. The kiss was so tender, so demanding, that she barely noticed when her feet touched the ground. After he finally let her go, he grinned at her, lowering his head to hers so that their foreheads were touching.

"So, we're together? We're facing the world together?" she asked.

His brown eyes were full of faith. "Absolutely."

"I love you too, Mac."

Strength returned to Shasa's legs. Maybe they'd carry her on to those new challenges. They descended the steps, entering the warm drizzle. Blindingly bright sun peeked through the heavy clouds, illuminating the tiny raindrops like crystals dancing in the air. Shasa opened her mouth at the sky, soaking in water and light.

Mac took her hand and twirled her on the pavement like they were dancing. An uncontrollable smile split her face.

"So happy," she said.

"So happy," he said.

It was the happiest she'd been in years.

Four Months Later

"Do we have more baked beans?" Shasa asked, tapping Lando on the shoulder.

The community house hall was packed with volunteers assembling donation boxes for struggling families. Lando cut the plastic wrap around the last pallet and peered inside.

"No, this is all tomato and creamed corn."

"We'll just have to substitute." Shasa blew into her freezing fingers and rubbed them together. The hall was difficult to heat in the winter.

She went to check on the volunteers. She didn't want to be seen to be playing favourites, but it was hard to ignore Mac. In a puffer vest and a beanie, he blended in but worked harder than anyone else, making sure both his and Lilla's boxes were filled correctly. The girl wanted to help but had the attention span of a squirrel.

"Wow, you're almost finished!" Shasa gushed.

Mac lifted the packing tape dispenser with an empty roll. "Is there another one somewhere?"

He got back to work, humming. At first, Shasa had thought he'd volunteered to impress her. But lately, she'd seen the spark in his eyes as he spoke about the families they were helping – the same families he'd wanted to help into home ownership. That plan was now on the back burner, but in the meantime, Mac seemed to enjoy connecting with people and helping in a tangible way, even if on a smaller scale. Shasa was so proud of him she got a lump in her throat every time she thought about how far Mac had come, from near bankruptcy to new focus and determination. If only she were able to share her life with him. Between busy schedules and complicated living arrangements, they didn't see each other much.

For the past four months, Shasa and Lilla had stayed in Elsie's guest suite while Mac rented an apartment in Hamilton. He'd decided to renovate the Tauranga house before selling it to get a better price. Since he was doing the work himself, he spent a lot of time over there.

Shasa entered the small office, looking for packing tape. Thank goodness for the play. Some weeks, the rehearsal had been her only chance to see him. Working with a large group of other actors wasn't exactly a date night. A couple of times, they'd snuck away for dinner afterwards, but it felt like their time together was a series of stolen moments.

Shasa's phone beeped. She pulled it out of her jacket pocket, struggling to tap on the message from Marnie with frozen fingertips.

About Sunday lunch ... are you bringing anything? Sue keeps saying 'just bring yourselves', but I'm pretty sure Elsie will bring some super expensive flower arrangement, and if you take something amazing, and I turn up empty-handed, I'll feel horrible!

Shasa chuckled at the row of terrified smiley faces following the message. She was even more terrified. This was the first time she'd been invited to Sunday lunch at Mac's parent's house.

She texted back to Marnie. *I know how you feel! We picked up some daisies. Mac says they're Sue's favourite.*

Shasa stared at the word 'we'. She wasn't used to talking about herself and Mac as a couple. Putting her phone away, she located a roll of tape on the desk. As she turned to go back, she nearly ran into Mac. He stepped in the office, blocking the doorway.

He smiled, sliding his hands around her waist, pulling her against him. "Found you!"

Shasa gasped. Okay, she'd allow herself a ten-second break. Fine, twenty-seconds. She slipped her hand through the roll of tape, the world's ugliest bracelet, and wrapped her arms around him. Her body responded to Mac like it had a secret on-off switch, going from zero to a hundred in seconds. He kissed her with passion and intensity, aware that their time was short.

Mac's raspy voice was hot in her ear. "Can you ask for someone to babysit so I can take you on a proper date? Or a weekend away?"

He loosened her purple scarf and bent down to kiss her

neck, lingering for a delicious moment. Shasa wanted to, badly. Now that she knew how he made her feel, she craved it even more. Since that first time in Tauranga, they'd only managed to get together in private four times, in his car or apartment after the theatre rehearsal and once on a long bush walk after Lilla had fallen asleep in the carrier. Every time she thought about that secluded spot behind large trees, her body flushed with heat. It was so good, but it wasn't enough.

"I will," she promised. "I just want to give everyone time to adjust. With us living at Elsie's…"

Mac groaned. "I understand she might need time. But why can't we ask Marnie?"

"She's already babysitting for every rehearsal and next week for the premiere."

"Let's pay someone. Or ask my mum. She loves Lilla." Mac brushed a strand of hair behind her ear. "It's almost like you don't want to date me."

Shasa bit her lip, her throat tight. He was right. She was holding back. She loved watching Mac bond with Lilla, but it also terrified her. She feared Mac didn't understand what he was getting into. The child would always be there, competing for their attention, complicating their lives. Everything required planning. Mac insisted he was okay to take it slow, but what if he got frustrated with all her baggage and moved on? Ollie had already sailed away to fight fracking in the Pacific Ocean, just as she'd expected. She had to protect her daughter. She had to protect herself.

If she was completely honest, dating felt wrong – something fun and casual that childless people did. For her, it had to be all or nothing. What if it ended up being nothing?

"Have you thought about moving in?" she whispered, breath catching in her chest.

Mac's smile was guarded, his lips tightly sealed. She'd asked him before, but he'd insisted Shasa focused on finishing the house to her liking. But how could she do that? She thought about him at every turn, wondering if he liked the colours and materials she picked. She'd included a lot of the charcoal and sandy tones she remembered from his house. They worked beautifully, although it would look different with her Pakistani cushions, chipped yellow teacups and the pink bedroom light.

Most of her stuff – the mouldy curtains, dream catchers with spider nests, and half-burned candles, had ended up in the skip. It had felt like an overdue cleansing ritual. Shasa didn't want her new home to look like a student rental that Ollie would feel comfortable bringing his ganja pipe into. No. This time everything would be higher quality, more considered. On a tight budget, it meant going without many things until she could afford them. She'd have to fight those urges in second-hand shops and learn to choose well. Maybe in time, Mac would be there to choose with her.

She placed her hands on his chest. "I know it's a huge decision, but it makes sense. Once you sell the Tauranga house, why pay rent for that place in town? I want you over every night … If you really want to be with us?"

A pang of pain clutched her chest as she searched for an answer in those deep, chocolate eyes.

Mac placed a quick kiss on her forehead and took the roll of tape off her hands. "Let's get this wrapped up so we can make it to that lunch."

She followed him out of the office, back into the hall. They worked as fast as they could, packing, prepping and cleaning. Once everything was in order, Shasa thanked the volunteers, locked the doors behind them, and they piled into Mac's truck.

Despite the cold, the sky was blue. Mac turned up the car heater, but it hardly had time to make a difference before they arrived at his parents' house.

"The house is ready!" Lilla yelled, jumping on the backseat.

"Wow!" Shasa cried.

With fresh paint and timber accents, their new cohousing community now looked like a real townhouse, dwarfing John and Sue's brick house. The fence between the two properties had been demolished, creating an enormous yard.

Shasa knew it wasn't quite finished inside. She'd opted for installing the kitchen and lighting fixture herself to save money – Mac's idea, like so many others. He'd also be the one to do the installations. Shasa had no idea what that entailed.

Whether either of them admitted it or not, Mac was already involved. They'd gone with the builders Mac had used for his own house and he'd done extra site visits, making sure they stayed on schedule and the work was done right.

"Do we have time for a sneak peek?" Shasa asked, glancing at the new house.

Mac smiled. "Absolutely. In fact, I asked Tony to meet us here."

Shasa's eyes widened. "The site manager? On a Sunday?"

"Don't worry. He's happy to, since he gets to hand over the keys. In record time."

"The keys?" Shasa squeaked, her voice nearly drowned out by Lilla's excited sounds. "I thought it was going to take another week?"

Mac looked out the window. "I lent them a hand to make sure it was finished a bit earlier. Come on!"

They got out of the car and approached the last unit, the one furthest away from the street that Marnie had promised to Shasa. Its yellow door beckoned her. It looked so happy.

As they reached it, Tony appeared from around the corner, holding a white folder. "Welcome to your new home!" he called, stroking his grey beard. "It's not quite move-in ready yet. We still have to finish the driveway and fencing. But you can certainly have a look."

He handed Shasa a shiny key.

Shasa gasped. "Wait! Shouldn't we wait for Marnie and Earl? Shouldn't we do this together?"

Mac shook his head and exchanged a look with Tony, who retreated down the driveway towards his car.

Mac nudged Shasa towards the door. "Come on!"

Confused, Shasa unlocked the door, letting Lilla sprint in

ahead. The girl ran from one room to the next, letting out
high-pitched yelps at every detail she noticed.

"My room!" she called from upstairs.

Shasa followed her up into the single bedroom right beside hers. It was pink.

"Did you already paint this?" Shasa asked Mac, who appeared behind her.

She'd been busy at work all week. As far as she knew, Mac
had only just arrived back from Tauranga after finishing his
renovations there. But it seemed he'd been busy at her house
instead. Everything looked finished.

Mac wrapped his arms around her. "I got back a bit earlier.
Well, a lot earlier."

Lilla threw herself on their legs, her eyes dancing. "I love
my room! I love it!"

Mac picked her up for a hug. "We can paint the unicorn
on the wall later." He let her down, and she skipped away to
explore the rest of the apartment.

Shasa whipped her head in astonishment. The walls were
painted, the kitchen installed. Only curtains were missing.
She shot a desperate look at Mac. "You can't do all this, it's too
much. Especially if you're not moving in. It's just ... wrong."

Mac stared at her and his eyes shifted darker, just like they
did on stage, right before a scene. "I don't want to be your
flatmate."

Shasa held back tears as he dug into his pocket.

"I want to be your husband." He held open a small velvet

box with a ring.

Shasa blinked several times, but the image remained. A simple gold band with fine scratches on the surface.

"It's recycled," he explained with a tiny smile. "I can make up a story of someone amazing it used to belong to if you'd like. Will you marry me, Shasa?"

She hadn't expected it. Ollie and she had never discussed marriage – he didn't believe in biblical covenants, or even legal contracts of that nature. Could she marry Mac? Shasa stared into his eyes and down at the ring. The scratches on it tugged at her heart. Staring at it, the shock wore off, gradually replaced by peace. It felt right, so much better than him moving into a house that was essentially hers. She wanted it to be theirs. She wanted to share everything with him.

Mac lifted her chin, forcing her eyes off the ring, back onto him. "I'm going to need an actual answer here. Even if it's no."

"No! No! I mean it's not no. The answer is not no. It's yes! Sorry, I'm ... in shock."

He laughed and kissed her shaky lips. "Wow, you nearly gave me a heart attack."

Shasa shook her head, laughing and crying at the same time. "I know! That was the worst response in the history of proposals. But I do love you."

He took her hand and slid the ring on her. Shasa didn't expect it to fit, but it did. Her legs trembled as they descended the stairs. They picked up Lilla from the laundry room and crossed the yard to his parents' house.

Shasa paused at the door. "Wait! How are we going to tell them?"

Mac didn't respond. Instead, he opened the door. Sue, John, Marnie, Elsie and Earl all sat at the dining table, engrossed in conversation. As they noticed Mac and Shasa, a deep silence fell.

Mac lifted Shasa's left hand. "She said yes!"

As if on cue, everyone started clapping and whistling.

Marnie was the first to rush in, hugging Shasa so tight she struggled to breathe. "Congratulations! I'm so happy for you both!"

"Congratulations!" echoed Elsie and Earl, both coming in for a hug.

John and Sue followed, smiling widely. Sue had tears in her eyes.

"What's happening?" Shasa asked, blinking in confusion.

Mac's hand curled around her waist, pulling her closer, claiming her to him. "I may have prepared them a little."

He winked and Marnie erupted in giggles. "I'm so relieved you said yes! We were all in knots over here. I know it's a big decision, especially when you have a kid ... but we've all got to know Mac." She glanced at Sue and John. "Well, some of us have a head start, but we've all got to know him and can't wait for him to join our cohousing community!"

"We held an emergency meeting, and I officially applied," Mac explained.

"To be honest, we're quite excited about the idea of living next door to Elijah," Sue said, her cheeks burning pink.

Mac nodded, pulling a face. "Yeah, that part is exciting for sure."

"We can take the unit on the roadside," John smirked. "That'll give the newlyweds a bit of privacy."

Newlyweds? He'd only just proposed. Had everyone else known about this but her? Shasa peeled herself off Mac's side and ran out the door, her heart pounding. All this time, she'd thought Mac didn't want to live with them, that he wasn't ready for that kind of commitment. She also had her own secret she'd kept from him. What would he say if he knew?

Shasa looked at the ring on her finger she'd just accepted, panic tightening her chest until she couldn't draw a breath. Not sure what to do, she retreated out the door, circled the house and sat down on at the outdoor table. She had to catch her breath. For the past week, Mac been so busy she'd thought he was pulling away. All the while, he'd been here, working long days at the construction site. He'd bought a ring. Shasa looked at the rough gold band on her finger, so absorbed by her thoughts that she jumped when Mac sat down next to her.

"Are you rethinking it?" he asked.

"No." The answer burst out of her chest. She wanted him, more than ever. But if this was going to work, they'd have to stop sneaking behind each other's backs. "You blindsided me. I thought you were going to break up with me. I—"

"I'm sorry. I never meant to make you think that! I was so focused on creating this perfect surprise that I got carried away."

"Yeah, I get it. But no more surprises, okay? Or secrets." She swallowed, her voice thickening in her throat. "That's why I have to tell you ... I'm the reason you lost everything. I snooped on your phone ... in the restaurant ... I saw what you'd offered and—"

"I know." A smile tugged at the corner of Mac's mouth. "For a spy, you're a bit sloppy. You didn't close the email. I figured you must have seen it."

Shasa's fingers curled around the bench as she thought back to that moment. Had she really been that careless? And how could this man still love her, still want to marry her? Mac sat down next to her, but she shifted away, her mind reeling.

"Were you not mad? That was such a horrible thing. You lost everything! I regretted it so much and I've been working up the courage to tell you..." She was fully crying now, wiping her nose with her sleeve.

Mac looked away, grimacing at the memory. "I was. But it's nothing I wouldn't have done, back when we first met. You didn't know how much I had riding on that deal. Only the bank did. I was gambling, and it's my fault I lost so much, not yours. But I want to do things differently from now on. Like you said, no more secrets. You're in my team now. If we spy, we spy together, right?"

Mac got up and pulled her up from the chair, against his chest. Her arms wrapped around him like a slap bracelet, activated by the contact. This is where she belonged.

"Sorry I messed up your proposal," she whispered.

Mac's arms tightened around her. "No, you didn't. As long as your answer is still 'yes'?"

Shasa nodded against his chest, a relaxing warmth spreading through her. "It is. I just didn't mean to snotty cry."

Mac stroked her hair. "All good. Besides, it's not over yet. We still have to tell Lilla and ask for her blessing. She might say no."

Shasa buried her face into his puffer vest, smearing the fabric with her tears. It warmed her heart that he wanted to ask her daughter. This is how it was supposed to be. Them on the same page, considering things together. Mac wrapped an arm around her and guided her back to the house. They found everyone around the dining table, waiting for them.

Marnie studied them with caution. "Are you still engaged?"

"Yes," Shasa said, a smile bursting through.

Lilla ran over to hug her legs. "Where did you go?"

Mac turned to Lilla, who stared at them, her eyes wider than Shasa had ever seen them. "Is it okay if I marry your mum? I promise I'll take good care of you both."

"Will you take me up in the unicorn balloon?"

"Oh, Lilla." Shasa sighed.

Mac gave her a grave nod. "I'll try to organise that."

"Then it's okay," Lilla announced with an exaggerated

shrug. She turned around and sat at the table.

Shasa held at the doorway, her whole body humming with happiness.

"Come on, guys. We're starving!" Elsie called from the table, making Marnie erupt in giggles.

The thick smell of roasted lamb lingered in the air. Mac turned to Shasa, cupping her face in his hands. She held her breath. He was going to kiss her here, in front of everyone, in bright daylight. No more sneaking around. No more secrets.

Shasa closed her eyes, letting out a breath she'd been holding for a long time, probably for years. As his lips found hers, her feet anchored on the flowery carpet. She was no longer floating, no longer lost. She was home.

Ready for your next read?
Sign up for my author newsletter and receive a digital copy
of *The Premiere* - the bonus epilogue for *Nest or Invest*.
Or jump straight into Marnie's story, *Hidden Gem*
– the book #2 in the *Love New Zealand* series.
enniamanda.com

CPSIA information can be obtained
at www.ICGtesting.com
Printed in the USA
LVHW091244190123
737417LV00006B/547

9 780473 562076